D0554667

ALSO BY
MATT RITTER

•

Plants of San Luis Obispo, Their Lives and Stories

A Californian's Guide to the Trees among Us

California Plants: A Guide to Our Iconic Flora

Rainwalkers

Something Wonderful

www.mattritter.net

Halo Around The Moon

A Novel

Matt Ritter

Pacific Street Publishing
San Luis Obispo, CA

This is a work of fiction. All the characters, organizations, and incidents portrayed in this novel are the products of the author's imagination.

For information about special discounts for bulk purchases, please contact Pacific Street Publishing at info@pacificstreetpublishing.com.
To request the author for a speaking engagement or book signings, please contact Pacific Street Publishing at info@pacificstreetpublishing.com.

Ritter, Matt.
Halo Around The Moon : a novel / Matt Ritter. — First U.S. Edition
p. cm.

ISBN 978-0-9998960-5-1 (hardback)
ISBN 978-0-9998960-6-8 (e-book)

Library of Congress Control Number: 2020925729

Thank you to Sarah Ritter, James Coffey, Kylie Mendonca, Sam Baber, Lucy Childs, Mike Garrett, Phil Jones, and Jenn Yost.

"Life's single lesson: that there is more accident to it than a man can ever admit to in a lifetime and stay sane."

—Thomas Pynchon

1
Beverly Hills, California
Present Day

The mutilated bodies of dead trees smell nothing like the mutilated bodies of dead humans. When a tree is torn apart and begins to rot, the air fills with the melancholy perfume of molasses and soil—the tangy smells of an old violin or a wet forest. By comparison, the human body is a disgusting thing. In the days shortly after death, the atrocious odors of a lifetime of accumulated sulfur and nitrogen bubble out in morbid flatulence.

These thoughts occurred to Marcus Melter while kneeling over the leg of a man who'd been run partially through a wood chipper. He poked at the transparent skin of the calf. It gave way, belching forth a stink so repulsive that he had to cover his mouth and nose with the back of his latex-gloved hand.

It was a warm sepia tone afternoon in a weedy vacant lot surrounded by mansions and high hedges. The September sun hung low, and everything appeared as if viewed through a jar of piss. With a pair of tweezers, Marcus extracted a pinky-sized shard of blood-stained wood from the upper portion of the severed leg.

"Who the fuck puts someone into a chipper?"

From his knelt position, Marcus looked over his shoulder at his long-time friend, Detective Jack Bratton, who was speaking to him from a safe distance.

Marcus shook his head and stood.

"I don't know."

Then he dropped the blood-coated splinter into a plastic bag that Jack held open for him.

2
Washington County, Arkansas
1905

Incredible as it may seem, earthworms are not native to North America. Their arrival on the continent wasn't marked by ceremony; a few hundred worms dumped with the wastewater from ballasts of the first European ships entering the Chesapeake Bay, sometime shortly after Columbus. Late in the fifteenth century, the worms began their generational migration westward through the thin, rich crust of the North American continent. During this slow and steady westward wave, earthworms irreversibly transformed the continent as they turned, rolled, and squeezed the topsoil through their transparent little bodies. Earthworms eat decaying plant matter, inadvertently swallow dirt, and accelerate the natural processes of decomposition in the soil.

Before their arrival, a thick mulch of rotting leaves blanketed the continent and fed the broadleaved trees of the great forests of the Northeast and Upper Midwest. The worms' movement through the landscape was slow and steady, but at the scale of geological time, they raced across North America consuming everything in their path, turning thick layers of rotting leaves into a thin veneer of nutrient-rich, loamy castings, better suited for pines and other fast-growing trees. In that geological instant after their arrival, the species composition of the vast forests of eastern North America changed forever; maples to pines, basswoods to cedars, and beeches to honey locusts.

Had the worms not committed this unintentional arboreal genocide, perhaps different trees would have dominated the forests on the western edge of the Ozark Mountains near the roadside between Springdale and Fayetteville. Perhaps, in the unusually cold winter of 1905, the vigilante captors of Obediah Bratton, Jack Bratton's great-grandfather, would have successfully carried out his hanging from a limb of a sturdier tree; but as it were, the earthworms had been by that very spot and accomplished their steady work many years prior, leaving only fast-growing, weak-limbed loblolly pines in their wake.

Obediah Bratton was neither a decent nor good man and deserved well to be hanged on that cold, full moon November night. He sat in the snow, watching white puffs of his breath dissipate in the blue moonlight, tears streaming down his cheeks. When no option for escape remained, he began to plead and grovel. He was hunched over, his hands tied behind him, his upper back resting on a tree, listening, but not making out the words of the hushed, angry conversation of his three captors. They quickly came to an agreement, and an old rope, no wider than a man's thumb, was knotted and thrown over a lower limb of a pine tree near the road shoulder.

One of the three men forcefully pulled Obediah to his feet and walked him to the hanging rope. The second man weaved the flaccid hoop over Obediah's head and cinched the knot down on the back of his neck. As the two men lifted Obediah off his feet, the third man pulled down hard on the rope. Obediah struggled and kicked violently in the empty air. Saliva glistened in the moonlight as it came trickling out of his mouth onto his blotchy beard. The rope pulled in hard on his neck, cut his skin, and crushed his Adam's apple. Obediah's face turned bright red, contorted, then almost purple. His vision darkened and narrowed to a tunnel, then went black in his left eye. The men stood stoically watching, waiting for the struggling to end. Blood covered their captive's neck and was dripping from his bulging eye.

A loud crack rang out in the night. Obediah, and the limb from which he was suspended, came crashing down. The noise of the broken limb echoed out into the woods, and silence returned. The three men looked down on their motionless captive. They could hear Obediah's difficult, short breaths. The rope was still around his neck, and the broken limb lay across the lower half of his body. Blood dripped from Obediah's face and landed on the snow.

"Should we haul him back up another limb?"

"Let him go."

"He'll live, though," said the man with both hands still gripping the rope.

"Not likely."

"We made all the effort. It'd be nice to see him dead."

"Let's go."

The man dropped the rope, and all three returned to their horses and rode off in the direction from which they had come.

Obediah was awoken from his unconsciousness by a biting pain in his neck and the cold of the snow on his face. He struggled to his knees. His hands were still tied behind him and the rope was around his neck. He rolled over the low snowbank onto the road, his breathing an involuntary quick panting. Confusion and panic were washing over him. He tried to take a deeper breath, but the air wouldn't come. The remaining vision in his right eye failed him, and he passed out again, falling face forward onto the edge of the snowy road.

On that dirty white slope, with the sterling moonlight on his back, for the second time, Obediah Bratton's short, 22 year-long life should have come to an end, nipped out by the elements while each of his organs spiraled down to a halt, but it did not.

3
Glostrup, Denmark
1941

The fat lady with the beard worked around the edges of a pore on her inner thigh. She could see the hair under the waxy plug of skin and she wanted, no she needed, to free it. With one leg up on the arm of the old maroon recliner she leaned back and strained to bend over the rolls of flesh on her torso. She prodded it gently with her long jaundiced thumbnail. With the concise pressure and accuracy of a surgeon, she forced the pore to give birth to a yellowish-brown plug of dirt and greasy sebum. With a second squeeze she brought forth a creamy custard afterbirth of puss, and the curly wet hair was reborn anew into the world.

"Shut the fuck up," she yelled over her shoulder. "You've been whimpering all night and I'm sick of hearing it."

She adjusted her stained underwear and took her foot down off the chair arm. She stroked the long straggly hairs on her cheek with the back of her fingers and turned to look at the gimp. "We're all sad he's gone, but enough's enough."

She would find out later that Otto Gillot Hort, the wondrous flying midget, the diminutive Danish devil, the daring dart, who died during the previous afternoon's performance, had been the gimp's clandestine lover for four wonderful years.

Earlier that day as Otto crouched into the human cannon, an untied leather bootlace lodged in a crack along the interior wall. When he was ejected with the smoke and powder, he spun sideways and fell short of the net by ten feet, breaking his neck on impact.

"I'm sorry, honey. Come over here. I know you're sad; we're all sad." The fat bearded lady stretched out her hand to the gimp, who limped to her like a hurt child. He curled up on her lap with his misshapen head between her hairy breasts and wept into her dress. The gimp wasn't only crying for the death of his lover, but because of what the ringmaster had said shortly after he was pronounced dead and they were deciding not to cancel the evening performance.

"The show must go on," he said. "The show must go on."

4
University of California at Los Angeles
Present Day

"Interesting," Marcus said, methodically scanning the bloody wood fragment under the lens of a microscope in his lab on campus.

"What is it?" Jack asked while anxiously looking over his shoulder.

"It's a bloody piece of wood!"

"Come on, dude, stop fucking with me," Jack said. "I've been on this thing for three days. I have nothing to go on here except for this splinter of wood."

"Nothing?"

"No. No ID on the body, no distinctive clothing, no face left. Except for the brand, no distinctive markings on the chipper."

"Alright, let's see what we have here."

Plants are strange. They have parts of their bodies that are completely dead, yet still functioning. The wood in a living tree is actually dead for the entire life of the tree and changes little even after the tree dies.

The thousand-year-old wood in the center of a thousand-year-old tree can remain unchanged as that tree begins to die and eventually fall. The body of that dead tree could wash down a whitewater river and out to sea and spend hundreds of salty monotonous years floating in giant circles in the Pacific gyre, like a ship in the night that eventually comes to grief on the shore of a distant island, only to bask in the tropical sun on the hot beach for several hundred more years. Some savage could come along and pick away at it with a rudimentary stone tool to gather enough of the tree's magnificent body to burn in a weary little fire. That half-burned fire and the unknowing humans sitting around it could then be buried by a wall of mud from a ghost tsunami from some distant earthquake. If all that happened, then thousands of years later, an archeologist could dig up the partially burned charcoal and identify the original tree.

"The wood's edges are dried and torn. The blood got on it much later."

"So?"

"So the wood must have been in the chipper a couple days before the person was put in it."

Marcus continued, "Since there are no seasons in the tropics, most tropical woods don't have growth rings in them, which are a tree's response to seasonal rain and temperature. When a tropical tree is grown in LA, which has seasons, albeit lame ones, the wood develops in a peculiar way."

"I don't get it. Do we have anything to go on?" Jack asked.

"This is clearly a piece of wood from a tree in the willow family. If it had a temperate growth ring pattern, I would have thought it was from a willow, but it doesn't. It has the growth pattern of a tree from the tropics."

"Does that mean anything in this case?" Jack asked.

Marcus smiled and said, "There's only one kind of tropical tree related to willows in LA, the Costa Rican Holly, *Olmediella betschleriana*, and they're mostly grown by collectors and in botanical gardens.

"Nice."

"We have a small line of them here, by the sculpture garden. Make some calls to botanical gardens, and I bet you'll find someone's missing a chipper."

5
Grajaú, Brazil
1930-1955

If one were to begin a question with: was there a human alive who has ever___? Or has there ever been a human who did___?, the answer is always yes, regardless of how those questions are completed. Billions of humans have lived out various lives—brief, insignificant, joyful lives—a quarter-million born and dying each day.

One may, for instance, ask, has a human ever been eaten by a snake? Has a human ever died in a pogo sticking accident? Has a human ever been born with a tail? Has a human ever made sweet, sweet love to a cantaloupe? The answer is always, yes.

Has a human ever died as roadkill? Has a human ever been hit by the indifferent bumper of a passing car and left to die on the pavement of the road shoulder, to rot and be picked apart by whatever scavengers pass by until their remains are nothing but bones and glistening sinew, like rust-colored taffy, inside torn clothing? One would think not. How could it be possible? A person missed by no one, rotting on the road? The scene of the accident untraveled by decent humans? Is it possible that someone could have died like that? The answer is always, yes.

Human roadkill wouldn't seem so unlikely after a visit to São Paulo, Brazil, in the 1940s and 1950s. The city, slow to recover from the widespread neighborhood bombings of the 1924 Tenente Revolt, had doubled in population between 1920 and 1940, without the necessary city services, infrastructure, or relevant law enforcement for such a population increase. Shantytowns stretched out in concentric rings from the dirty brick buildings of old town São Paulo. It was a city overcrowded with a swirling, sweaty, suffering, and striving mass of humans, a few short generations past the end of Brazil's brutal 300-year experiment with slavery, left to their own devices by coffee barons and the sugarcane and banana plantation owners.

Marcus Melter's grandfather, Joseph, came to São Paulo in the late 1930s from a dreary suburb of Munich, Germany. While still a teenager, his uncle told him of a South American timber-trading ship that left from the docks at Bremerhaven each March. There was work on the ship, and as a European, young Joseph would be granted a piece of land from the Brazilian government to help with what was called "bleaching the race." The Brazilian government was wary of the possibility that slaves brought from West Africa a century earlier would outnumber other ethnicities, and Europeans were enticed to Brazil with land.

Three springs after first hearing his uncle's story, Joseph Melter, who had earned a fair bit of money working on timber trading ships, stepped down the gangplank onto the docks at São Paulo. After a visit to city hall and payment of a nominal application fee, he was deeded a piece of the land outside the southern Grajaú region of São Paulo. There he met Mãe Paciência, Marcus's grandmother, a sixteen-year-old black girl whose freed slave parents had immigrated to São Paulo from the poor sugar-growing northwestern corner of Brazil. So happy were they to marry her off to a European that they paid him a hard-earned dowry of six burlap sacks filled with sweet manioc root, which Mãe lovingly prepared and Joseph graciously ate for the first six months of their marriage.

Each night, while muttering unintelligible German expletives, Joseph Melter made every effort to bleach Mãe Paciência's race, and in the summer of 1939, Marcus's father was born. Joseph Melter's bleach was weak and Marcus's father, Alexander Melter, was born black, as black as if he'd been secretly fathered by one of the men working for Joseph. Joseph's fears of a cuckolding were relieved by the baby boy's perfectly straight, slender nose and almond-shaped eyes. Joseph and Mãe went on to spawn several more hybrids of varying shades, but none as dark and none as beautiful as Alexander.

Life on the outskirts of São Paulo for a German farmer, his black wife, and their children was difficult at best. Joseph Melter's land grant was barely enough to support his family in hard times, and as World War II came to Brazil, it accentuated the poverty in São Paulo and put the farmlands at risk of being overrun by the starving masses in the nearby slums. With each report of yet another Brazilian ship sunk by a German U-boat submarine in the Southern Atlantic, Joseph Melter's paranoia and distrust of his fellow Brazilians heightened. As the war continued, food was rationed, commerce slowed, and the Melter family learned to survive on little.

These were the times in which Alexander Melter lived his first years, surrounded by degrading poverty and the fear and paranoia of his father. In 1952, at age fourteen, he found the remains of the July 1st, 1946 issue of Life magazine. Its greasy color drawings of women in bikinis on the beaches of Southern California hit him like a revelation. The coincidental magazine discovery and his recent entrance into the puzzling and shameful world of puberty were almost too much for young Alex to bear. He kept that magazine hidden, and a small fire ignited in him for a place called Los Angeles; a fire that apparently existed in his penis, which he stoked regularly and vigorously.

The magazine solidified his vague idea of escaping Brazil. He was neither German, nor was he truly Brazilian, not white nor black, and had always been treated differently because of it. Now the bikini-clad women reclining on their beach towels under tall palms in the golden Santa Monica afternoon provided him with a clearly defined destination.

Along with his strikingly attractive features, Alex Melter was graced with natural intelligence, good humor, and a mild detachment from the world around him, all traits he would eventually pass on to his son. These traits made him sought after by his peers. The less Alex seemed to care about their companionship, the more they tried to impress him.

He was sixteen when some friends led him to a scene that would reinforce Alex's desire to escape Brazil. They brought him out past the unfinished masonry, rogue power lines, and corrugated steel of the local slum to a discovery they had made the previous day. Lying twisted half in the ditch, half on the exposed red dirt of the road shoulder, was a rotted human body. A shudder moved through Alex in the moments after he realized that the pile of hair and dried skin were the remains of a human. He looked down into the brown face of the corpse, and the open eyes with their raisin eyeballs stared through him at the sky.

A car had struck this person low and hard across the waist, which had broken and distorted the hips and several lower ribs, leaving some intestines exposed through a large gash. In the crotch area, the clothing was twisted and torn open by the impact of the bumper. Some animal had come by, possibly a rat, and partially ate the inner thighs. As the body dried and shrunk in the sun, the teeth marks were well preserved.

Unanswered questions about how a person could come to rot in such a public place troubled Alex. Why had no one claimed the body or buried it? Was the victim still alive while being eaten? He, too, was guilty of gawking at the body, but not reporting it to anyone. Was all of Brazil so busy trying to survive each day that they would step over the rotting remains of human roadkill?

The thought of that body, its leathery skin stretched over slender bones, was there as a reminder of where he didn't want to be. The scene of the human roadkill was still clear in his mind two years later while feeling the dull pains of loneliness and fear in the cargo bay of a ship leaving his family and São Paolo for Manzanillo, Mexico. The memory stayed strong during his years working on fishing boats in Mazatlán, where during his daily walks to the dock, he occasionally saw a dead animal lying on the roadside. Alex's mental images of that body finally faded several years later as he lay under a tarp in the bed of an old pickup truck, crossing the U.S. border south of San Diego, headed for the beaches and women of Los Angeles.

6
Westwood, California
Present Day

"What'd you find out?" Marcus asked Jack.

They were at the bar of D'Amores Pizza in Westwood, where they regularly met for lunch. D'Amores served Jack's desire to be surrounded by UCLA undergrads and inexpensively buy Marcus a slice while discussing the details of cases.

Marcus sat on a stool facing the window out to the street, eating his pizza, and Jack was standing next to him with his back to the bar.

"I think I called every botanical garden in LA following up on your tree. They all thought I was crazy and no one was missing a chipper."

"Did you try our campus? Remember I told you we have a line of the Costa Rican Hollies near the sculpture garden."

"No, who should I call?"

"Hold on," Marcus said while looking at his cell phone. "Call this guy. Scott Truebly, he's the head of campus grounds."

"Okay, I'll be right back."

Jack stepped out into the golden midday sun to dial the number, while Marcus turned his attention to his remaining pizza.

A few minutes later, Jack returned to the bar, smiling. "Guess what? The guy can't find one of their three chippers."

"What do you mean he can't find it?" Marcus asked. "How do you lose a chipper?"

"That's what he said. Missing. Can you believe it? That was a UCLA chipper with the dead guy in it. Good call, dude. Apparently the gate on the storage yard was fine, with the lock on it, and no one on his crew knew where it was."

"Who had access to the storage yard?"

"He said all the grounds workers have a key. One of them, some new guy, hasn't shown up for work in a week." Jack looked at the notepad he had scribbled on during his phone call. "One Lars Ostergard.

His last reported address was over in the valley. Reseda."

"That might be your guy."

"I know. It's the first real break I've had since catching this case. I'm going to look in on Ostergard tomorrow. You should come with me."

"Sounds good to me," Marcus said. "Don't you guys have rules against working on a case with a civilian?" Marcus smirked. They'd had many versions of this same conversation.

"Oh, I'm sure we do." Jack smiled. "But if I take you, we might actually get something done," Jack said, scanning the room, no longer looking at Marcus.

"See those two girls at the table by the register? They've been looking over here at us for the last couple minutes."

Marcus swiveled nonchalantly on his stool, pretended to look around the pizza shop, and saw two dark-haired women in their early twenties; young, attractive, and laughing. When he looked in their direction, one of them smiled, made eye contact with him, and turned to say something to her friend.

"Watch this," Jack said with a tone in his voice filled with bravado, which Marcus had come to enjoy over the years. Jack's willingness to enter the fray of any given situation was typically preceded by those two words; watch this. It was the same *watch this* Jack said to Marcus many times during college. It was the same *watch this* that Marcus heard before Jack won a bet by eating eight bags of WOW Brand Olestra fat substitute potato chips in ten minutes. The label on the side of the bag read: This product contains Olestra and may cause loose stool, especially after excessive consumption in a short period of time.

"There's no need to bother them. Maybe we should just finish our pizza." Marcus said, suspecting that some Jack Bratton variety of embarrassing situation may soon befall him.

Jack was already stepping away from the bar saying loudly "Hey, yeah you, hey, ladies, come over here," nodding, waving, and pointing at the two young women. Although ladies, when used improperly, can be one of the creepiest words in the English language, Jack seemed to be able to pull it off in a clueless, almost cute way.

The two women stood from their table and walked toward Jack and Marcus. The one who had made eye contact and smiled at Marcus reluctantly trailed her friend. Jack returned to his position leaning back, with his elbows up on the bar. His white Oxford button-down was tucked into a pair of khakis, his yellow tie was loose, with his police badge displayed prominently on the front side of his leather belt. Marcus was now turned on his stool facing the approaching women. He sat up straight.

"We saw you looking over here."

"That's right," answered one of the women without hesitation, barely taking the time to look the two of them over. She made a brief fake smile at Jack and didn't seem intimidated by him nor particularly interested. She was wearing a tight, gray button-down sweater, with the top three buttons undone. Her breasts were prominent enough to make it difficult for Jack to maintain eye contact while speaking with her. When she smiled, slight wrinkles in her young skin formed two inward-facing crescent moons just outside the corners of her mouth.

"Are you UCLA students?" Jack asked.

"Yeah, are you guys?" she responded, looking down at the badge on Jack's belt, then turned to look at Marcus. She stuck out her hand to him and said, "I'm Stephanie."

"I'm Marcus. This is my friend Jack."

"I'm a detective in the LAPD," Jack said, seeing that Stephanie was entirely focused on Marcus. "Homicide." Jack was shaking her hand, but she was looking at Marcus.

"Sounds exciting," Stephanie said with a sarcastic tone.

"Well maybe, but there's lots of paperwork. You know, intellectual stuff," he responded.

Stephanie smiled and asked Marcus, "What about you? What do you do?"

"Why are you asking him that? You know what he does," said the second girl to Stephanie. She had been standing behind her friend during the conversation, but now stepped forward and extended her hand to Marcus while saying, "Dr. Melter, I had you for intro botany two years ago. Amy Butler; do you remember me?"

"You had him?" asked Jack under his breath.

Marcus smiled and said, "Oh, there's always so many students in the lecture. Sorry I didn't recognize you. How did the class go for you?"

She had a star-struck and mischievous look in her eyes, like she had just seen Tom Cruise buying a pack of adult diapers at the local drug store. "I loved that class, you were great," said Amy.

"I bet he was great," Jack said.

"What?" said Stephanie.

"Nothing," Jack replied.

"Thank you. I'm glad you liked the class. We'll let you go back to your lunch now," Marcus said, turning his glance to Jack.

"Of course, you two could join us for dinner tonight, if you're interested," Jack said.

"Although we'd love to, we can't. It's laundry night," replied Stephanie.

"Okay, we'll let you go then," Jack said quickly. After a brief and awkward silence the two girls returned to their table.

Marcus said to Jack, "You gave up on that one easily. Uncharacteristic of you. Was it because she was one of my students?"

"Are you kidding? No. They had to do laundry tonight." When Jack said laundry he made two large quotation signs in the air with his fingers.

"So?" Marcus asked.

"So, that's code. It can only mean one of two things. They're lesbians or they're on their periods," Jack said. "I thought you were hipper than that."

"You're ridiculous," replied Marcus.

"Whatever; I know what I'm talking about."

"Right," Marcus said.

"When do you want to go to Reseda tomorrow?"

"Let's go early. Pick me up at seven at my house and don't be late."

"Late? You know I'm never late," Jack said as Marcus shook his head.

7
Century City, California
Present Day

Jack Bratton awoke from a deep sleep and sat on the side of his bed, with his elbows on his knees and his head in his hands. A day that would end poorly for him began like most others. Thoughts came unhurriedly to him about what day it was and what he was supposed to accomplish. It was 6:54 AM. He had hit the snooze button on his alarm six times, and the bright blue light of the Los Angeles basin slid through slits in vertical, white plastic blinds.

Jack lived alone in a sparsely furnished apartment in Century City. Home furnishings didn't occur to him as important. Anything in the apartment that wasn't of utilitarian value was the result of a visit to the Burbank Ikea taken against his will with an overzealous girlfriend, now ex-girlfriend, in her futile attempt to domesticate him.

Jack was tall, with a fair complexion and blond hair, with just a hint of strawberry to it. The sharp curves of his bulky shoulders, which had been so prominent in college, were now softened, giving him the appearance of being slightly overweight. Jack was strong, but lumbering, and a little doughy; features that many women found attractive, but that other men felt compelled to mock. His eyes were hooded, his forehead proud, his teeth white and straight, and his smile was clear. He had learned to carry himself upright with confidence and authority, even if at times he didn't feel endowed with either.

After his unhurried morning rituals Jack picked up Marcus fifty minutes late. They drove north on the 405 Freeway into the San Fernando Valley. Jack was distracted by his hunger, and a vision floated into his mind as they drove. A large breasted waitress wearing a low-cut V-neck T-shirt of thin material that exposed the perfect skin of her cleavage would place a huge omelet on the fake wood Formica table in front of him. Nat's Early Bite Coffee Shop in Valley Glen was the nearest location to realize his vision, so he talked Marcus into stopping for breakfast. Nat's turkey, bacon, cheddar, and avocado omelet didn't disappoint, although it was brought to their booth by an unshaven middle-aged man in a dirty apron. As the man bent to pick up a used napkin that had fallen from an adjacent table he revealed to Jack the less than perfect skin and cleavage of his ass crack.

With Jack's morning vision half-realized, they drove toward Wyandotte Street in Reseda. Although Reseda sits in the low, fertile center of a beautiful valley named after the celebrated Saint Ferdinand, it is crowded with ugly little houses hastily built in the late sixties, and those on Wyandotte were no exception. This was a working-class San Fernando Valley neighborhood, nothing charming about it. Jack drove slowly while Marcus checked addresses until they arrived at 18900 and pulled the metallic blue Crown Victoria to the empty curb opposite the house. With the car's engine still running, Jack checked his watch to see that it was 9:20 AM.

The Wyandotte house was a typical Reseda architectural abomination. The one-story house had a light brown Dutch hip roof with wide overhangs and bulky eaves, giving the house the look of a rotten mushroom. A white RV camper trailer sat in the concrete driveway. The property was clean, with no obvious signs that someone was living there. Except for the grass on the front lawn and a lone thirty-foot tall Mexican fan palm in the back corner, the property was without landscaping.

"You stay here. I'll knock on the front door," Jack said to Marcus, while turning off the car.

He stepped out of the car and slammed the door just in time to look up and see a blond man in a white tank top and blue sweat pants exiting the trailer parked in the driveway. He was carrying a propane tank. Upon hearing Jack's car door, the man looked up at Jack and saw the badge and gun on his belt. He dropped the empty tank he was carrying and turned to run. The noise from the metal tank hitting the concrete driveway was still ringing out as he disappeared along the right side of the house.

Jack scanned the front yard. He put a hand out to Marcus to signal to him to stay in the car, drew his gun, and yelled, "Hey, stop right there."

Holding his gun in front of him, he pursued cautiously. As he came around the right side of the house he saw the man's back as he jumped over the tall wooden fence into the adjacent backyard. By the time Jack got to the wooden fence, holstered his gun, and pulled himself up to look over it, the man was gone. Jack was panting, mouth open, with a toothpick still stuck to his lower lip from breakfast.

As Jack stepped down off the fence and turned back toward the house he saw the brief flash of a wooden 2 × 4 swinging toward his face. As the board met his forehead with a dull thud, he saw electric white light, then darkness.

8
Washington County, Arkansas
1905

Obediah Bratton lay unconscious on the snowy road bank, his lungs still drawing shallow breaths, for all of forty minutes, when Uncle John McAlester came by, returning from town in the wooden bucket of his heavy one-horse cart. After Uncle John lit a lantern and surveyed the scene of the failed hanging, he slipped the noose from Obediah's neck and lifted his limp body, with much difficulty, onto the open back of the cart and continued toward home.

Obediah recovered from his near hanging on the living room floor of Uncle John's cabin. The sight never returned to his left eye, his head had a permanent dull ache, and for the remaining ten years of his short life, as air passed over his broken windpipe, his voice came forth as a low, breathy growl.

Uncle John McAlester lived on a wooded lot in southern Washington County, a short distance from where he had found Obediah. He was a skilled carpenter and devout Christian, who never remarried when, many years earlier, his wife died of a fever on the wide floorboards of their half-built cabin shortly after they were wed.

Out of some combination of loneliness and a pious call to serve the less fortunate, Uncle John allowed Obediah to share his cabin and work with him after his long recovery. Even though Obediah was slow and careless in his work and took Uncle John's patient suggestions begrudgingly, he helped Obediah build himself a small cabin in the back portion of the McAlester lot.

Several years after his aborted hanging, Obediah met Minnie Holmsley, the rebellious daughter of the Washington County postmaster. Against the objections of her father, whom she had grown to vehemently hate, Minnie moved to Obediah's cabin. In the fall of 1910, as the trees on the Ozarks' western edge once again turned a brilliant red in preparation for feeding the awaiting worms, Levi

Bratton was born. Minnie birthed him in a pool of lukewarm water and blood in the claw-foot bathtub on the cabin's freshly built wooden back porch. It was a difficult, breech birth, with a labor long enough for Uncle John to fetch a midwife from Fayetteville. Levi's strenuous entrance into the world, which Minnie barely survived, left her without the ability to conceive another child.

During Levi's early years on the McAlester lot, Obediah was around less and less frequently. Obediah would come home to the cabin after he was gone for days, sometimes weeks at a time, either with a new suit of clothes and gifts for Minnie and Levi, or scraggly and beaten up, like he'd been on the run. He would beat on Minnie for the slightest transgressions while the boy watched.

On one of his longer stays, Obediah hatched a plan, which had been incubating in his slow mind for years.

"You know he's got all them folded bills squirreled away in that case under his bed," Obediah said to Minnie as they lay awake in bed.

"He's a kind old man who don't mean us any harm," Minnie replied.

"It doesn't matter. That's enough money for you, me, and the boy to move on and live proper, somewhere nice."

"It ain't our money, and besides, I don't want to move on. I like it here, and Levi's gunna start school soon," Minnie said.

"Well, it ain't up to you," Obediah said, then he was silent.

Several weeks later, on a warm night in early October, shortly after Levi's seventh birthday, Obediah lay in bed waiting for everyone to fall asleep. Bright moonlight streamed through the small windows of the one-room cabin as he quietly left Minnie and little Levi asleep in bed. He walked along the narrow path by the light of the moon toward Uncle John's house. For no apparent reason, he stopped halfway and looked up at the moon through a clearing in the pines. A concentric ring of light, half again the radius of the moon, faint and frayed, clung to its outer edge.

Obediah could hear Uncle John snoring as he crept onto the back porch and quietly opened the unlocked door. Uncle John's deep sleep wasn't disturbed by the creak in the floorboards as Obediah approached his bed. He lifted the pillow near Uncle John's head, and as he placed it over his face, he bore down on him with all his weight. Uncle John struggled violently under Obediah, but his arms were trapped under the sheet.

Obediah was lying nearly horizontal on Uncle John, bearing down hard on him, waiting for the old man to suffocate, when a hot flash of pain shot through his back. He turned to see Minnie standing over him, her eyes and mouth wide open. He reached feebly for the kitchen knife that she had plunged into his upper back. He gasped for air and coughed a mouthful of blood onto the bed. Uncle John took a deep breath as he pushed Obediah onto the floor. Obediah lay there still, gulping for air, suffocating on the blood filling his lungs. A bewildered look crossed his face as he gazed up at Uncle John, at Minnie, then at the seven-year-old Levi, who had seen the whole scene from the corner of the room behind his mother; then Obediah Bratton was gone.

9
Reseda, California
Present Day

Jack regained consciousness slowly and painfully on the backyard lawn of the house in Reseda. He'd been unconscious for several minutes and was dazed and confused as he awoke. He lay on his back for a few seconds, looking up at the tall palm tree arching into the bright blue morning sky above him. He wondered if trees could see, what that palm would have witnessed over the last few minutes. He had a vague sense during the time of his partial recovery of consciousness that the tree was watching him. It was a silent witness to all the ridiculous activities of the desperate creatures below. As that realization faded permanently from his mind, Jack saw the backlit face of Marcus, saying something.

It took him some time to regain his ability to hear anything or remember why he was lying on his back. An aching pain spread out across his forehead. He felt the humidity of the lawn, and the steamy smell of dog shit wafted up around him. His hearing faded back in.

"Hey, hey, hey," Marcus kept repeating. "Wake up, are you okay?" Marcus knelt over him pushing on his shoulder. "What happened? I saw you take off. I waited. I shouldn't have waited."

"It's fine."

"Are you alright? Should I call someone?"

"Help me up." Jack's voice cracked as he said the words and his own voice sounded foreign to him.

Marcus helped Jack to his feet. He was shaky at first but regained his steadiness momentarily. He reached for his gun, which was still in its holster, and quickly looked around the backyard.

"What happened?" asked Marcus.

"I got hit with that piece of wood," Jack replied, pointing to the abandoned 2 × 4, the length of a baseball bat, on the lawn next to them. "Did you see anybody come out the front of the house?"

"No. Nobody."

"What did you see?" Jack asked.

"Nothing. I got out of the car and came around back to look for you and found you lying there."

"The second guy, the one who hit me, must have jumped the back fence, too. Come on, let's get back to the car."

Once they were seated in the Crown Victoria, Jack probed his forehead with two fingers. "Goddammit, that hurts," he whispered to himself.

"Shouldn't we call for backup or something?" asked Marcus.

"No, we're going to search that camper and the house," replied Jack.

"You sure that's a good idea? What if somebody is still here?"

"There isn't anybody still here. We'll be careful," Jack said while reaching into the glove compartment box for a bottle of ibuprofen. He swallowed a handful of four pills without water and stepped out into the street next to the car. He opened the trunk of the car and extracted a large black flashlight.

"You can stay here if you want."

"No way. I'm not sitting out here while you get knocked out again."

Marcus followed him across the street, up the driveway, to the entrance of the trailer. Jack unbuttoned the holster of his handgun and knocked loudly on the metal door with the flashlight. The thin aluminum of the door rang out and caved in around the heavy flashlight with each knock. When no answer came, Jack turned the handle and pulled the door open. Two steps led up into cramped living quarters, which smelled of cooked beef and onions. Jack stepped into the trailer while Marcus held the door open.

He could see the remnants of a half-cooked meal on a Coleman camp stove. Dirty clothes lay on the built-in bed, and there were others on the floor. A small sink was full of dirty dishes. A booth table and upholstered bench sat on the opposite end of the trailer from the bed. A pair of jeans with the leather belt still in them lay on the bench.

"What do you see?" asked Marcus, looking around behind him toward the car, still holding the door open.

"This dude lived in squalor," Jack replied.

Jack went through the pockets of the jeans and laid out their contents on the table. "Here's his wallet. Lars Ostergard," Jack said, flashing the California driver's license at Marcus. "Also a UCLA staff badge.

Here, check to see if this works on the door."

Marcus grabbed the key, slid it into the lock on the outside of the trailer door, and it turned smoothly. "Yup. What's the address on his driver's license?"

"18900 Wyandotte," Jack replied.

"Strange. Why would he be living in a trailer in the driveway?" Marcus asked.

"I don't know. We'll check the house next," replied Jack.

"What's that?" Marcus asked, pointing to a green neon work vest hanging on the post near the bed.

"Probably the guy's work vest at UCLA."

"I don't think so. Not that color. Grab it and throw it over here," Marcus said.

Jack pulled the vest from the hook and threw it to Marcus. In black writing on the back of the vest read Solina, with a large oval around the letters.

Jack stepped back down out of the trailer into the midday sun. He leaned unsteadily against the door as he closed it and touched his forehead gently with his fingers.

"You okay? Do you need to sit down?" asked Marcus.

"I'll be alright, just a little light-headed. Let's check the main house."

Jack crossed the upper portion of the driveway from the trailer to the front door and tried the handle. Locked. They circled around the house, where the 2 × 4 still lay on the lawn near the fence. The back door was also locked. By peering through a crack in the poorly fitting blinds, they could see an empty kitchen inside. Jack stood back and gave the door a hard, swift kick. He grunted as the heel of his shoe landed firmly six inches below the handle. A crack formed along the wooden frame, and Jack's second kick pounded the door open, sending a shard of wood onto the linoleum floor inside.

As soon as the door flew open Jack and Marcus both smelled it.

There are three categories of foul smells immediately recognizable by the human nose. Millions of years of evolution and selection have created a keen sense of revulsion to these three types of smells in normal humans. Those without this innate sense got sick, didn't reproduce, and were selected out of the gene pool long ago. One; the smell of feces. Shit is dangerous and full of things that will make a person sick. Flatulence, rotten eggs, and other nastiness containing a significant level of hydrogen sulfide all fall into this category. Two; the smell of vomit. Vomit and other humans vomiting means illness, move away, immediately. Some rotten foods, dairy products, and anything with butyric acid falls into this category.

What they smelled when the door flew open was in the third category; decomposing flesh—an altogether different type of bad smell than vomit or shit, but so easily recognizable; roadkill, gangrene, death.

10
Bakersfield, California
1936

Walnuts are California's heritage. Not the sinister little half brains that go about their business ruining perfectly good brownies, cookies, and other dessert items, but the wood; that fragrant, maroon, hard, yet easy to carve wood. The large nuts come from the English walnut, but the wonderful wood, that is purely Californian. Deep in the San Joaquin Valley, where walnut trees grow in endless rows, the English walnut's roots are too feeble for the tree to prosper in the rich New World soils. The California black walnut, however, evolved in the San Joaquin and grows vigorously in the chocolate loam. Even though the tree produces such wonderful lumber, California walnuts are smaller than a cat's testicles, equally as shriveled, and probably more bitter on the tongue.

Human ingenuity and the miracle of grafting eventually spawned a tree that produces the vigorous roots and beautiful wood of the California black walnut and a cash crop of large nuts from the English walnut. When two trees are young, their trunks no wider than pencils, they can be forcefully joined. An English walnut branch is skillfully inserted into the top of a California walnut stem. In a short time, their tissues grow together, and the two are married for life—a perverted and unnatural chimera of two species. Abundant nuts are reaped as the unnatural love children of these unlikely unions.

In the walnut's marriage, the Californian is the workhorse; no glory, just work, a vigorous life beneath the soil, searching and searching for water and nutrients, transporting them heavenward into the body of the English walnut that rides on his back. The English walnut is pruned, sprayed, picked, cleaned, and doted over, while the workhorse chugs away down below, his body in complete darkness, fending off fungi, nematodes, and the occasional mole. That life of toil in service of the English walnut makes the California walnut hard, gives him character; beauty earned through adversity.

Like a Japanese sword maker, pounding and turning steel, the constant weight of the English walnut misshapes the California walnut below it. Eventually, the point of their awkward union, their life-long attachment and conflict, begins to swell and expand. In his attempts to push upward under her weight, the California walnut swirls and interlocks on himself, the density of his wood ever increasing. From this marital quarrel, which rages across the decades, a ground-level California walnut burl is formed—a swelling of twisted wood with unequaled beauty. The dense, purple, sinuous wood of a California walnut burl makes the best gunstock.

The old man knows all this, as he sits hunched over a stool behind his bench, rubbing Danish oil into the newly shaped California walnut shotgun gunstock. The dry wood pulls the liquid in greedily. As it fills the hollow cells, the wood takes on a luminescent glow. He sees the iridescence as he turns the stock under the single light bulb above the bench in his small shop.

He hears someone step onto the front landing and returns the half-oiled gunstock to his bench. He reaches under it to feel for the Colt .45 that sits on a shelf. A ring comes from the bell.

He takes a long breath, keeping his hand steady on the gun, and yells, "Come in, it's open."

A tall, dark-haired man of about thirty in denim work clothes cautiously pulls open the door of the shop and steps inside. He looks around briefly and sees that the old man is alone.

"Glad you're still open. Sorry to come by so late."

"Stand over here closer so I can take a look at you," says the old man, raising the Colt into clear view of his visitor.

The young man lifts his hands and steps under the light bulb where his proud brow casts dark shadows in his eye sockets. "I was sent here by Jim Johnson at the general store down on Main. I was told you sell guns."

"Jim sure likes to run his damn mouth." After a long pause he says, "Hand me that knife on your belt. Careful now."

The young man reluctantly slides the weapon from the leather scabbard on his belt and places it gently on the bench.

The old man returns the Colt to its hiding place behind his bench. "Sorry to be anxious, son. I seen a faint halo 'round the moon earlier tonight, which always puts me on edge. My grandma said them halos were bad omens. I think she was right 'bout that. Something terrible always seems to happen when they're around."

"No problem. Just lookin' to buy a gun."

"You see that halo?"

"I didn't, sir."

"Hmmm. Maybe I'm wrong. Sure as shit think I saw it though."

"Well I wasn't looking for it, so maybe you did."

"If you see one of them, you're dancin' with damnation, or will be soon."

"Yes, sir."

"This here's an interesting knife," says the old man, twirling it in his hands. "What do you know about it?"

"Not much. Got it from an old man who watched out after my mama and me when my father died, back in Arkansas. He was like a grandpa to me. Said he got it from a man who got it from a man who was a well-known blacksmith."

"Arkansas, huh?" says the old man, more interested than before.

"Yup, Arkansas."

"I spent my life makin' and repairin' guns, but I much prefer a well-made knife. The thing about guns, even though they's useful tools for certain situations, they ain't discreet. If discretion is what you seek, and you should in most matters, a little skill and a razor-sharp blade is all you need."

"I was hopin' you'd be able to sell me a handgun."

"A handgun?" replies the old man, laughing a little to himself. "You want a handgun? Everybody wants a handgun. Sure, I could sell you one, got plenty of them lying around; just don't know if I want to. Let me tell you a bit about this knife of yours. Maybe you'd be interested in a trade."

"Yes, sir."

"What we got here is a Bowie knife, the handgun of knives. Your knife comes from a long history of man killin' knives. They ain't got no intended function outside winnin' a fight and effectively killin' a man. You may have this knife because your granddaddy gave it to you, but that knife exists because of a long line of hard men looking for a better way to win a fight."

The old man moves a thumb along the distance of the knife-edge. "Looks like it ain't been sharpened properly in years. Bet you been usin' it as a can opener. It don't matter. You see right here, how the tip of the blade tapers along the back and is sharp on both sides? That's called a concave clip point. You see how it looks like a little sword, balances nicely in the hand, the cross guard at the base of the blade protects your hand in a fight."

The old man pauses, pulls a cigarette out of the front pocket of his flannel shirt, lights it with purpose, and takes a long drag.

"Supposedly Bowie ground down an old file to make the first version of this knife. Bowie's brother, Jim Bowie, got ahold of it and used it in a duel on a sandbar in Natchez, Mississippi, killin' several famous men with it, making himself and the knife popular in the process. Jim Bowie had a blacksmith make him a fine version of that old file knife, which was still on his hip when he died at the Alamo a few years later, but that's beside the point. That blacksmith made hundreds of them, improvin' a little on each one, some of the finest knives ever made. My guess is that what you got here, son, is one of the original Bowie knives, probably from the 1850s or 60s. I only seen one other in my life. Don't know how your granddaddy ended up with it, but a lot of them old timers in Arkansas had one lyin' around."

Leaving the knife sitting on his bench, the old man reaches into a drawer behind him. "This here's a Smith and Wesson .22 revolver. Ain't worth shit compared to that knife of yours, and it's a whole hell of a lot less discreet. Smith and Wesson made a million of these. They're loud and ain't that powerful, but they work every time."

The young man picks up the revolver and studies it. "A .22 revolver. It'll do. How much you want?"

"I ain't sellin' you no handgun. Don't have a license to sell guns in this town. I'll make a trade for your knife, though. You sure you need a gun that bad, son? You'd be a fool to trade me your knife for this revolver," says the old man.

"You got bullets to go with it?"

"Yup, got a box right here," says the old man, rifling through the drawer below his bench.

The young man picks up his knife once more, and for the last time, runs the flat side of the blade across the palm of his hand. "Nice to know the history of it. Wish I would have known that stuff before. Wouldn't have changed much, but woulda been nice to know." After a long pause, the young man says, "Alright, it's yours."

While shaking his head, the old man takes the knife and slides the .22 and box of bullets across the bench. "Might as well give me that scabbard, too."

The young man slides the leather scabbard off his belt, re-buckles it, puts the box of bullets into one pocket of his overcoat and the gun in the other.

"Thank you, sir."

"Now you don't get in any trouble out there, you hear. You're under a halo," the old man says.

As the door to his shop closes once again he stares down at the knife, still shaking his head. "Somethin' ain't right with the world these days. The country ain't like it used to be," he quietly says to himself.

Placing the knife to the side, he picks up the walnut gunstock and begins to oil it once again. As the swirling iridescence of the chocolate wood continues to reveal itself he smiles and takes refuge from the world in a thing well-made from material forged by suffering.

11
Reseda, California
Present Day

It was such an intense smell that Jack wondered how he hadn't smelled it before. As soon as it reached him, he reconsidered entering the house. To move farther in the direction of that smell was to fight against some deep human nature.

"Watch yourself," Jack said to Marcus with a look of disgust. He covered his nose with his hand. "Stay here in the back, and I'll look in the front rooms."

"What do you mean, watch myself?"

"Just stay here, you'll be fine."

Jack proceeded cautiously with his gun drawn through the kitchen and down the hallway in the center of the house toward the bedrooms. Off the hallway were two bedrooms, one on each side, and a bathroom. All the doors were closed to the hallway. To the side of the kitchen was a carpeted living room area, completely devoid of any furniture.

Jack opened the first bedroom door, stepped inside, and slid back the mirrored closet door to see that it was empty. He moved back into the hallway to the next door, opened it, and saw an empty bathroom without a shower curtain. The intensity of the smell increased as he approached the remaining room. He became aware, briefly, that his head throbbed and an aching pain stretched down across the back of his neck. With his gun in one hand, he reached for the handle with the other and pushed open the door.

Jack had seen dead bodies before, many of them, and this one was no different. A wave of intense smell hit him as he pushed the door all the way open. In the middle of the carpeted floor lay a body that had been decomposing in the warmth of the Southern California fall for several weeks. The body was face up with its arms crossed over the chest. The mouth and eyes were wide open, as if he'd lain on his back in the middle of a room, saw something surprising on the ceiling, and never got up. The skin on the hands and face, the only skin visible, was purplish-brown and shiny.

As a body decomposes, all the cells are initially poisoned and acidified by high levels of carbon dioxide no longer exhaled. Enzymes, which continue to work after death, digest and rupture cell membranes causing tissues to liquefy and leak. All the rich fats in the membranes begin to melt and putrefy. This process had softened the body, which leaked and spread out an aura of brown stain on the light blue carpet. This greasy caramel-colored halo left where an undiscovered body decomposes has come to be known by some coroners as the grandma glow.

Jack holstered his gun and stood looking at the body for as long as he could stand the smell, then turned to walk back into the hallway. As he turned, Marcus was standing in the doorway.

"Dude, you scared the shit out of me. I thought you were still in the kitchen."

"I wasn't going to stay back there," Marcus said, looking at the body. He lifted his hand to his mouth.

"This guy's clearly been dead a while, though obviously not long enough for the smell to die. Looks like a white guy, maybe in his forties."

"Look, he's still got his wedding band and watch on."

"Yeah, and no blood or anything. No real obvious signs of what killed him either."

"Did you check for identification?" Marcus asked.

"No, we'd have to roll the body to get his wallet. We shouldn't touch anything yet. Come on, let's get back to the car. Now I need to call this in."

Jack left the bedroom, unlocked the front door, and went out, leaving it wide open. Marcus paused briefly at the doorway of the bedroom to look again at the body, then turned and followed Jack out onto the sunny driveway.

"Weird that the house was totally empty. Strangely clean," Marcus said once they were back in the car.

"Yeah, and who was the second guy? The one who hit me. No sign of him at all."

12

An unmarked Crown Victoria similar to Jack's rolled down Wyandotte. A uniformed officer lifted the police line so the car could drive under it, then up on to the driveway next to the camper trailer. As the car arrived Jack was talking to a young female officer on the front lawn, retelling his story and rubbing his head while Marcus sat waiting in the front seat.

Jorge Vargas, a large Hispanic man with slumping shoulders, stepped out of the car. His white collared shirt fit poorly, and he had to work constantly to keep it tucked. Certain body shapes were never meant for modern men's clothing. He pulled up his pants and slid a hand under his belt as he exited the vehicle.

Vargas spoke in a sarcastic tone with a kind smile, "Bratton, what did you do this time? The commander sent me over to take care of another one of your messes." Vargas was a hard-working, skeptical, and thorough detective. He had an instantly recognizable kindness and patience about him.

"LA's finest," Jack said. "Really, thank you for coming out here to save me. Now that you're here some real police work can happen."

Vargas turned to the female officer and put his arm over Jack's shoulder and asked, "You know this guy's a real hero? More cases solved than anyone who's been a detective for the same amount of time? Can't seem to work by himself, though. Always brings along his professor friend who does the thinking for him."

They turned to see Marcus crossing the road to join them.

"How's it going, Professor? You solve this one yet?"

"I'm good, Jorge. How you doing?"

"Good enough. Let's take a look," Vargas said, gesturing toward the house.

"Alright," Jack replied, then turning to the young woman said, "We'll talk more later."

Jack and Vargas began up the driveway toward the front door. Vargas called to Marcus, "Come on, Professor, you might as well see it, too."

"No, it's okay. I already saw it. You go ahead without me."

The two detectives entered the house, past a uniformed officer at the door and into the front bedroom. All the windows in the house had been opened, and the smell of rotten flesh had gone out into the dry valley air. The flash from a crime scene photographer's camera momentarily lit up the room as they entered. Vargas put on a pair of blue vinyl gloves and offered a second pair to Jack.

Vargas squatted next to the body. He poked it on the hip to test its solidity, then with two hands, he rolled the dead man onto his side. As Vargas rolled the body, Jack could hear the faint sound of air escaping the dead man's lungs. Vargas reached into the back pocket of the brown chinos, extracted a black leather wallet, and handed it to Jack.

"James Lindster, born September 14, 1970. The address on the driver's license is on Pico, near Mid City," Jack said. He paused while reading a second card in the wallet. "Wow, this guy's a government employee. He's an investigator at the EPA. Says right here on his ID badge."

"The EPA, no shit," Vargas said, looking up at Jack. "I'm sure he's got a missing person's report then. Let's call it in."

"What happened to your forehead?" Vargas asked Jack.

"I came here following a lead on another case. Chased a suspect into the backyard. Out of nowhere somebody hit me with a piece of wood."

"Did you get a look at him?" asked Vargas.

"No. Didn't see him at all before I got hit." Jack said and touched his red forehead gently.

Vargas nodded, looked down at the body, and snapped off his latex gloves. "Let's check the rest of the house and the trailer and get this place printed and cleaned up. You better get looked at, make sure you're not going to become retarded or something."

The two men left the house by the front door, and Jack rejoined Marcus on the lawn while Vargas made a phone call.

"The dead guy worked for the EPA," Jack said to Marcus.

"Really?"

"We got something on James Lindster," Vargas said after his short phone call. "He was reported missing by his wife a week or so ago. He was last seen in his office at EPA headquarters downtown. We'll look into that tomorrow."

"Sounds good," Jack said, rubbing his forehead.

"You better get some rest. I'll follow up with you on anything we find around here."

13
Provo, Utah
1999

In a quiet neighborhood in a town at the base of the Wasatch Mountain Range, between 9:34 PM and 9:42 PM, a cockeyed man with a large mole on his cheek murdered his whole family. First, he strangled his wife, then each of his three young children while they slept. He went to the garage where he found a crowbar, returned to the porch, and beat his dog to death where she laid. On his way back into the house to collect his fake identification, money, and other provisions, he saw the goldfish. Floating in his bowl, motionless, gills pulsating in the murky water, the fish looked at him with its damn knowing glance. He knew what he had to do next. For completeness, he pulled it out of the bowl and crushed it under his boot. When the fish's body gave way with a muffled click, for the first time in many months, he felt a slight twinge of guilt. Completeness matters, he told himself, but that fish was the only one he liked.

Then he disappeared, but not to some far off exotic land. He created a new life, if one could call it that, right under the nose of the authorities in America's second-most populous city, Los Angeles. There he lived, a dim reflection in a dark windowpane, a shadow in the backyard, a curious figure, avoiding eye contact in a crowded place, an unknown and emotionless face, numb to the confused whimpers of the soon to be dead.

14
Downtown Los Angeles
2015

It was 7:12 PM, and nearly everyone had gone home when James Lindster stood from his desk. After the argument with his boss, he had worked frantically through the afternoon hours. This argument was different and more hostile than those they'd had before. He had to get it all down, had to make his case, and now it was done. In his daily leaving ritual, he closed his computer down completely, locked his desk, and checked each of the file cabinets to make sure they were securely locked; then, he walked past the abandoned cubicles to the elevator and rode it down to the underground parking garage. He could hear the echo of his hard-soled shoes on the concrete in the nearly empty garage while he walked. He slowed his steps and approached his car cautiously upon seeing a man in a gray suit leaning against the hood.

"Can I help you?" Lindster asked the man.

The man turned to look at him and stood away from the hood. He was in his late forties with graying chestnut hair, a proud chin, and a barreled chest. "Is this your car?" the man asked Lindster.

"Yes, it is."

"Sorry about that. Excuse me," he said and flashed a cold smile.

He stared at Lindster while he spoke. There was something askew, something creepy, about the man. He stared without necessarily making eye contact. As he got closer Lindster wondered if he was actually looking at him or through him. Even though the dark brown mole on the upper part of his cheek was the most conspicuous feature on his otherwise attractive face, his lazy eye left people with a chill. The color in that iris was lighter, serpent-like, and caused people who got close to him a tinge of fear, perhaps as a relic of millions of years of evolution for a primal wariness of snakes. The man with the mole stepped back, holding tight the venomous smile, and continued to watch as Lindster reached into his pocket for his keys.

As Lindster drove away, he peered into his rearview mirror to see the man with the mole standing, still as a statue, watching him leave. Lindster was relieved to be out in the late summer evening streets of downtown Los Angeles, headed home for the weekend. He was tired and wanted to see his two young girls. Next week was going to be a stressful week at work, and he needed the break.

In the traffic along Pico Boulevard, just before turning into the parking lot of a grocery store, Lindster thought he saw the face of the man with the mole several cars back in the red LED glow of a traffic signal. When he looked closer, he didn't see him again.

Twenty minutes later, Lindster emerged from the grocery store carrying a heavy brown paper bag.

"I should be there in less than twenty," he said into the phone tucked between his ear and shoulder. "Tell Sarah to leave out the drawings, and I'll go through all of them with her when I get home."

Standing next to his car in the crowded parking lot, he switched the side on which he was carrying the bag, fumbled for his keys, and opened the driver's door. After placing the bag on the passenger seat, he closed his door and started the engine. When he looked up from the dashboard into the rearview mirror, adrenaline bathed his muscles and momentarily stopped his breathing from the shock of seeing the man with the mole in the back seat.

"Drive," the man said while flashing his cold smile.

15
Crawford County, Arkansas
1928-1936

None of the supposed wealth and opulence of the 1920s came to western Arkansas, the McAlester lot, nor Minnie Holmsley and her son Levi Bratton. They lived simply and in poverty. Uncle John, in his mid-sixties, did his best to provide for Minnie and help raise Levi in the years after Minnie and Uncle John buried Obediah in a bloody bedroll in the woods behind the cabin. Minnie was strong, caring, and loved Levi like the mother of an only child, but there was something in him that she didn't understand and couldn't control. He grew up independent and restless, and at times reminded Minnie of his father.

On a summer day in 1928, Uncle John used two horses to drag home a broke down 1916 Cadillac Model 53 that he took as partial payment for re-roofing a neighbor's house.

"It's yours if you want it," Uncle John said to Levi as he jumped down off the hood and untied the horses.

"Does it work?" Levi asked.

"Nope."

"What's wrong with it?"

"Don't know. But if you get in there and fix 'er, I'll teach you how to drive it."

Levi's self-education began the next day when he cracked open the hood of that Cadillac for the first time. In the weeks that followed, Levi learned the empowerment that came from taking something apart, figuring out how it worked, and putting it back together. He spent months under the hood, finally getting it to turn over and lurch forward in a furious cloud of black smoke. As the smoke cleared and the engine continued to chug with the fire of forty horses, Levi was overwhelmed with a sense of pride and confidence that he could fix anything.

Two days before his eighteenth birthday Levi took his mother on her first car ride. It was less than a year later that he had left home and was working in a service station south of Fayetteville in the pass-through town of Alma, along the road that headed west to Oklahoma City.

In the spring of 1935, Levi stood in the parking lot of Armer's service station, futilely wiping grease onto his blue coveralls from his blackened hands. He gazed up at the orange afternoon sky to the west. Hundreds of miles over the western horizon, the scorched earth had coughed up a coffee-colored wall of dust fifteen thousand feet high that was moving in his direction.

"Something ugly's headed this way," Levi said.

"Best roll down the doors and tighten up the pumps," said George Armer, standing next to Levi, squinting into the distance.

What they were witnessing was the first of many dust storms that made Alma and other little towns like it nearly uninhabitable, and it was Joe Glidden's fault.

Joe Glidden, a man who died four years before Levi was born, would be partially responsible for driving Levi out of Arkansas, to the western United States for the rest of his life.

Joe Glidden invented barbed wire. Through an accidental and serendipitous discovery, Glidden figured out how to cut small wire hooks with a refurbished coffee grinder and grip them between two strands of braided wire. It was a simple little invention that not only changed the life of Levi Bratton; it changed everything.

Throughout the history of the tree-less landscape of the American West, everything capable of movement—wild animals, livestock, Indians, and the occasional pansy French explorer—had roamed free. There were boundaries, of course, though these were mostly ineffective and irrelevant, drawn all over the West by rich white men drooling over maps and claiming ownership of land they would never see. Upholding these boundaries with quality fences, in the absence of trees and other raw materials, was expensive and unfeasible. Keeping cattle required cowboys, cattle drives, little campfires, and starry nights on vast landscapes of solitude. Barbed wire changed all that. It killed the cowboy, and the Indian, and irreversibly changed the landscape of the West.

While Levi spent the last years of the 1920s repairing cars in the greasy metal service station in Alma, barbed wire was gripping the land to the west of Arkansas, ruthlessly latticing it, strangling it, making it manageable, making ownership easier—allowing man to control the land in ways not previously possible. All those interconnected, thorny metal sutures across the swollen grasslands caused a change to brew and churn across the West. Cowboys, with their hard-earned dignity and freedom, were demoted to fence custodians, riding and repairing the mortal coil. A rancher is nothing but a cowboy tamed by barbed wire. They settled, everyone settled, and with their ambition, their fenced-in animals, and their tractors, they took everything they could from the land until it refused to provide anything more. Then the rains stopped, and the soil dried to fine dust, and the real suffering began.

As Levi rolled down the garage door, he looked up at the dust wall to the west, blooming and rolling in on itself. Dust would soon sail on the prevailing winds from Oklahoma all the way to the eastern seaboard, but before it made it that far it settled in hard on Alma and blanketed everything.

Had Joe Glidden not been born, had his awful barbed spawn not been invented, Levi may have lived out a reasonable life in Western Arkansas, fixing cars, earning a share of George Armer's service station, and eventually finding his way out of bachelorhood. Maybe Joe Glidden didn't cause the dust bowl. Maybe it was the colder than usual ocean surface temperatures at the equator or shifts in the warm subtropical North Atlantic currents that caused several years of La Niña weather conditions that brought drought and deserts to the American West. Maybe. Barbed wire definitely didn't help the situation.

Less than two years after they had stood in that parking lot gawking at that brown wall of dust, the service station was closed. By 1936, towns all over the West were dying. On the farms, dust swirled and settled between long runs of rusty barbed wire. It settled and moved and settled and moved again in dry ashen ripples, and no water came, and nothing would grow, and dust blew over the carcasses of starved cattle. The barbed wire rusted and broke, and the weak fence posts—tree limbs hastily cut and driven into the ground, with their knots and branch stubs still visible—began to lean and fall. The land had abandoned the people, and the people had to move on to survive. They collected themselves and whatever they could take with them and streamed off the dead farms on little tributaries of dirt and pavement and coagulated and pulsed westward in the main artery called Route 66. Everyone was moving to the west, escaping the dust, the drought, the hunger, the past, headed to new land, to fertility, to hope.

And here's a story you can hardly believe, but it's true, and it's funny and it's beautiful. There was a family of twelve and they were forced off the land. They had no car. They built a trailer out of junk and loaded it with their possessions. They pulled it to the side of 66 and waited. And pretty soon a sedan picked them up. Five of them rode in the sedan and seven on the trailer, and a dog on the trailer. They got to California in two jumps. The man who pulled them fed them. And that's true. But how can such a courage be, and such faith in their own species? Very few things would teach such faith. The people in flight from the terror behind—strange things happen to them, some bitterly cruel and some so beautiful that the faith is refired forever.

Although that well-told story was true, and some sentences have been read a billion times, it was like most true stories—a simplification of the truth, a shadow of what actually happened. Even though the story was hardly believable, it wasn't the whole truth. It was Levi Bratton who drove the sedan that hauled that family of twelve to California. He didn't haul them out of kindness or anything that would affirm one's faith in their own species. That family paid dearly for the ride, and so did Levi.

16
Northwestern Los Angeles
Present Day

Jack rode with the passenger seat leaned way back, and watched Marcus as he navigated the Crown Victoria in an unbroken stream of cars backed up along the 405 Freeway down into the Los Angeles basin. The afternoon sun was low in the sky, casting a dirty, mustard-colored haze over the river of traffic. The cars idled and pushed forward, one after the other, in a synchronized crawl on the hot asphalt.

"How's your head?" Marcus asked.

"Hurts."

The dull ache across his forehead had moved to his neck and upper back. The Day-Glo green Solina work vest sat at Jack's feet.

"Why didn't you tell Vargas about the vest or Ostergard's wallet?" Marcus asked.

"No need to give him too much information. I'll follow up on it. See if it leads anywhere," Jack replied.

"You should find out who owns the house."

"Right."

"Clearly it was taken care of. The lawns were green and freshly mowed. It's not like the place was abandoned. Just empty." When Jack didn't respond, Marcus went on. "What I can't figure out is the motivation behind keeping a body in a house like that. Of all the places to dump a body, a suburban house; seems like a terrible idea, especially if you're living in a trailer in the driveway."

"Yeah." Jack's eyes were closed.

"And an EPA inspector? Does this have something to do with his job or does he just happen to work for the EPA and just got caught up in something bad? What does the missing chipper and the unidentified guy in it have to do with the dead guy we found today?"

Jack shrugged. "It's strange. I don't know."

He opened his eyes then closed them again, wishing for the dull ache across his forehead to subside. In the vibrating comfort of the warm car, he couldn't resist sleep. The afternoon light flickered on his face and became a fading flesh tone on the back of his eyelids. As he entered a dream, he was consciously reminded of familiar and comforting places from his time in college.

Jack met Marcus as an undergraduate while they were serving individual community service sentences. For three Saturdays a month over a four-month period, they were required to report to the Surfrider Foundation beach cleanup volunteer coordinator. When Marcus arrived on the beach the first Saturday, Jack knew he was something special and instantly took a liking to him.

While scraping by as a business major at San Diego State University, Jack's attention was directed at his social chairmanship of Sigma Chi. One August, when everyone was returning for the new school year, he had what he thought was a stroke of genius. He conceived of a prank that he and his fraternity brothers could laugh about all year long, but like so many other ideas generated by young men surrounded only by other young men, it turned out to be inadvertently misguided and mean-spirited.

He and his fraternity brothers sent the girls of Gamma Phi Beta two dozen donuts with a note welcoming them back to school, saying that the men of Sigma Chi were looking forward to spending time with them during their annual social events. The girls enjoyed the donuts with guilty pleasure and were happy to receive the all too rare friendly greeting. The next day a manila envelope arrived on the brick doorstep of the light brown stucco sorority house. The contents of the envelope were revealed, with horror, to be glossy black and white photographs of Jack and his fraternity brothers balancing the recently consumed donuts on their hard cocks. One particularly disturbing image portrayed Jack on his back with his legs over his head with several maple bars meticulously placed along the crack of his ass.

The thought of her delicious maple bar having touched the balls of that overly confident, pretty boy Sigma Chi social chair was enough to motivate the Gamma Phi Beta chapter president to press charges against him. The Greek Life Disciplinary Action Board recommended that Jack write an official apology letter to the sorority and serve fifty hours of community service for having been the architect of the prank. The incident provided Jack with real feelings of guilt and remorse. He wrote the letter and tried several times to apologize in person, but was never allowed into the sorority house again.

Jack was sound asleep when they arrived on the curb in front of Marcus's house on the south end of Westwood. When the hum of the engine turned to a tremor, then stopped, Jack awoke.

"We're here. You alright to drive?" Marcus asked.

"I'm fine. I feel better," Jack responded, getting up and coming around to the driver's side.

"Alright, get some rest then."

17
The American Midwest
June 3rd, 1936

Summer rains over Kansas, Nebraska, and Oklahoma are not rare occurrences, but in the summer of 1936 they were. At that time, the entire Midwest was in the grip of the longest and most severe drought in its recorded history. The earth was tragically parched, what crops remained were failing, and the pervasive dust whipped up with the slightest breeze. Rain hadn't fallen in months, and the summer sun beat down on the High Plains, turning everything green to brown.

On the especially dark night of June 3rd, when the moon was just a sliver, a thunderstorm centered over Morris County, Kansas welled up and pounded an area several hundred miles in diameter for eighteen minutes; then the storm was gone as quickly as it had come. During the downpour, water droplets collided with the dusty ground sending microscopic particles airborne. As the thunderstorm dissipated and the air warmed, dust was carried high into the atmosphere. Inside each particle, a microscopic colony of *Pseudomonas syringae*, hitchhiked into the sky.

Pseudomonas syringae, a bacteria that lives on the skin of plants, has the remarkable ability to produce ice. They can freeze plant tissue and then feed off the frost burned material. During those eighteen minutes on the night of June 3rd, 1936, large numbers of *Pseudomonas* found their way into the atmosphere and ultimately had a profound effect on the climate. Because they can freeze water, each bacterium becomes the center of tiny ice crystals in the upper atmosphere. If the conditions are right, these bacterial ice crystals grow, become heavy, and fall from the sky, melting along the way, causing rain. *Pseudomonas syringae* is a bacterial rainmaker.

Not all atmospheric bacterial particles, however, rain back down to earth. *Pseudomonas* can also live for decades, potentially centuries, in the inhospitable environment of the upper atmosphere, drifting over the continents, feeding only on the small organic molecules found in clouds. Occasionally the conditions are just right for each bacterium to form a hexagonal ice crystal that, on a clear night, focuses the moonlight into a diffuse halo.

18
Shawnee, Oklahoma
June 4th, 1936

As Levi Bratton sped westward through central Oklahoma, the waves of beige sand reflected on the uninspired voluptuousness of the chrome grill of his 1928 Model 62 Chrysler sedan. Like the round-edged pyramid atop Manhattan's Chrysler building, the grill blazed in the morning sun as he overtook another jalopy filled with a displaced farm family limping westward under the weight of their worthless possessions. He'd occasionally slow to make brief, but uncomfortable eye contact with family members—dirty children smiling with missing teeth, fathers glancing up with disdain, focused, working the wheel, listening intently to the engine, attending to their precarious situation. Then there were the mothers, some no older than Levi, but already with four or five, or good God, even six children.

He overtook twenty such trucks in an hour and was approaching his twenty-first, an old Ford pickup, the bed stacked high with cases and dirty blond children. The father was hunched behind the wheel, denim overalls stained brown, greasy creases in his cheeks, and an unlit cigarette perched on his lips. Levi came up beside them, slowed, and looked to his right. As they were coming over a low hill, he let his eyes linger on the young mother long enough to watch her lick her dried lips and look at him disapprovingly. On the other side, a tractor was crossing the road in the oncoming lane. Levi braked hard, swerved to his left, narrowly missed the tractor, and hit a bank of soft dirt on the road shoulder. The truck puttered onward, and Levi could see the smirk on the father's face in the truck's dusty side mirror. Save his pride, he was uninjured, but the Chrysler's grill was smashed, and the radiator was leaking.

It had rained briefly the night before, a rain that brought the farmers onto their porches in the morning, squinting at their dampened fields with renewed dreams of the future. Rain in the summer of 1936 in central Oklahoma was an uncommon event. In that land, at that time, moisture meant hope. One farmer fired up his old tractor and kindled his futile hopes by busying himself with crossing the interstate to drive around his damp fields.

Levi exited the Chrysler in the bright Midwest morning. The air was heavy with the smell of grass and diesel exhaust. In the distance, he could hear the engine of the jalopy hobbling westward and the purr of the tractor, now off on a dirt road between quickly drying fields.

He heard a hiss from under the large black hood of the Chrysler, saw steam rising from the front grill, and coppery green fluid pooling momentarily, then percolating into the porous red sand below the car. When the hissing had stopped, he opened the hood to release a small mushroom cloud of steam and discovered radiator fluid leaking from a crack in a broken hose. He touched the hose with his outstretched middle finger and stroked the crack up and down. A trickle of warm chartreuse fluid, only slightly more viscous than water, ran down his finger and glistened on the back of his hand. He raised two thick, moistened fingers to his nose, closed his eyes, and breathed deep while memories of his time at the station came rushing over him.

Over the preceding two years, since that first dust storm, Levi had become all too familiar with the farm exodus. People poured off the dried up and dying farms on the plains to the west and came east through George Armer's gas station in Alma.

As the unlucky farm families streamed through, Levi witnessed how indiscriminately unfair life was. These people thought they could take care of each other, that the world was kind and would take care of them, and they were wrong. They had nothing to show for their hard work and suffering.

The families migrating east through Alma showed up with nothing. Nobody could pay for anything, and it wasn't long until Levi was without a job. He had $450, a single case with all his possessions, and a full tank of gas on the day he pulled out of Armer's for good. He had no destination. The last time he'd seen his mother was at Uncle John's funeral, several years prior. He turned out of Alma and headed north in her direction, but five minutes from the station, he turned west, away from the McAlester lot, and away from his mother, whom he would never see again.

19

Levi was standing in the morning sun awaking from his momentary reverie with the realization that his wrecked Chrysler would go no farther without damaging the engine. He decided to leave it on the roadside and walk to Shawnee for a replacement hose. By the early afternoon, Levi was returning to his car with a new hose in hand, walking with purpose in the center of the road. So few cars passed over the road's surface that it had become nothing more than two tire tracks beaten into the weak pavement. Dust and sand covered the shoulder and slid into the ruts, obscuring the delineation between the road and sandy fields that lined it. As he walked, he left footsteps in the fine dust behind him. The moisture from the previous night's brief rain was gone, and he could smell the escalating dry heat with each breath.

Levi came upon a small farm, like many he'd seen at sixty miles per hour in central Oklahoma—an unpainted wooden house, a dilapidated barn, and a rusted tractor with its black rubber tires hardened and cracked by the sun. Everything was partially covered in dust and its larger, abrasive cousin, sand. Out in front was a lanky man in clean, dark brown coveralls and gray overcoat, loading a homemade trailer, skillfully welded together from tractor parts and other farm equipment.

"Salutations, my friend," said the man to Levi, pushing up the brim of his hat.

"Afternoon," Levi said back, looking up from the road, surprised and confused that the man had said anything to him.

"Can I assist you with something? It appears that you're endeavoring to carry out a repair," said the man, pointing at the radiator hose in Levi's hand.

"Got it taken care of; just a cracked hose, 'bout half a mile up the road on the interstate," Levi said.

"I'm Tom, Tom White," he said, extending his hand to Levi.

"Levi Bratton."

"Pleasure to make your acquaintance," Tom said, still looking at the hose. "I'm proficient in most cases of automobile repair and would be willing to service your vehicle for a meager fee. I have all the necessary tools."

"Kind offer, but I think I can manage. Should be no trouble," Levi said.

"Are you in possession of a sufficient volume of water to recharge your radiator?" asked Tom.

"I'm not sure what you mean," responded Levi.

"Have you enough water to top off your drained radiator?" asked Tom again, trying to speak slowly for him. Levi hadn't thought of that, and he could tell Tom knew.

"I can see that you're mindful of an expedient departure from our deteriorated farm, but if you briefly humor my windy conversation, I'll provide you with the water you need to be on your way," Tom said.

Levi looked at him blankly.

"We haven't been able to access a suitable quantity of groundwater of late, but on account of the brief but substantial rains our recent luck has afforded us, our well may yield enough to fill those two metal cans to satiate your radiator and retain enough for our afternoon's drinking."

Tom picked up two large tomato cans that he was loading onto the trailer and turned toward the house. "Join me if you will," he said, turning back to Levi.

Without a word, Levi followed Tom through a wood and wire fence gate. They walked between the house and the barn toward the windmill, a short distance behind the barn.

As Levi stood on the road talking to Tom, in his peripheral vision, he saw children begin to appear from around the house and out of the field and barn. They stood barefoot, with dirty faces and torn clothing, shyly staring at him, half-hidden, as if they were afraid to be seen. As Levi and Tom walked toward the well, more children appeared, older children holding babies, toddlers running to hide behind their older siblings, and teenage boys in overalls stood looking at them from the dusty field in the distance.

"Are these your children?" Levi asked when they were standing at the base of the windmill.

"Yes, they are. All mine and Patsy's. No fewer than ten of them in total. There's my bride, many years past the altar now, but still as lovely and delightful as the day we wed," Tom said, pointing to a woman in the house standing with her back to a dirty window.

"Ten children?" asked Levi.

"You heard me correctly, my friend; ten. And Patsy is nearing her forty-second year. Seems like nary an instance of us lying together occurred without producing a child." Tom smiled. "The occasions for that vital enterprise grow in rarity each year, however, now that our bed is populated with sleeping children." He paused awkwardly.

"Our youngest is baby Thomas," he said, pointing to a naked baby held by what looked like an eight-year-old girl sitting on the back porch of the house. "He'll be turning one next week. Our oldest is Ella Mae. A constant reminder of the regrettable speed with which the years have passed, she'll be nineteen in a few months."

As Tom spoke, he absentmindedly rubbed the point of his shirt collar between his thumb and forefinger. He leaned down to fill the two cans with the trickle of water that ran from the spigot at the base of the windmill. As Tom filled the second can, Levi stood looking out over the dried-up farm. A small blond boy saw the running water, and cautiously came closer. He stared at Levi, then at the large knife on his belt.

"Come nearer, child; have a drink," Tom said, and the little boy ran to the spigot and drank hastily and thirstily like he'd not had a drink in more than a day.

"How long you been on this farm?" Levi asked.

"Patsy and I began our occupation of the lovely strip of land nearly twenty years ago, after our marriage in Shawnee. Her father extended us the kindness of a no-interest loan for the purchase of the land, which we farmed prosperously and largely according to plan until the rains ceased and the dust descended upon us."

"You both from around these parts?"

"My lovely Patsy was born and raised in a proper manner, just a short, yet comfortably suitable, distance from here. I hail from what many would call the dreary east. After university, I undertook a brief, but not brief enough, spell as an engineer avoiding Kraut U-boats aboard the USS New York. After returning home and trying to salvage my father's ruined empire, I finally had the good sense about me to head west. On that journey, I was struck by the great fortune of meeting Patsy at the train station here in Shawnee."

Levi stood looking into the distance, nodding his head while Tom went on.

"That was so many years ago now. More to the matter currently at hand, nature's disparagement of our little piece of heaven on earth has been without mercy of late, and last year we were forced to part with most of our agricultural implements, our newest and only functioning tractor, in addition to our truck. We sold it all just to continue to reside in our home. As the spring and summer months passed with the rains still refusing to commence, it became apparent that selling the whole farm, nearly thirty days ago now, was the only course of action that would enable us to garner the resources necessary to travel west," Tom said. "We are now in the precarious situation of being seven days beyond the date on which the bank had originally intended us to vacate the property."

"How you going out west without a truck?" Levi asked.

"Our prospects for transportation are meager. I'm currently loading everything onto our trailer with the hope of hitching it to something moving westward."

As Tom spoke, going on about the nuances of high-quality trailer construction for proper load-bearing, Levi heard what sounded like a distant metallic rhythm of a hammer hitting a piece of tin. He looked up at the windmill above them, to see that it wasn't moving, yet the rhythm continued. He looked off into the distance where the metallic ringing was speeding up and getting louder.

Tom handed one of the two full cans to Levi and said, "Don't mind that peculiar noise. You're just hearing Ella Mae coming around the house."

20

Nearly fifty years earlier, on the cold and clear afternoon of January 5th, 1881, George Humphrey Herrington entered the Sedgwick County Courthouse in Wichita, Kansas, with three handwritten pages and two hand-drawn figures in an old leather folder. Meticulously drawn on those pages was a new design for what he called the adjustable spring stilt, a version of what would ultimately come to be known as the pogo stick.

The events of that cold Wichita afternoon and the resulting patent issued to Herrington were unbeknownst to Tom White when in 1927, he made his oldest daughter a toy spring jumper from old tractor parts. It was a simple and elegant device, one which he would never get credit for inventing. His spring jumper was easy enough to make, and Tom reckoned it had been made many times over by other farmers and tinkerers. A greased rod welded to a spring, slid inside a cylinder, was nothing new, but Tom White's great innovation in pogo design was the peddle and handle crossbars. George Herrington's adjustable spring stilts lacked them, relying instead on awkward foot straps, yet the handles were ultimately what made the pogo stick comfortable, easy to use, and widely popular.

Many years after Tom made his first spring jumper, a German baby furniture designer in Chicago saw a photograph of Ella Mae White in a work camp in the San Joaquin Valley jumping on her father's handled spring stick. He patented the design and went on to form the SBI company, the world's largest producer of pogo sticks.

The metallic bouncing sound continued to ring out as Ella Mae rounded the corner of the house. She bounced into Levi's full view, and he was awestruck. She was a precocious eighteen years old, wearing an old dress that fit her at fourteen, but was now too tight for her voluptuous frame. It clung to her and wrapped tightly around her moist, olive oil skin, struggling to keep it all in. As she bounced, time expanded. Levi saw her in slow motion. Her taut and supple flesh pulsed under her dress, straining to obey gravity as she descended, compressing and expanding upward, whirling, and undulating, an engorged pink balloon, guava jelly, pawpaw cream pie. To see Ella Mae pogo was to watch Kamala consume a fig; it was to observe Salome shake her hips, to get lost in Sharbat Gula's deep green gaze, to receive a flirtatious glance from Bette Davis. It was to prostrate oneself before Cleopatra as she ruled from her pharaoh's throne.

Tom watched Levi watch Ella Mae, then turned to the little boy and said, "Run along and get your sister to come introduce herself to our guest." The little boy licked the remains of the well water from his lips and ran to Ella Mae, who followed him back holding her pogo stick. As she came closer, she grew more beautiful. Levi stood with his mouth half-open, not breathing as she approached.

"Ella Mae, say hello to our new friend Mr. Levi Bratton," said Tom.

"Hello, Sir, I'm Ella Mae," she said in a low gravelly voice—a voice that sounded as if it were going to be lost, that these were the last words that beautiful throat could muster. It was the sexiest sound Levi had ever heard. As she introduced herself, she extended her left hand, as the right was holding her pogo stick. Out of habit, Levi extended his right hand to meet her left, and when their two opposite hands met, a brief awkwardness ensued. Her slender fingers wrapped around the side of his forefinger. He pressed down on them gently with his rough thumb.

The shape of the human fingernail varies greatly. A nail's evolutionary history is that of a horn-like claw, except that it's flattened, softened, and does not, in cases of good hygiene, extend beyond the digit, whose tip it protects. The longer the appendage on which that nail sits, the faster the nail grows, forefinger faster than pinky, fingers faster than toes.

Levi made eye contact with Ella Mae, then briefly looked down as their hands awkwardly folded together. He noticed the length of his fingernails in contrast to hers. Whereas his were long, too long, slightly curved and compressed side to side, hers were flat and delicate, and strangely luminescent.

Each human fingernail has a whitish crescent half-moon at the base, seen most easily on the thumb. The Romans called it the lunula, the little moon. As Levi glanced downward, Ella Mae's lunulas sparkled in his view and were ringed with a second subtle, white halo.

"Afternoon, ma'am," Levi said after a long and dumbfounded pause, still awkwardly pressing her hand. "What's this you're hoppin' on?"

"It's a bouncing stick Pa made for me when I was younger. Been riding it for years now, almost bottoming out the spring," Ella Mae replied and looked over to her father.

"Looks like fun," said Levi.

"I like how bouncy it is. I like riding it for hours. It makes me feel like I'm flying, like I can go anywhere," Ella Mae said with a sweet and mischievous smile. "You want to give it a try?"

Levi looked down at Ella Mae and smiled. "No, thank you, ma'am."

Tom stood watching them look at each other in silence. As he was never one to let a gap in a conversation last, he said to Levi, "Can I suggest that you and I undertake the excursion to the highway and your malfunctioning automobile, reconnoiter your situation, carry out the necessary repairs, then return here for the evening?"

"What? We're coming back here after? Sure."

"Yes sir. When we return, Patsy and I will engender you with a generous hospitality. Tomorrow, in the light of a new day, we can discuss fashioning a substantial hitch on your automobile."

"I'll be staying here tonight?" Levi said, still smiling at Ella Mae.

"Affirmative."

Levi hadn't paid attention to nor understood Tom's plan, but he replied with, "Sounds good to me."

Ella Mae and Tom White exchanged a brief, knowing glance.

21
Laguna Canyon, California
June 6th, 1962

"This is where the ride ends, no vamos mas." The driver leaned into the bed of the truck and folded back the stiff olive tarp.

His backlit face took shape as Alex Melter's eyes adjusted to the orange late afternoon light. Alex stood, took a long look around, and jumped down from the back of the truck. The smell of rotting flesh was in the air, and a shadow moved quickly across them. The driver looked up at the two vultures sailing low in the sky.

The syrupy thick stench came in waves. At first it was overbearing, then it was gone, then it was back again in a few breaths. Alex knew the smell well. There was no mistaking it. His thoughts returned to years earlier when he had seen the human roadkill that hastened his departure from Brazil. Coyote, deer, raccoon, squirrel, or human, they all smelled the same in death.

"You'll have to walk from here. Tienes que andar," said the driver, still looking skyward.

"Thank you," Alex said in a deep accent. The Mexican driver assumed, like everyone had during his time in Mexico, that Alex spoke Spanish. He did, but only poorly, and his English wasn't much better. What English he knew was slurred at him by a drunken expatriate doctor in Mazatlán to whom he gave the occasional fish so he would be allowed to sit and listen to the doctor's bitter and often unintelligible rants about the country with which he was so disappointed—the same country with which Alex was completely infatuated.

Alex was as easy to look at as he was easy to be around. He was hardworking, and even though he didn't speak much, people often took a ready liking to him. While in Mazatlán, Alex had little difficulty proving himself a valuable asset to several fishing boat captains, and jobs came easily. He earned enough money in three years on the boats to survive for many months after crossing the U.S. border. Eventually one of his employers, El Capitan Santana, a kind, blond bearded man who was missing the tip of one ear and who drooled while speaking, gave Alex the name of a relative in Tijuana who would smuggle him across the U.S. border for a price.

"Make sure you get to this address in Atwater, in northern Los Angeles," the driver said as he handed Alex a piece of yellow paper. "You'll need to find Poncho Meisenheimer. He'll help you with your papers. ¿Entiendes?"

"Yes, I understand. Thank you," Alex replied.

The driver looked at Alex as if seeing him for the first time. His bright green eyes, the straight pointed nose of his German father, his milk chocolate skin, and kinky black hair were often met with a mixture of confusion and admiration.

"You don't have any family in this country?"

"No."

"You have money?"

"Some."

"You're a long way from Atwater. Don't get in trouble in the meantime." The driver gestured toward the west. "Follow this road into Laguna Beach and spend the night there."

Alex gazed beyond the driver's outstretched hand across the olive green patchwork of vegetation. The chaparral hills abutted the edge of the road and crowded the narrow shoulder on each side. Raised peninsulas, blanketed in dark green and silver, interlocked like fingers on opposing hands, and Laguna Canyon Road flowed along the dry creek that had once cut through the hills on its way to the beach.

"You're going to be just fine. No vas a tener problemas."

The driver hastily shook Alex's hand, returned to the truck, made a U-turn on the dirt turnout, and headed back toward the freeway.

As Alex watched the truck go, the smell of freshly raised dust and sage competed with the reek of carrion. Alex stood, all his possessions in the green Army bag on his back, looking at the address scribbled on the small yellow square of paper. He watched the truck disappear in the distance just as he realized that he had forgotten his favorite brown flannel shirt in the bed of the truck. Alex shrugged, smiled, tucked the paper deep into his back pocket, and set out toward the beach.

22
University of California at Los Angeles
Present Day

Two days after the dead body of James Lindster was discovered rotting in the house in Reseda, students sat in a lecture hall on the UCLA campus. This was a room of learning, a well-worn room. Little stains of human grease formed dark blotches on the sidewalls where weary heads had lain against the raw concrete.

Humans seem to be willing to pay for four things, and not much else; sustenance, shelter, protection, and entertainment. To make it economically viable, modern higher education has been marketed as entertainment for young people, and protection from their otherwise inevitable future financial ruin. So what? Marcus thought. Maybe universities have become extended summer camps for entitled upper middle-class kids without an academic bone in their body. He tried to teach, or entertain, and often he didn't know nor care which was which. He enjoyed himself.

There have always been great teachers, some greater than others. Through revolving eons, something is always created as something else is destroyed. Creation evolves from beginning to end; the end is predicted in the beginning, the same way a new beginning is inherent in the ending. The blue, ash-covered Lord Shiva, the destroyer and transformer, with his glorious love handles, saw the ego-consciousness of this cycle of creation and sidestepped it. Buddha, his scalp knobby and clean, like polished wood, saw the bitter cycle of birth, the agony of life, old age, death, and rebirth, and rose above it, but Krishna, Lord Vishnu incarnate as a beautiful young man, he became the cycle, turned people on to it, helped them discover it as a revelation for themselves. He was a great teacher. Knowledge of self is the ultimate aphrodisiac, and women swooned in his presence. With his steely-gray dolphin-like skin, garlanded in orange tropical flowers, the color of freshly opened birds-of-paradise, and his cloth-wrapped flute, wielded like some mysterious phallus, Krishna attracted young men and women from far and wide to be seduced by his child-like curiosity, to fall prey to a playful ruse and be turned on by his insight into the world around them.

Marcus Melter was a modern-day Krishna, viewed by a select few of his students as a wise prince and an avatar for knowledge itself. In the confines of soul-sapping university lecture halls, with their smell of new carpet and ugly fluorescent lights, he was still glorious, still funny, and still turned young people on to the mysterious and cyclical world around them.

"There is sacred in the mundane, potentially unanswerable questions inherent in everyday objects that we take for granted," he said in the middle of his botany lecture. "Mysteries are all around us; we just have to train ourselves to look for them. We have to cultivate our curiosity."

He went to his bag behind the lectern and held up a banana. "The banana, for instance. Have you thought about the banana? Really thought about it? For many of you, it's your favorite fruit, the first food you were fed as you were weaned from your mother's breast and the last food you'll be fed before you die, but you haven't truly considered it. It's the most eaten fruit in America, the most commonly purchased item in grocery stores. They're so common we don't even think about them anymore. But have you ever observed, over your morning breakfast, that there are no seeds in the banana? Never have been, never will be. A banana seed is the size of a pea, and rock hard. Yet the kind we eat has none. How are fields of bananas planted if there are no seeds?"

A student in the front row raised his hand. "By chopping up plants?"

"Yes," Marcus continued. He was briefly distracted by his cell phone buzzing in his pocket. "By chopping up plants. A banana plant has a huge underground stem the size and shape of a beach ball. By chopping that ball up with a machete and planting the pieces of it, farmers all over the tropical world can turn one banana clump into twenty, twenty into one hundred, one hundred into a whole plantation. But here's the difficult and profound question, if a farmer has a banana plant for ten years, then cuts the clump in half and plants those two halves, how old are his two new clumps? Do they become zero years old when he cuts the original clump in half? Are they still ten years old?"

For a long moment, he let a silence fill the room. The silence was interrupted by his cell phone buzzing once again in his pocket.

"Careful how you answer this question," Marcus went on. "If you say the two clumps are zero years old, that means you believe a machete has some magical power to reduce the age of a banana. That's fine if you want to believe that. People believe in stranger things, but there's no evidence that a machete can turn back time."

"Then they're ten years old," a student said from the back.

"Well, if those two clumps are ten years old, and the clump they came from was several years old, as was the one before it, then what that means is every banana you've eaten is about 4,000 years old. That's when the seedless banana, the kind we eat, was discovered in the New Guinea highlands. Four thousand years ago, and it's never made a seed since. It's been living with humans for all that time, cut and multiplied by them, living on and on, producing its age-old bananas."

Another student raised her hand and said, "Every banana can't be 4,000 years old. It may grow off a plant that's 4,000 years old, but the banana is probably only a couple months old."

Marcus smirked. "Are the leaves on a one-hundred-year-old tree one hundred years old? How about the branches? The trunk? What is 100 years old on that old tree? How old are you?"

"I'm nineteen."

"What is nineteen years old on you, for that matter? Is your skin nineteen years old?" Marcus waited silently, so the student would understand that it wasn't a rhetorical question.

"No, I guess not. It's replaced all the time by new cells."

"Is your finger nineteen years old, even though it's made of new cells all the time as well? If you could be cloned by splitting you in half, what should be considered the true you? What is actually nineteen years old?"

"I am."

Marcus's phone buzzed a third time.

"But what are you? What is a banana? Is it just the underground stem or all the parts of the whole that make up that plant? Is the banana immortal? Age, youth, death, mortality. These words may fail us when we try to capture the complexity of how certain organisms exist, even ones that we interact with on a daily basis. The banana isn't just a simple breakfast fruit; it's a philosophical challenge and a window into a way of existing in the world that we don't understand well."

Marcus smiled. "Alright, we'll pick this up again next time. I'll see you all on Wednesday."

As the students filed out of the room, Marcus packed up his materials and looked at his phone. He had four missed calls from Jack.

With his bag around his shoulder, Marcus stepped out into the midday Los Angeles sun. He stood at the top of the brick steps of the science building and the opulent and vast lawns of the UCLA campus, an obvious sign of wealth and power in water-stressed Southern California, stretched out below him. He paused to put on his sunglasses and noticed a small group of women had gathered on the steps below him.

"That's him," one of them whispered.

"Hi, Dr. Melter. This is my friend Angie. She's not in your class, but the rest of us are."

"Hi, Angie. Nice to meet you."

Angie giggled and put out her hand. "Hi."

Marcus stood silently, waiting to see if Angie had anything to say to him. She didn't. "Well, I'll see you all later then," Marcus said as he passed through the circle of women, walked down the rest of the steps, and took his phone out of his pocket once again.

"Bye," several of them said in unison as he walked away.

Since he began teaching, he'd always had an effect on his female students. Marcus figured it was the power dynamic—when forced to listen to a person long enough, lusting after him is a likely consequence. He wasn't a rock star. It wasn't as if the glory of his Amazonian blowdart of knowledge, the tender teeming tendon, Peter Pan in loose tights, filled them with squealing awe. No, these were sophisticated and ambitious young women, but they *did* lust after him, and they all knew it.

As Marcus walked away, he returned Jack's calls. "Jesus Christ, Jack. Four calls in the last hour? I was in lecture. What's up?"

"We have some great leads on the chipper case. I'll come pick you up."

"Pick me up? I'm headed to my office, and I have meetings this afternoon."

"Cancel them. This is exciting stuff."

Marcus was silent while he considered his afternoon and what he could miss.

"Alright, sounds like fun. I think I can get out of the meetings."

"Good, 'cause I need your help," Jack said. "I'll be outside your office in twenty."

23

Half an hour later Jack saw Marcus standing on the curb talking to a young woman. When he pulled up, he honked the horn loudly, flashed his badge, and waved for Marcus to get in the car.

"That's funny, dude," Marcus said sarcastically as he got in the passenger seat.

"Thought she'd find it impressive."

They drove north once again on the 405 through the chaparral-covered Santa Monica Mountains.

"Where we headed?" Marcus asked.

"It's a surprise."

"What did you find out about the Reseda house?" Marcus asked. "How's it connected to the chipper?"

"Oh, I have no idea. I was just kidding about that on the phone. There's no new information," Jack said and turned to smile at Marcus.

"Very funny. You better start talking," Marcus said.

"Did you give one of your little speeches today?"

"It's called a lecture. Tell me what you know," Marcus demanded.

"Alright, I'm just fuckin' with you. Man, I got a whole rash of shit about all that," Jack started. "I broke a bunch of procedural rules for the department. Shouldn't have entered the house without callin' it in first, shouldn't have had you with me if I was on official police business, shouldn't have been following up on a lead on a day off. Shouldn't have done this and shouldn't have done that. I spent all of yesterday doing paperwork, on a Sunday, and hearing all about how bad I fucked up. They even made me see a doctor this morning about my head."

"Are you all good?" Marcus asked.

"I'm fine. The commander kept me on the case. Said I'm supposed to share all my findings with Vargas, who's taking the lead on Lindster, the dead EPA guy. And we all have to report to Ana Zaragoza, the department's new FBI liaison."

"Why?"

"I don't know. Maybe because of the EPA thing. We also put out an APB on Lars Ostergard. Nothing on him yet."

"What about the house?"

"That's the interesting part."

"Who owns it?" Marcus asked.

"Turns out the title to the house is held by a company called Van Nuys Properties. When I looked into it further, Van Nuys Properties is a subsidiary of the Solina Chemical Corporation."

"Nice. The green work vest in the trailer," Marcus said.

"Yup. We're headed to Glendale. The Solina headquarters. I'm hoping we can talk to Jeff Hoerburger, the owner."

"Does Vargas know you're following up on this?" asked Marcus.

"Not yet. I didn't tell him that we found the vest. If we find anything out at the Solina headquarters, we'll report it back to Vargas," Jack said.

"What about the dead guy?"

"Not much to tell. Lindster was a family man, a wife and two children; worked in the downtown EPA office. Vargas is following up with his family."

Jack drove down West San Fernando Street in Glendale. The road was edged on one side by black fencing made of vertical wrought iron bars, each with a spearhead point, curving toward the street. Behind the fencing was a large complex of single-story warehouses with a new three-story glass front office building.

"Jack Bratton, LAPD," Jack said, showing the receptionist his badge. "This is my colleague Marcus Melter. We're here to see Jeff Hoerburger."

"Do you have an appointment?" asked the receptionist after thoroughly studying Jack's badge and looking the two of them over.

"No, we don't."

"Have a seat over there, I'll call upstairs and see if Mr. Hoerburger has availability."

They crossed the awkwardly large space between the receptionist desk and a group of modern looking recliner chairs arranged around a coffee table backed by a large indoor ficus tree.

"This place is brand new," Marcus said as they sat down.

"You can still smell the paint."

They could hear the receptionist having a muffled conversation on the phone. She hung up and sat staring at a computer screen. Marcus and Jack waited for nearly ten minutes before Jack grew impatient. Finally, he got up and went back to the receptionist's desk.

"What's going on? Is Hoerburger here?"

"Yes, Mr. Bratton, he's here. He's in a meeting and will be with you shortly. Someone will be along soon to show you up to Mr. Hoerburger's office," then she added in a stern tone, enunciating each word, "Please sit down."

Jack paused, looking at her, then turned to join Marcus, who was shaking his head and smirking as Jack sat down.

"Ouch. How does that feel getting scolded by a secretary?" Marcus asked quietly.

"It feels kinda good. I was going to tell her that it turned me on, but I thought she might get up from behind that desk and attack me."

Across the wide entrance area, the elevator door rang. A massive Northern European man in his late twenties got out of the elevator and walked to the reception desk. He was wearing black slacks and a short-sleeved black polo shirt that was far too small on him. He was so big, though, it seemed as if a polo shirt had never been made that could contain him. The sleeves strained and stretched as they wrapped his bulging upper arms. His skin was a glowing, hairless veneer, coating slabs of pure muscle beneath. His forearms were lined with veins the diameter of pencils, running down to his thick wrists and gigantic hands. From the shoulders up, his youthful, radiant skin, fine blond hair, and baby face gave him a prepubescent quality. He was beautiful.

"Mr. Bratton, Mr. Melter," the receptionist yelled across to them, "Rem will show you up to Mr. Hoerburger's office now."

Jack and Marcus stood and walked in the direction of the receptionist. Without introducing himself, and before they arrived at the receptionist's desk, the large man turned and walked toward the elevator, apparently expecting them to follow. For all Rem's gigantism, he was well-proportioned. From a distance, he looked like a normal-sized man, but when Jack approached him, he was taken aback by his size. At six feet tall Jack looked up at Rem at least eight inches. He also noticed the lump where Rem's untucked polo came down over his pants in the back, the unmistakable shape of a concealed handgun.

"Rem, huh. You work for Solina, Rem?" Jack asked when they got into the elevator.

Rem looked down on Jack, and in a startlingly low, accented voice that sounded as if someone had recorded Arnold Schwarzenegger, then played it back at half-speed, he asked, "What happen to your brow? It's purple."

"Rem; is that short for something? What's your last name?" Jack asked, ignoring Rem's question as he had ignored Jack's.

Rem stood silently as the elevator passed the second floor and arrived on the third. The door opened, and Rem walked out without a word.

"Rem, hmmm," Jack said loudly as they followed him down the hallway. "I think it's short for Remmy. That's it. I'm going to call you Remmy."

Rem reached the corner office, opened the door, and allowed Jack and Marcus to enter. As Jack passed, they shared a long moment of eye contact. Rem was shaking his head, Jack was smirking. "Remmy," Jack said under his breath.

24

Marcus entered the office first and saw a man in his mid-fifties get up from behind his desk. Too many hours on a tanning bed and too many cigarettes had aged him beyond his years. The leathery skin on his cheeks showed cavernous vertical lines when he greeted them with a smile.

"Mr. Bratton, Mr. Melter, welcome to Solina. Jeff Hoerburger," he said, offering his hand. He had the bushy, dirty-blond mustache of a veteran police officer and stood straight and tall with dignity as he shook his guests' hands. His clothing didn't match his demeanor. He was wearing a blue t-shirt with a faded yellow Pac-Man on it, a brown blazer one size too small, a pair of new blue jeans, and white sneakers. He looked to be awkwardly experimenting with his fashion, as if someone much younger than he, dressed him in the look of a billionaire CEO from a Silicone Valley computer company.

"I'm Marcus," Marcus said, shaking his hand, wondering how he could look in the mirror and not feel absurd.

"And I'm Jack, Jack Bratton, with the LAPD."

"Marcus, Jack, nice to meet you. Please sit down. I see you met my associate Rem," Hoerburger said, nodding to Rem, who silently turned to leave the room.

"Not really," said Jack.

"Well, he's not the best conversationalist, but useful at times."

"Oh, yeah. Like what times are those?" Jack asked.

Hoerburger seemed surprised by Jack's question. He thought for a moment. "You know, when you need to reach something on a high shelf," he said with a smile that squeezed out deep wrinkles along his temples. His teeth were artificially bright white. "How can I help you today?"

Hoerburger returned to his place behind his desk while Marcus and Jack sat in the two chairs facing him. A tinge of artificially sweet air freshener poorly disguised the smell of new carpet in the office.

Jack removed the pad of paper from his shirt pocket and looked at it.

"Thank you for taking the time to see us. We just have a few questions for you. Can you tell us what you do here at Solina Corporation?" he asked.

"We're a chemical manufacturing company. Solina has been in my family for many years. My father started the company after the war. He was a mechanic in Germany during the war, and when he returned to California, he worked as a pool cleaner around Los Angeles."

"What kinds of chemicals do you manufacture?" Marcus asked.

"My father experimented with making different stain removers with chlorine and eventually found a way to manufacture high-quality trichloroethylene."

While Hoerburger spoke, Marcus glanced over at Jack, who toyed with something lodged into the gum of his canine tooth. He fished for it with his tongue, conspicuously distorting his mouth in the process, then slid it off the tooth with his thumbnail. Hoerburger turned toward Marcus and began speaking to him.

"Trichloroethylene. It's a solvent, right?" Marcus asked.

"Yes, it's that and so much more. Trichloroethylene is a wonder product. It's used in everything from metal degreasing, to stain removing, to carpet cleaning, and whiteout. My father made his fortune, our fortune, on that one chemical."

"Is it still made here on-site?" Marcus asked.

"We have several manufacturing plants. The main one is in Burbank, where the company used to be headquartered. Since my father passed away, we've diversified the company a great deal and moved here to our new building."

Hoerburger stopped and looked at Jack, who was doodling in his little pad. Jack asked, "Can you tell us about Van Nuys Properties?"

"We have business interests and investments in several areas, and real estate is one of those. You're a homicide detective, am I correct?"

"Yes."

"What do my business interests have to do with homicide?"

"We found a dead person in one of your houses," replied Jack.

"One of my houses?" asked Hoerburger, looking surprised. "I live in Beverly Hills."

"One of the houses you own. A house owned by Van Nuys Properties."

"That's horrible. Who got killed?"

"I didn't say anyone got killed. We just found a body in the house. Because the investigation is ongoing, we're not able to share any details," Jack said in an official tone. "Do you have a man named Lars Ostergard employed here at Solina?"

Hoerburger waited before speaking. "I've never heard of him, but we have several hundred employees at the different plants. I'd be happy to direct you to our head of human resources so they can provide you with the information you need."

"Yeah, we'll need to get a list of employees."

"Give me a little time. I'll have one waiting for you on your way out." Hoerburger picked up the phone. "Doris, can you have Diane produce a complete list of employees and have it at your desk for the detective on his way out. Yes, just printed. Thank you."

Hoerburger looked at a piece of paper on his desk. "And Dr. Melter, the biology professor at UCLA; what's your purpose here?"

"Sounds like you did a little research on us. I'm just along for the ride. Call it a field trip day, a ride-along," Marcus replied.

"Well, as you can imagine, I'm a busy man, and I don't want to break up your field trip, but if that's all, I have another meeting in a few minutes," Hoerburger said, standing from behind his desk.

"That'll be all for now then," Jack said.

"Okay then, I'll have Rem show you down to the receptionist's desk so you can pick up the employee list."

As they shook hands, the giant Nordic opened the office door and stood silently waiting for Jack and Marcus to exit. "Just one more question. Will Rem's name be on the employee list?"

Hoerburger hesitated as if caught off guard by the question. "He's a private contractor, so you may not find him on there."

"So he's not technically an employee of Solina?" Jack asked.

"No."

"Hmmm. Alright, thank you for your time."

During the elevator ride down Jack asked, "So, Remmy, how long have you been Hoerburger's hit man? Do you have a permit to carry that weapon?"

Rem didn't answer. Instead, he just stared down at Jack.

"You know I'll find out about you, and I'll be back," Jack said as he and Marcus stepped out of the elevator.

"Perhaps," Rem replied. Then gave Jack a closed mouth smile as the elevator door closed in front of him.

25
Laguna Canyon, California
June 6th, 1962

Juan Santana watched his passenger disappear in a cloud of dust in the dirty rearview mirror of his old pickup. Juan was in a hurry. His son was due to be born any day, and he'd been away from home too long. He sped around the sweeping corners of Laguna Canyon Road, where the buckwheat and sage grew in clumped lines of pink and gray-green, like varicose veins on a flesh-toned landscape.

He'd had three passengers in a week and was tired of driving. His eyes felt swollen and watery, and he longed to stop for a short nap. Juan reached up to steady the mirror and get a closer look at a brown shirt fluttering in the back of the truck bed. His last passenger must have forgotten it there when he jumped down out of the truck. The shirt filled like a sail, floated in the wind, then lifted off. Juan watched it fly out of the bed and onto the road behind him.

While Juan distractedly watched the shirt flutter away, his right front wheel caught the edge of the narrow road and the truck was instantly pulled toward a deep ditch. He jerked hard on the steering wheel, lurched off the shoulder, crossed the lane, and ran head-on into an oncoming truck. Juan Santana took his last two breaths, full of hot sage and dust, eight seconds later where his broken body skidded to rest on the asphalt roadside.

Three days later, upon receiving the news of her husband's death, Rosaria Santana entered a fourteen-hour labor resulting in the birth of Juan Santana Junior. As a baby, his eyes were dull and grayish-blue but quickly grew into bright aquamarine, the likes of which Rosaria had never seen. Rosaria thought he was the embodiment of an angel sent from on high to care for the family in her husband's absence. Angel was all she ever called him. Though others in the family adopted the name, they saw it as a gross misnomer. Even as he spent most of his teenage years in juvenile detention centers and later in prison for a string of poorly executed crimes, Rosaria never saw him as anything but an angel.

26
Shawnee, Oklahoma
June 5th, 1936

Before their journey began, Levi Bratton helped Tom White jerry-rig a steel hitch to the chrome rear bumper of his dented Chrysler while Tom went on about his time studying engineering at Harvard. By early in the afternoon, Tom had the trailer loaded and Patsy had readied the family. All the children were on the trailer, and their parents stood together facing away from them, surveying their lost farm. They stood there talking quietly for a long time.

"Everything ends, but this was too soon. I'm sorry I couldn't make it work. I did what I could," Tom said while putting his hand between the blades of Patsy's shoulders as she looked at the ground.

"I'm so sorry," Tom kept repeating. Patsy didn't reply.

As the sadness washed over them, Tom and Patsy took the few minutes before departing to console each for the loss of their place in the world, for fear of the unknown days ahead, and for the vulnerable situation in which they found their family. As they spoke a shred of light, a wave, a particle, passed between them. Simultaneously millions of others like it crashed over all the earth's inhabitants. Light encircles our planet 500 hundred times each second, but like simultaneous events, sad events only happen relative to each other. There is no sadness, or simultaneity, except in time, relativity, and perception.

At the very moment Tom and Patsy stood looking at the brown acres of their dead farm, a little girl in a bamboo hut outside Kolkata, West Bengal, 9,350 miles away, sat confused and hungry, waiting for a third day for her dead mother to wake from her bed. At that same time, 7,138 miles away, hot tears streamed down the brown freckled cheeks of a Somali man who had returned from the front of the Second Italo–Abyssinian War to his burned village and discovered the crib and charred remains of his only son. While he wept, an old Italian woman, 2,345 miles to the north of him, adjusted a crooked cross on the wall above her son's bed, thinking, had she only straightened it earlier, possibly he would still be alive. While she rested on his bed, a man sat in a café in Boedo, Buenos Aires, 4,467 miles south of Tom and Patsy. He sipped a glass of Douce Noir, tried to swallow the knot in his throat, and waited for a woman who would never come back to him. Just under 1,500 miles to the east of Shawnee, a homeless man sitting on the curb at 41st and Broadway spilled his last cup of coffee. As he bent to lick up the rivulet of steaming brown liquid coursing in the gutter, a lighthouse keeper in Weihai, Shandong Province, China, 7,765 miles across the North Pacific Ocean, stumbled home drunk, enveloped in the dull early morning light, thinking of his widow, his empty house, and wishing he could hear her voice in it once again. At the same moment he fell across the threshold of his front door, back in Oklahoma, at the Oklahoma Crippled Children's Hospital in Oklahoma City, only thirty-eight miles away from where Tom and Patsy stood, a mother and father hunched over their frail and bony eight-year-old daughter. She was as pale as the sheets of her hospital bed, trying not to disappoint her parents, smiling, even while taking her last few breaths.

While these sad things came to pass, other occurrences were bathed in a different light. Simultaneously joyous events transpired, full lives were lived, wishes were granted, kind words were exchanged, corporeal passions satisfied, and people sacrificed for one another. An older generation failed so a younger one could succeed. Lovers met, a young woman felt saved, a young man found his way. Time stood still, then sped up, then returned to a reasonable pace, and only an echo remained.

These things happened, and Tom and Patsy were ignorant of them. They returned to the loaded trailer, Tom helped Patsy up to her seat, and took his own next to her, still holding her hand. His face was still, the cavernous hollows of his cheeks shadowed by the afternoon sun, and he squinted into the distance. For the time being, as a calmness descended upon him, he stopped rubbing his shirt collar. He nodded at Levi, who opened the passenger door of the sedan for Ella Mae and placed a hand on her lower back as she took her seat. Thirty seconds later, the trailer was pitching and yawing, shaking and creaking its way westward.

27

In the hot afternoon of June 12th, 1936, one week into their journey, Levi Bratton and the Whites were crossing the Southeastern California desert. That morning, as they broke camp in eastern Arizona, Levi hadn't been careful when reloading a box of tools on the trailer. He left a screwdriver sitting atop the toolbox that eventually bounced off the back of the trailer and landed on the road shoulder as he and the Whites rolled westward through the creosote scrub desert.

Timmy White, a smart and resentful fourteen-year-old, who had ridden on a small flat area above the vibrating trailer wheel for the last week, saw the screwdriver hit the road, slide along behind and roll onto the shoulder. His father did not see the screwdriver fall, as there is little doubt that he would have made Levi stop the rig so he could retrieve it. Tom had a peculiar respect and nostalgia for tools, especially ones he had spent a great deal of time with. Timmy didn't say anything. He looked around, saw that two of his brothers seated near him hadn't seen the tool fall, and didn't say anything to anyone. Timmy wanted to be riding up front with Ella Mae and didn't understand why she was the only one who got to be in the front car. He wasn't that much younger than she. Anything that prolonged this terrible journey, like stopping for a screwdriver, was out of the question as far as Timmy was concerned, so he watched silently as the tool faded on the horizon, then was gone.

There it lay on the road shoulder, a simple flathead screwdriver with a cracked, yellow, plastic handle, the result of Levi Bratton's few seconds of carelessness and Timmy White's resentment toward his sister. The forces of sun, water, and rust are the enemies of ostensibly indestructible objects. An old screwdriver lasts a long time in the California desert, but not forever. This particular screwdriver, however, wasn't subjected to the elements for long—nine years, seven months, and twenty-five days to be exact, a short time in the life of a screwdriver.

On the morning of February 6th, 1946 Eddie Pike woke on a cardboard bed and exited a parked boxcar on the Burlington Northern Santa Fe Railroad, crossed the small patch of granite sand desert between the rail line and Route 66, and stood on the road shoulder, singing quietly to himself, intending to hitchhike west into Los Angeles. A hobo with whom he'd shared the boxcar shit himself the night before, and Eddie had to get out. As he stood waiting for a sympathetic car to pass, he spotted Tom White's screwdriver lodged in a crack in the pavement. He would have missed it completely, as many others did in the years since the screwdriver had fallen from the trailer, but by happenstance he was standing right above it. Eddie Pike bent down, wiggled the tool free of its temporary home, and placed it in an external pocket of his knapsack. Shortly after, he landed a ride into Los Angeles.

Eddie and the screwdriver made their way down to the Long Beach Harbor, where he was looking for an uncle who had shipped out to the Pacific Theater in '42 and supposedly had returned earlier that year. Eddie slept under an overpass on New Henry Ford Avenue with some newly found friends, one of whom robbed him of his knapsack just before dawn and escaped with it to the shipping yard before rifling through it for food or other items of value. Due to its disappointing contents, the knapsack was discarded between two shipping containers where it was discovered three days later by two Mexican ship hands setting out that evening for Salina Cruz, Mexico. As their freighter floated out of Long Beach Harbor, Eddie Pike's knapsack was searched for the second time. This time the screwdriver was found and pocketed by one of the sailors before jettisoning the whole knapsack, which sunk to the bottom of Long Beach Harbor, where the more durable portions of it remain today.

Ten days later, the screwdriver left the cargo hold of the Aliança Freightliner in the pocket of Martine Morales, the ship hand who had acquired it in Long Beach. Morales discovered that he was still in possession of the screwdriver later that evening while putting on his nicer pants, the same ones he had worn while boarding the ship in Long Beach. He was readying himself for a night in the port bars of Salina Cruz and decided for no particular reason to keep the screwdriver with him. That night, during what should have been a routine bar fight, Morales, who was known for his excessive drinking, stabbed the screwdriver through the neck of a bartender, piercing his jugular vein and killing him almost instantly. Morales spent the rest of his life in the Centro Federal de Readaptación prison in Toluca, while Tom White's screwdriver spent eight years in the evidence locker of the Tehuantepec municipal police station in central Salina Cruz.

There it was eventually found, cleaned of the remaining dried blood, and used to pry open the broken desk of Roberto Tinto, the officer in charge of police evidence at the station. After storing the screwdriver in his desk drawer for nearly three months, Officer Tinto eventually brought it home to his son, along with several other tools he had collected. The gift was an ill-fated attempt to masculinize his son, whom he correctly suspected of having homosexual tendencies. The eleven-year-old boy, Roberto Tinto Jr., who liked the chipped, plastic screwdriver handle and the way it felt as he rubbed his thumb and lips over the jagged indentations, brought it with him a year later as he and his mother, who had immigrated to southern Mexico from Brazil, traveled south to visit her parents.

On September 8th, 1954, Roberto Tinto Jr., his mother, and Tom White's well-stroked screwdriver, reached the Grajaú Bus Terminal in southern São Paulo, Brazil, where his uncle was awaiting their arrival. Roberto's uncle, Gabriel Gama, was a fat, sweaty, despicable man who had grown moderately wealthy during the São Paulo real estate boom of the early 1950s. When Gama arrived at the bus station that afternoon, he was distracted by thoughts of a large real estate deal in which he was over-leveraged. Lost in devious thoughts and emerging unscrupulous plans, he turned the key too hard while turning off the car, and one-quarter of its distal end broke off in the ignition. Upon returning to the car with his sister and her son, Gama was unable to restart the vehicle. Roberto Jr. offered his uncle the screwdriver, which by chance slid nicely into the ignition, pushed the remaining portion of the broken key into place, turned smoothly, and started the vehicle. Gama kept the screwdriver, with a false promise to his nephew that he would return it after having the ignition fixed. For three months, Gama used Tom White's screwdriver to start his car.

On an early afternoon in the same year of his nephew's visit, after again over-eating at lunch, sweating profusely, and stinking of fish and rotten tomato soup, Gama was speeding along a side road outside Grajaú. He glanced to his right and saw that the screwdriver had fallen to the floor in front of the passenger seat. He was late for a meeting with a potential investor and wanted to be able to turn his car off quickly when he arrived, so he looked down, struggling to reach for the screwdriver. As his sausage-like fingers clawed at the floor, he heard a terrible noise, a thud, a pop, the ring of metal, and a crumbling sound as something soft rolled under his car. Gama sat up, looked into his rearview mirror to see a human somersaulting onto the red dirt road shoulder.

Gabriel Gama was never discovered for his vehicular murder, and Tom White's screwdriver sat in the glove compartment when he sold the car a week later. It remained there for nearly a decade, discovered but unused by the new owners until the car was sold again, stripped of the useful parts, and crushed into a tidy scrap metal cube at the São João landfill. Eventually, that metal cube and the screwdriver deep inside it were shipped to the Gerdau steel mill where they were shredded and melted at 2750°F for low-quality steel feedstock that was extruded into thin sheets from which disks were punched and formed into bottle caps. The steel from Tom White's screwdriver was dispersed throughout South America in the crimped bottle caps of Bohemia brand beer.

Never mind about screwdrivers and bottle caps and how one of those Bohemia caps was responsible for the death of Gama's only son, and the end of his thin bloodline. Twenty-eight years earlier, seven days after they first met, Levi Bratton and Ella Mae White crossed the border from Arizona into California, a state which neither would leave again. As that screwdriver hopped off her father's makeshift trailer on which the other eleven Whites rode, deep inside Ella Mae, a blob of 256 cells rode a peristaltic wave of ciliated flesh fingers through one of her fallopian tubes—a two-day-old fertilized egg. The blob lodged in the upper reaches of her uterus and over the next eight months and thirteen days would gestate into Willie Bratton, Jack Bratton's father.

28
Laguna Canyon, California
June 6th, 1962

The blanket of shrubby vegetation that dominates the hillsides of Southern California has the perverse misnomer, chaparral. When the dry, hard Majorcans came north into the state to set up their shabby missions and collect the native souls, they incorrectly and lazily named many of the new plants and animals with the same old name of organisms found in their homeland. Father Junípero Serra, who cared little for anything that didn't instantly reveal itself as useful to him, having spent the long and arduous previous day limping across the Tijuana River Estuary, hiked up the low hills above their camp at Mission Bay on the morning of July 1st, 1769. He took his first look at the seemingly endless scrubby vegetation of his new home in Alta California and dismissed it with a derogatory Basque word for stunted, chaparro.

Like similar plants in the Padre's native Spain, chaparral shrubs have strange leaves, some barely recognizable as such. Having been brutalized for millennia by the fire and drought of the Mediterranean climate, many chaparral species have evolved impossibly small leaves—stunted little sausages no longer than the copulatory organ of a male water skeeter. Even though the leaves of California's chaparral and the penis of an insect that can walk on water rarely meet, they may have converged coincidentally on the same size and shape for the perfect performance of their seemingly unrelated functions.

These and all manner of other wonderings distracted Alex while he walked on the road shoulder toward the beach. He had an insatiable curiosity about his natural surroundings, a trait he would pass on to and eventually help cultivate in his only son. Curiosity entertained and sustained him. He was happy to be in a strange land filled with new organisms. He reached out to one side of the road to rub an unfamiliar, shiny, three-lobed leaf and smelled the spicy sting of herbal volatiles released from its bruised surface. No leaf he encountered in

Mexico smelled like that. Two minutes later, he did something he would come to regret for several weeks afterward. He stepped off the road behind a large oak with low arching branches, unzipped his brown chinos, pulled back the wrinkled foreskin of his Kielbasa-sized penis, and urinated.

As Alex Melter neared Laguna Beach and the shade was beginning its ascent of the hills around him, he noticed the soil along the road getting sandier; then he smelled the familiar marine air as it drifted up the canyon from the Pacific.

In none of Alex's fantasies of California was it so dry. The summers in Mazatlán and São Paulo were wet and humid; this new home was parched. He wasn't seeing the roadside puddles and water skeeters that had been so common in the summer on his daily walks to the fishing docks. He often stopped to watch closely as the male skeeters slid, pulsated, and whirled on the water, banging their genitals against the dark surface, creating the little love ripples that drove females in the area crazy with desire. Most copulation in water skeeters, like humans, only happens with female consent, yet she has to hear just the right rhythm on the ripples from her potential suitor to drop her exoskeletal genital shield.

Like a successful male water skeeter, Alex gave off just the right rhythm because consensual, human mating had always come easy to him. During his time in Mexico, several women, including one forthright captain's wife who liked to stick her finger up his butt, dropped their genital shields at the first sight of him.

The sun had set, and dusk was taking hold of the coastline as Alex Melter took his first steps onto a Southern California beach. Behind him, a weak light came over the low eastern hills from whence he had come, and the first lights were coming on in the beach town. Alex found a flat rock on the sandy bank above the beach and sat to triumphantly remove his shoes and watch the waves. He reached into his knapsack and removed the tattered pages of his 1946 issue of Life Magazine, with its beautiful women in frumpy bikinis on the golden beach. He studied the pages, as he had so many times in the past, then looked up from the magazine, smiled, and tossed it onto the sand behind him.

The sea had turned chocolate brown as the light faded to the west and, a warm inland breeze, smelling of the canyons, floated over him. Alex relaxed, and his eyes filled with tears of joy. He remembered the truest and most beautiful poem that had ever been recited. He whispered it to the ocean.

I belong to no one.

I have something inside me that cannot be taken.

The past can't hurt me.

29
Southeastern California
1936

The seven days between Shawnee and the California border were slow going, long days. Levi Bratton pulled the Whites' trailer over a thousand miles, nearly directly west along the 35th parallel. At forty miles an hour, the old truck tires began an uncomfortable wobble. Levi and the Whites made six and seven-hour days with brief stops for food, urination, pogoing, and repairs to the trailer. Tom had outfitted the rig well for the trip, with enough rationed supplies for nearly two weeks for the whole family, not imagining at the time that all those supplies would eventually run out.

At the end of the first day's drive, Levi pulled the Chrysler and trailer to the side of the road on the edge of a field.

"This spot will suffice for the night," said Tom to Levi as he came down off the trailer, then looking into the distance he yelled, "You be mindful of snakes in that assemblage of rocks, child."

Levi opened the hood of the Chrysler and looked across the dusty intersection where Ella Mae was pogoing while the small children watched. She was barefooted, smiling, and giggling, with her thin skirt hiked up above her knees. She had the vertical bar of the pogo stick tightly gripped between her thighs, and her hands were waving wildly in the air as she hopped without holding the handles.

Levi smiled to himself. Ella Mae was a light bulb in a room that had been darkened for years. From the moment he first saw her bouncing toward him in Shawnee, an unfamiliar feeling rose inside him, not of lust, but of something like purpose. His feeling wasn't the same ephemeral burn he experienced for some beautiful adolescent farm girl or young Oakie mother at Armer's service station. He was starting to feel protective of her and her family.

She didn't need him or his help, that much was clear, but he wanted to serve her. To serve Ella Mae was to serve her family, and even though he was initially reluctant, he took a liking to the Whites.

Tom and two of the older boys raised two large dome tents that could have easily slept twenty. The multi-pole geodesic dome tent was another Tom White invention for which he would get no credit. With no knowledge of Walther Bauersfeld nor Buckminster Fuller, Tom invented a way to use bent steel rods and lightweight tarp, in which Patsy had sewn a door, to raise waterproof, comfortable sleeping space for the whole family.

"Son, you're welcome to sleep inside the tents with us," Tom said to Levi when he realized that Levi was watching intently while they raised the tents, and may have been sleeping in his car while traveling.

"No, thank you. The night's plenty warm, and I have my bedroll," Levi replied. "Where'd you get those structures?"

"Patsy and I fashioned them ourselves," answered Tom, looking up from his work.

"Seems like your whole trailer is well outfitted," said Levi.

"That's true. We benefited from the substantial time frame during which our farm was ossifying. Although we hoped for a reversal of our fortune, we had the advantage of many months of preparation for this trip." Tom massaged his shirt collar for a moment, then stepped closer to Levi.

"Instead of despairing, we set to work on the accommodations necessary for our dislocation, so as to extemporize in as few ways as possible during our journey to a better location. You, my boy, were the final component," Tom said with a smile.

"As to the dome," Tom continued, "it always seemed to me the most efficient use of space, and the shape promotes a natural cooling airflow. Patsy's insights were the rollup door and the affixation of the canvas to the inside of the bent pole exoskeleton with small ties, which greatly expedites the ease of erection." Tom paused and smiled. "As it turns out, she's particularly industrious in helping the ease of an erection."

Levi, who stood with his mouth open while Tom spoke, looked at Patsy, who was shaking her head. As always, Levi had understood the gist of Tom's response, but few of the words.

Levi was impressed by Tom and hadn't met someone like him before. In watching him rig the trailer, use tools, and carry out minor repairs on the Chrysler, Levi could tell that Tom was better than he was with cars and machines. Levi had learned a great deal about automobiles from George Armer, but he knew nothing compared to Tom. Automobile repair and general handiness were the only currencies that Levi knew for respect and admiration, and in that regard Tom was wealthy.

After a long second day on the road, they made camp in the late afternoon outside Amarillo, Texas. It was the beginning of a long summer evening. The sun was down, the heat of the day subsided, and the Whites busied themselves with dinner, exploration of their roadside camp, and erecting their two domes. Levi was kneeling on the ground near the Chrysler, spreading out his tarp and padded blanket when he sensed someone watching him from behind.

"I thought I heard the bouncing stop," he said without looking up.

"You know I appreciate what you're doin' for us, we all do," Ella Mae said in a serious voice.

"I'm glad to help. I like to drive, and pullin' a trailer doesn't slow you up much." They both knew he was lying.

"I'd like to learn to drive someday. Pa taught me to run the tractor, but I never drove a car," Ella Mae said.

"Here, sit down. Get a feel for it." He stood and opened the driver's side door so Ella Mae could sit down. Levi kneeled back down next to the driver's door and watched her pretend to drive. As she wiggled back and forth in the seat, her legs were outstretched, barely reaching the pedals, and her faded floral print skirt sat high on her thighs. Levi was hyperaware of the slight line made by her underwear beneath the thin material, so subtle and so low on her hips. Her thighs were muscular, her shins thin, and her knees knobby. He let his eyes rest on the plump side of her breast, pressed under her bra, and she turned to look down on him.

"How'd you get those scars on your ankles?" he asked her softly.

She swiveled in the seat, turned her legs away from the pedals of the Chrysler, and placed them on Levi's thigh. He could see matching scars on the inside of her slender ankles.

"When I was just getting good at bouncing, the insides of my ankles rubbed against the bar just right. They've all healed up now," she replied, still looking down at him. "Go on, it's okay, you can feel 'em."

Levi held her foot between his two rough hands and softly ran a palm over the inside of her ankle. Her skin was cool and smooth. Her feet were dark and tiny in his large hands, and the scars were a shade lighter than the tanned skin around them. He rubbed her calf and brought it closer to his face. Ella Mae smelled familiar to him, like the sweet loam and worm castings on the forest floor around his childhood home on the McAlester lot. She scooted forward on the edge of the seat, rolling her pelvis, pushing herself in his direction to make it easier for him to access her thighs. It was such a simple gesture, meaningless out of context, but in that moment it was her surrender, her request.

Levi saw the thin, dark cracks in the calloused skin on the outer edges of his two thick forefingers as they pressed into her inner thighs and slid firmly up from her knees. His fingers found her cotton underwear, the wetness of freshly cleaned and ringed out laundry. He stroked her, with soft, long touches up and down and could feel the swollen folds of her skin underneath the wet material. She closed her eyes, tilted her head back, and placed her hands on his shoulders as he reached underneath her underwear. Her skin was slippery and wet, and he pressed solidly against her with the soft pads of three large fingers as she rolled her hips back and forth, allowing his hand to slide on her at the right pace. After a few moments, Levi pulled his hand from her dress, and they both smiled as they saw his fingers glistening in the remaining light. Levi lifted his hand to his mouth and wiped the shiny, viscous fluid from his fingers onto his lips. It was an awkward gesture, but the awkwardness only lingered briefly as he sat back on his bedroll and pulled her onto him.

30

On their seventh day, Levi and the Whites crossed the California desert, accidentally changed the future course of several lives in Mexico and Brazil, and crested the southernmost finger of the Sierra Nevada in Tehachapi, where they stopped for water and to rest from the heat. Seventeen miles to the west of Tehachapi, near the intersection of Bear Mountain Road and Route 66, Levi pulled to the side of the road as the sun was setting. He eased the trailer down an embankment and brought the Chrysler to a stop. As soon as the trailer had ceased its lurching, before the dust could settle, the White children were scattering.

As the family made their camp, Levi was once again under the hood of the Chrysler.

He looked up and called out, "Timmy, come help me."

Ella Mae's younger brother was the only White still sitting on the trailer. "I need you to hold this hose while I tighten down a clamp."

Timmy approached him nervously. "Grab me the yellow handled screwdriver out of the toolbox," said Levi.

Timmy looked through the metal box on the side of the trailer, pulled out a different and similar sized flathead screwdriver, and handed it to Levi, who used it without hesitation.

Timmy held the hose while Levi worked on the clamp. "You're doing good watchin' out for the younger ones," Levi said when they were done.

He reached into his pocket and pulled out a caramel hard candy in a transparent red wrapper, which he had bought during their stop in Tehachapi. Timmy smiled, took the candy cautiously, and quickly put it into the back pocket of his denim overalls. He quietly thanked Levi and went off on his own to savor it. As Timmy left, Levi looked up to see that Tom had been watching their whole interaction. Tom nodded approvingly at Levi.

Later that evening, as their roadside camp grew dark, Levi and the Whites gathered around a fire that Patsy made for the cooking. The children had eaten well, and tired eyes reflected flames as they died down to embers. From the west, a distant hum turned into what Tom and Levi recognized as the sickly purring cluck of a diesel engine. As the sound grew louder and oncoming headlights could be seen in the distance, Tom handed the small child in his lap to Patsy and stood.

A rusted, forest-green, flatbed Ford truck pulled onto the shoulder near their camp, raising a cloud of dust. The truck stopped a short distance from the trailer, the headlights turned off, but the engine remained idling with a loud rattle. Levi stood to join Tom, and they approached the two men in the truck.

"Can we do anything to help you gentlemen?" asked Tom as he approached the truck.

"What y'all doin' here?" asked the driver. He was younger than the large bald-headed man who sat silently looking disinterestedly forward in the passenger seat.

"We're camped for the evening. We were under the impression that we were only briefly occupying public property and didn't need to announce our presence to anyone. Have we transgressed some premises over which you have dominion?" replied Tom.

"What?" said the driver, looking at Tom disgustedly.

Levi stepped forward next to Tom. "He means to say we thought this was public land. Y'all own this spot?"

"Where you headed?" asked the driver to Levi.

"We're headed down to Bakersfield in the morning, lookin' to settle for a bit and get some work," replied Levi.

The driver laughed sardonically, and the large man in the passenger seat still hadn't looked at Tom or Levi, but could be seen to shake his head. "No you ain't. Bakersfield's closed right now," said the driver.

"What'd you mean, it's closed? Ain't like you can close a town," Levi said. His irritation with the two men was beginning to rise.

"For you, Bakersfield's closed," said the driver with a sarcastic smile. "Best you head left at this intersection down into Arvin. There's a labor camp out there."

"We'll head wherever we want to," Levi said and started to back away from the truck.

At that, the large man in the passenger seat turned to face Levi, who paused in his tracks. In a voice that was as much a growl as it was a hiss, he said, "You go on and try that, but we'll be waiting on the road." He looked Levi directly in the eye, then let his eyes wander to the campfire behind them. "Y'all got women and children with you, right? You should be careful."

The large man nodded to the driver, who pulled on the headlights, revved the engine, forced the truck into gear with a loud grind, and headed back down the road toward Bakersfield, leaving Levi and Tom in the settling dust.

They stood there for a long time not saying anything. Finally, Tom let out a strained chuckle and said, "I've never heard of Arvin, but it sounds delightful compared to Bakersfield."

"Are we just going to let them intimidate us after all that distance we come?" asked Levi.

"I don't suppose we can proceed to Bakersfield at this point. Those gentlemen were quite persuasive," replied Tom.

"We shouldn't stand for it. They're probably tryin' to scare folks off and keep work for themselves," said Levi.

In as plain language as he could bring himself to use Tom said, "Levi, look at me son. It's irrelevant. We're not going to Bakersfield. Those two men, no matter their motives, stand to lose far less than we do. We have the kids to look out for, Patsy, Ella Mae." In the low-light of the moon, Tom tried to gauge Levi's response at the mention of his daughter's name. "If you continue into Bakersfield, you'll have to leave the trailer and all of us here." Tom paused for a long moment, "all of us."

Levi looked up at Tom, then back down to a small stone he was toeing in the dust. He didn't respond for a long time. Finally, he said, "Alright, alright. We'll head south from here tomorrow morning. But tonight, I want your help unhitching the trailer so I can drive down into Bakersfield. I'll be back before dawn."

31
Los Angeles, California
Present Day

Jack pulled the sun visor down to block the western light. He and Marcus traveled against the traffic, moving swiftly westward along the edge of a river of oncoming cars. The sun was behind a strip of diffuse chocolate clouds, and the light was changing fast. At the same time, in the office they had just left, Jeff Hoerburger spoke to his bodyguard in a hushed voice. Meanwhile, Jack and Marcus exchanged some words of their own.

"Why would the head of a chemical company need a huge bodyguard, or whatever that guy is?" Marcus asked.

"I don't know. He seemed vaguely familiar to me though."

"Which one?"

"The big guy, Rem."

Marcus looked over at Jack, then the oncoming traffic. They sat in silence while Jack focused on driving. Jack tapped the steering wheel with his forefinger, beating out the rhythm of some song in his head. Ever since they had met, Jack drove in that way, never with the radio on, but always with a song in his head. The gentle cadence of Jack's finger and the sway of the car had a soothing effect on Marcus, and he began drift off.

Marcus was a PhD graduate student at UC San Diego, teaching a microbiology class, when he was accused of making racial slurs in front of the students. The associate dean responsible for checking student evaluations called Marcus into his office and read aloud what a student had written, "Marcus has an interesting vernacular, he once said to me, 'You rocked that slant's world.'"

The associate dean knew that Marcus was half black, and had learned at one of his several sensitivity trainings that race relations are tenuous between Blacks and Asians.

Upon hearing the comment on the evaluation, Marcus smiled and replied with, "What's wrong with that comment?" The associate dean responded by launching into a long speech about tolerance and not creating a hostile environment for students. As he spoke, Marcus became more and more confused. The associate dean ended with, "the use of derogatory racial terms like slant in front of students is unacceptable."

Marcus, who until that point considered himself a connoisseur of all things inappropriate, including racial slurs, had never heard the term slant used to describe an Asian. He explained to the associate dean that a slant was a commonly used tool in microbiology—a glass test tube placed at an angle in which liquid media cools and solidifies inside, forming a large slanted surface for bacterial growth. In an attempt to inoculate the delicate gelatinous surface, that student had likely wrecked it.

By then, the associate dean was already worked up and proud of himself for having identified the type of subtly racist student whom he had learned about in the race relations seminars. Marcus confirmed his suspicions that black people disliked Asians, and whether slant actually referred to people or microbiology equipment didn't matter. If Marcus wanted to continue as a student and not have this incident appear on his official record, he would have to carry out community service. The volunteer coordinator for the Surfrider Foundation, who just happened to be the wife of the associate dean, would be signing off on twenty-five hours of beach cleanup by Marcus.

Jack Bratton, the orchestrator of some stupid fraternity prank, was already on the beach the following Saturday when Marcus reported for duty. Marcus and Jack laughed a lot during their hours together, each with their Day-Glo orange, netted vest and 36-inch trigger-handled trash picker. Based on their outdoor custodial experience, one would deduce that the typical Southern Californian beachgoer was a McDonald's-eating litterbug and staunch believer in safe sex. Jack was fascinated by Marcus's explanations of the likely path that each item had taken to the beach. For Marcus, driftwood pieces weren't just sticks on the sand; each was a mystery, an opportunity to hone his skills of careful observation. While Marcus studied the different types of wood that had washed in with the tides, Jack worked on a way to use part of a discarded cinderblock and his trash picker to make a seesaw type catapult whereby he could jump on one end and launch a dirty diaper out to sea.

32

Jack pulled the car to the curb, and Marcus got out.

"Thanks for the pizza. Look, I'm pretty busy on campus for the next few days, so I'll see you after that."

"Alright, thanks for coming out there today."

Marcus lived in a rented house on a quiet street a few miles south of the university. It was built during the 1940s Los Angeles Spanish Colonial architecture revival, with smooth white stucco walls and a low-pitched clay tile roof. The inside had white-washed plaster walls that arched gracefully into the ceiling at the corners, and the floors were covered with oak and terra cotta tile. Marcus always thought it was far too nice of a house for how little time he spent there, and he felt some guilt about how unfurnished he kept it.

He walked along the sidewalk that bisected the patch of lawn between the curb and the front of the house, then up onto the steps of the concrete porch and to the front door. As he came onto the porch, he noticed a light coming from the house that he hadn't left on. He cautiously checked the front door, and it was locked. Maybe I did leave that light on, he thought. He inserted his key into the lock quietly, turned the lock, which made a conspicuous click, then pushed the door open quickly.

"Hello?" Marcus called.

"It's me, Elizabeth," a woman replied from the kitchen. "I hope you don't mind; I let myself in."

"You have a key?" Marcus asked as he came into the kitchen.

"You never asked for it back."

"What are you doing here? Last time you said you didn't want to see me like this anymore."

Elizabeth Shackleton was holding a half-full glass of wine. "I brought a bottle of Pinot. Do you want a glass?"

Without waiting for an answer, she turned around and reached above the counter into an upper cabinet to retrieve a wine glass.

Elizabeth wasn't tall, and the glass cabinet was a stretch for her. As she reached up, the light blue tank top she was wearing slipped up and exposed a spiral tattoo on her lower back, an artifact of her exuberant years as an undergraduate. Her skin and the tattoo hadn't degraded in the slightest now that she was in her early thirties. She was compact, firm, youthful, slender but round at the same time.

When Marcus saw that dark blue vortex, which he had stared at many times before, perfectly centered between a pair of slight dimples, a small but controllable urge grew within him. Though he tried to hide it from her, she knew that she became irresistible to him with even the slightest exposure of any part of her body.

Elizabeth's shoulder-length hair was effortlessly beautiful, dirty blonde, with tawny waves flowing through darker patches. On that particular night, she had it hastily tied up with several clumps refusing to cooperate. Marcus could tell by her hair that this was an unplanned visit. She was much shorter than he and had to stretch her neck back to make eye contact while coming close to hand him the glass of wine she had just poured.

"I know what you're going to say, and I'm sorry I'm here again. I had nowhere else to go. Richard and I had a big fight."

"You know you're welcome here anytime. Where does Richard think you are?" Marcus asked.

"I don't know. I walked out during our fight and didn't tell him where I was going."

Marcus went to the window that faced the street and looked out to see a dark car parked across the street a few houses down. He couldn't tell for sure, but it looked as if there was someone seated in it.

"Richard wouldn't follow me here. Don't be so paranoid," Elizabeth said in a nonchalant way.

Marcus realized it would be ridiculous for him to think someone was outside the house watching them. He came away from the window, noticing that he hadn't yet put down his shoulder bag.

"I'm not paranoid," Marcus said. "I don't care if he finds out anymore. I love you and want to be with you. You know that."

"And you know that it would never work," Elizabeth said, looking into her wine glass.

"We could leave here. There are other jobs out there for me."

"Here, come sit down next to me on the couch," Elizabeth said, enticing him with a look that was all too familiar. Marcus hesitated, but not for long.

Marcus's house was warm, and he was disheveled. He removed his bag and coat and sat down. His necktie had loosened to a point as to no longer serve any purpose. Once they were seated, Elizabeth reached over and pulled on the knot to remove it. "You look like you've had a long day."

"Yeah, it was interesting. After my lecture, I drove out to Glendale with Jack to look into something we're working on."

"Why do you go with him?"

Marcus shrugged. "I love it. It's an opportunity to affect the real world. Two people with lives and loved ones are dead, and we don't know why. In this case, my tree knowledge actually mattered. Jack cares about what I know more than any of my students." Marcus smiled a little to himself. "Plus, I like Jack. He's funny and easy to be around. Why did you and Richard fight?"

"It doesn't matter. He's such an unresponsive prick."

"I know you think because he's my department chair you have to be careful, but really, I'll let it all go for you. We can leave here and never come back."

"I know, I know. I want that too. Let's work toward that," Elizabeth said while turning sideways on the couch to face Marcus.

She set her wine glass down and leaned back against the edge of the couch. "Take a load off," Elizabeth said with a deviant little smile. "Come over here and lay on me."

It was an offer that, had he wanted to refuse, he probably couldn't have. With a clink, Marcus set his wine glass down on the coffee table and leaned over onto her. She wrapped her arms around him and pulled him tightly down onto her.

33

"Where's my underwear?" Elizabeth asked Marcus fifteen minutes later.

Marcus enjoyed watching her dress herself. Each time it was as if she was getting dressed for the first time and didn't quite know how each garment was meant to fit on her.

"They're under the coffee table. You don't have to get going yet. Why don't you stay the night?"

"Richard is going to wonder where I've been," Elizabeth said, then thought for a moment. "Or maybe he won't wonder at all."

"Why did you marry him?" Marcus asked.

"I can't remember. I really can't," Elizabeth said, studying her underwear, making sure to get it on the right way.

"How do you stay with someone who just doesn't care?"

In the orange lamplight of Marcus's living room, her blond hair contrasted with her thick, dark eyebrows, which formed perfectly matching oblong crescents around her eye slits. She stood, wearing nothing but her black panties, staring at him, where he was seated on the couch. She didn't answer him. In the glow of the room, her skin was matte brown and didn't reflect any light. He wanted to sit and look at her for hours. She was a wildfire that burned everything up inside of him. All his carefully tended dreams sat like dry tinder ready to ignite in the shifting winds of her temperament.

"Alright, well, it's probably best that I get back soon," she said.

As she reached up to pull her hair together, her breasts lifted on her chest. They were flawless—perfectly round, taut, just the right amount of fat, nipples like pencil erasers, surrounded by darkly pigmented areolas, each just smaller than a quarter. Marcus looked down at his own dark-skinned naked body and thought, this is it, this is your body, your pleasure vessel, and it doesn't get any better. Try to enjoy it more. Allow yourself to be pleased. You may be content but try for happiness. For a moment, when she smiled at him, he was happy.

"Come sit with me on the couch," Marcus said, patting the cushion next to him.

"I have to go," Elizabeth said, putting on her remaining clothes.

Once they were both dressed, Marcus stepped out onto the front porch behind Elizabeth. The outside air was cool and humid. Ocean fog was rolling in over Santa Monica, heading east, where it would eventually dissipate against the warm inland mountains. Marcus looked up to see the quarter moon showing brightly through the fog that blew inland below it.

"Look at that," Elizabeth whispered to Marcus on the porch, "there's a little halo of fog around the moon."

"Yeah," Marcus said. "You don't see that often. The air must be pretty cold up there."

"Okay, thanks for letting me come over."

"When will I see you again?"

"I don't know. Soon, maybe. I don't know," Elizabeth said, trying to be reassuring.

Marcus held out his hand to her. She looked around, then briefly touched his hand while mouthing the words, thank you.

Marcus stood on the porch while she walked to her car. After she pulled away, he went back into the house, put his wine glass in the sink, and stared at the empty living room before returning to the porch. On the front stoop, Marcus noticed that the car he had seen earlier was gone. He listened to the street, vaguely hoping to see Elizabeth's car return while staring up at the peculiar halo around the Los Angeles moon.

At that same moment, scientists in Norway were analyzing the center of large pellets of hail that had fallen and been collected along the coastline of the Barents Sea months earlier. The odd halo in the warm Los Angeles night sky above Marcus and the large lumps of fallen ice in Norway were both caused by a new strain of the bacteria *Pseudomonas syringae*, whose accidental evolution occurred in a wheat field in Morris County, Kansas in the summer of 1936.

This newly discovered strain of *Pseudomonas* would eventually be at the center of several breakthroughs in bio-precipitation, enabling scientists and farmers to control local rain and weather patterns by seeding the atmosphere with genetically modified bacterial rainmakers. This elegant innovation, and all the subsequent discoveries in the field of aeromicrobiology, would stave off the effects of global warming and the inevitable meteorological calamity that awaited the human race several centuries later. With the ability to exploit *Pseudomonas* to create rain, humans lasted for 178 years longer than they otherwise would have.

34
Kern County, California
1936

On the eighth day of their journey from the east, Tom White stood in the rosy predawn light fidgeting nervously with his shirt collar and looking down the highway to the west. He thought about how the sun had already made landfall on his Shawnee farm two hours earlier and its light was sweeping westward across the continent at 1,000 miles an hour. As the light began to blaze on the hilltops and creep along the ground in his direction, Tom was momentarily struck by his surroundings—a beautiful blanket of stubbled, lion colored grass interrupted occasionally by stunted bluish-green oaks. Why had he not noticed this place the night before? What were these new and unfamiliar organisms?

The Sierra Nevada foothill landscape receded quickly from his mind, and he returned to calculating the probability that Levi would actually be coming back. He had to make plans for getting the trailer pulled by someone else if they never saw him again. He watched a low-slung jalopy putter by, carrying a groggy family and all their possessions toward Bakersfield and wondered about their fate.

Moments later, the children were streaming out of the geodesic domes. Sticks cracked, pans clanked, Patsy and Ella Mae tended a morning fire, and Tom turned from the roadside to return to camp. He heard a car racing up from the west and turned to see, with great relief, the chrome grill of Levi's Chrysler reflecting the morning sun like a star rising over the western hills.

Tom helped Levi back the Chrysler up to re-hitch it to the trailer. "Everything alright?" he asked when Levi got out.

With a distant look in his eyes, Levi replied, "Yup, everything's fine, but we should break camp soon and head out."

"What did you see?" Tom asked.

"Ain't much to see down there. Never saw those men again," replied Levi.

Tom shrugged and looked at Ella Mae, who was listening to their conversation.

And for the second time, Tom White hitched his family to Levi Bratton. They ate breakfast, broke camp, and were on the trailer in just over an hour. The Chrysler strained under the weight as Levi eased it up the embankment and back onto Route 66, where they drove a short distance to the west, then turned south along Bear Mountain Road.

The sun was behind them as they descended into the great hazy valley below—a valley named in 1805 for the feast day of Saint Joachim, the grandfather of Jesus, as Gabriel Moraga and his cavalry crested the Pacheco Pass and looked down upon an abundance never before seen by Europeans.

The trailer shivered and pulsated beneath them as they went. First, the oaks disappeared, leaving only a blanket of short, sandy-brown grass, then the smell hit them. It was a familiar smell to Tom and Patsy; wet loam, a smell that had left their farm in Shawnee many years before. The dried grass yielded in a sharp line to a verdant patchwork of fields, vineyards, and orchards. The brakes on the Chrysler were relieved as they rolled onto the valley floor. Humidity rose from the plants, and they were surrounded on both sides by green as far as they could see and ditches running with water.

Levi drove with the window down and his left elbow resting outside the car. He was excited about the lushness of their new surroundings. In the fifteen hundred miles he'd come from George Armer's service station in Arkansas, he'd seen nothing like it—dried up farms in Oklahoma, dust and dirt in Texas, heat and sand of New Mexico and Arizona, the California desert, and now this. They had arrived. His right hand was on Ella Mae's thigh, and she held it tightly with both her hands.

The road led through a tunnel of tall vineyards into the town of Arvin. The night before, Levi had used most of the remaining gas, so he slowed the rig and pulled the Chrysler into a one pump service station.

An older black man in a grease-stained dark green jumpsuit emerged from the station with a scowl, waving at Levi to drive on. "If y'all don't have any money for gas, move on. We can't give away no more free gas," he yelled.

"Free gas?" Levi replied with a confused look. "We got money and we need gas. Do you have it?"

The man approached the Chrysler. His scowl turned into a look of skepticism. "You have money?" he said, looking at the trailer and all the Whites.

Levi turned off the car, got out, and approached the old man, who was hunched over and much shorter than he. Levi stood uncomfortably close. "Why do you think we'd stop here if we didn't have money to pay for gas?" he asked with clear irritation in his voice. He was close enough that he could see white stubble emerging from the man's dark brown chin. Many pores from which wiry black hair had once emerged vigorously were now nothing more than dormant craters, never bound to erupt again.

"No offense meant, sir," said the old man, looking up at Levi and taking a step back. "Lots of folks like you come through here lately without no money, askin' if I can spare them a gallon of fuel. Desperate to move on. Lookin' for work."

"Well, we ain't them. Now fill it up," Levi said.

"You don't mind if I see your payment before fillin' it up, do you?" asked the man sheepishly.

"We don't mind at all," Tom said from the top of the trailer. He could sense Levi's hostility rising. "Levi, pay the man so we can move on."

Levi reached into his back pocket and extracted his billfold, which was becoming much thinner than he would have liked. The money he saved at Armer's service station was disappearing, and the thought occurred to him that he was going to need work again eventually. He handed a five-dollar bill to the old man, who strained to move quickly to fill the tank.

Turning from the pump, trying to be friendly, he asked Tom, "Been in town long?"

"Nope, just got in this morning. We're looking to settle down and find work."

"Like I said, lot of folks is lookin' for work right now. Ain't much to be harvested for another month or so. You come down here cuz you know someone hirin'?"

"No, we got no connections out here," Levi said.

"Y'all been to Weedpatch?" asked the old man with his hand still on the nozzle as it dispensed gas into the Chrysler at a painstakingly slow pace.

"Never heard of it," replied Levi.

"Weedpatch is a camp outside town about a mile that way," he said, pointing to the west. "The government just finishin' makin' it. I ain't been by there lately, but I heard they put up nice sites, showers and washbasins, too, and folks gunna come by offerin' work when it's available."

The rolling number counters on the gas pump stopped at $3.24. The old man swung the metal lever and returned the nozzle to its slot in the pump. "There you go, nearly eighteen gallons." He reached into a little box of coins on top of the pump and handed Levi his change, then unfolded a dollar bill from the back pocket of his coveralls.

"Much obliged," Levi said.

"Alright, y'all come back soon," said the man with a nod and turned back to the service station office.

A mile farther along the road to the west, they could see the camp in the distance as they approached. There were over a hundred large tents with white and tan canvas roofs arranged in straight rows behind a tall chain-link wire fence. Scattered neatly among individual groups of tents were freshly painted white wooden buildings with low, red roofs. Everything was clean and looked as if it were just built. Levi pulled the trailer off the road, through a wide opening in the fence where four men were building a significant speed bump just near the entrance. One of them waved Levi forward to another man who was standing on the running board of a guard station. He held a clipboard and wore the cleanest white shirt that Levi had ever seen tucked into neatly pressed khakis.

He came around to the driver's side, held his hand out for Levi to stop, and presented him with a friendly smile. "Morning, sir, how can I help you?" he said.

"We heard you may have campsites here we could use," Levi said.

"Yes sir. We just opened a few months ago, haven't even finished the fence yet. It's filling up fast, though. We have a few sites left. Why don't you pull around back toward unit three; there's a site there. Folks just left two days ago. Someone will be around in a bit to fill out your paperwork. Dan Collins is the camp's director. All the sanitary buildings are fully operational. Do you have all the bedding you need?"

"Yeah, we got plenty of bedding. What's a sanitary building?" Levi asked.

"The buildings with the red roofs have showers, washbasins, and toilets. All with running water. Hot water sometimes, too," said the guard, like the proud owner of a new house.

"How much is it going to cost us?" Levi asked skeptically.

"Dr. Collins will arrange that with you. He's over in the administration building now." He stood back away from the car to allow Levi to pull forward. Levi looked at Ella Mae, who looked surprised and smiled. As a little girl, she had used a toilet in the general store in Shawnee when she and Patsy went for supplies.

With a clank of the loose hitch, the trailer lurched and shook as they pulled ahead onto the grounds. Along the tidy rows of tents, throughout the camp, hundreds of young sycamore trees no taller than a man, freshly planted and staked, lined the dirt roads. At the base of each tree was a delicately formed soil basin that had been recently watered. The wide, clean roads were swept down and sprinkled with water.

As they drove through the camp, they passed an old woman bent over, watering a newly planted tree with a small watering can. She held her lower back and stood with difficulty to look at the Whites on their trailer. She shook her head, and Tom recognized a look of pity on her face. The crunch of gravel under the tires and the creaking of the trailer was too loud for Tom to make out what she said, mostly under her breath, as they rolled by, but it sounded like, "Move on, just move on."

They passed a campsite where a beautiful young woman in a blue dress sat with her sister. Her hair looked as if she'd just come from a salon, and her dress was immaculate. To Levi, she looked like a large piece of perfectly cut sapphire that had dropped from the cool heavens into the drab dust and heat of the camp. The young woman's white teeth shined in the early afternoon's bright light as she looked up from the table and smiled while watching the Whites roll by. Her hunched-over sister shook her head and scowled.

They pulled into a site with a beige circus-style tent and wooden lattice shade structure a short distance from a sanitary building. Levi turned off the Chrysler. The journey was over; the distance had been covered.

Tom and Patsy came down off their trailer while their children jumped from their riding spots and scattered, looking for new territory to explore. Levi stepped out of the Chrysler and went around to the passenger door to open it for Ella Mae.

As he opened her door, he looked back across the camp toward the administration building. He stood still as a chill ran through him. The same rusted, forest-green, flatbed Ford truck that had visited their camp the previous night was parked in front of the building.

35
Laguna Beach, California
June 6th, 1962

In the early 1960s, in a quiet coastal town in Southern California, a Mexican fan palm towered over the beach. A mature palm is an organism with freaky proportions. It is impossibly tall and thin, one hundred times taller than wide, with a thousand crosshatched scars left by each fallen leaf on its telephone pole trunk. High above the beach, the starburst sphere of bright green leaves swayed, danced, and bent with the breeze. On the occasion of September 25th, 1939, during the only known tropical cyclone to make landfall in Southern California, it nearly bent to the ground, but because it bent so well, it didn't break, and over twenty years later, it still stood awkwardly tall against the elements.

For decades the palm witnessed the narrow coastal strand while waves, like furious and unrelenting hands, beat the shore, pushing sand up then pulling it back again. In that palm's long life, its viewpoint getting taller each year, the beach was fluid, folding in on itself, expanding and contracting—never still. Rocks noticeably shrunk as the edges were pounded into sand.

Like busy little ants, humans scampered about the beach. With eyes squinted and red faces turned to the west, they briefly sat still on the rocks under the palm's slender trunk to watch the sun go down. In the human time frame, the beach was static and the sun took its time setting, but for the palm, the sun fell like a golden dagger, stabbing the ocean with a green flash.

As the dusk turned to night on a warm June evening in 1962, the palm witnessed a young man sitting near its trunk waiting for the last arc of sunlight to fade on the Pacific's purple western line. As the evening set in and the canyon breeze warmed the air, the man didn't leave the beach. He was smiling the unmistakable smile of joy and possibility. He laughed quietly to himself and shed a few tears of happiness for his arrival in a new world, for his journey, and for his family, which he had left long ago in a distant land. As he looked at his bare feet, two tears fell free from the bulge of his lower eyelids and hit the sand with an inaudible thump. Several minutes later, the salty water in those tears was pulled by osmotic forces into the awaiting roots of the palm tree and began its ascent to the top. It would be late the next morning by the time the upper reaches of the palm tasted his tears, and by then, the traveler would be long gone.

The moon finally rose over the eastern hills. Light rippled off the sea foam and cast a long russet shadow from the palm's body down onto the sand and water beyond. The tree watched as two young women walked hand in hand down the beach. They approached the traveler on the rocks and introduced themselves.

Audrey, Kate, meet Alex Melter. He's smiling. He's young and beautiful. You're young and beautiful. He's what you've been looking for. He does not speak English well, but that's alright; he will soon. Take him with you. He can help you with your experiments. You don't yet know what it means to be truly free, but you're trying. It has something to do with openness to new experiences and foreign people, realizing your growth edge, then moving beyond it; manifesting your abundance, as the Swami would say. It's okay, take him with you.

A brief conversation involving a good deal of body language and some confusion ensued. The palm, from atop its lofty and scarred pillar, witnessed the three moonlit youngsters, soon to be lovers, walk the length of the silver strand and out of its sight. As they walked away, the traveler was holding his green canvas backpack and worn shoes, smiling all the while.

36
Westwood, California
Present Day

Forty-two minutes after awaking on his thirty-first birthday, Marcus was at his kitchen counter, eating his breakfast while standing and answering emails on a laptop folded out in front of him. His cell phone rattled on the tile countertop, and he picked it up to see that it was Jack calling.

"Morning."

"Did I wake you?" Jack asked.

"Dude, it's 7:30. I'm just headed off to campus. What's up?"

"Is everything alright? Are you at home?" Jack asked. Marcus could hear noise from the cell phone in the background. Jack was clearly driving somewhere.

"Yeah, I'm fine. What's up?" Marcus asked for the third time.

"Stay there. We need to talk. I'm on my way over. Are you still seeing that Elizabeth woman, the wife of the guy you work with?" Jack asked.

"She came over last night. Why, what's this about?"

"She was found dead in her car late last night a few streets over from your house. I got the call this morning," Jack said.

"What? What happened?" Marcus asked, suddenly holding on to the counter in front of him.

"I was hoping it wasn't her, but I remembered the last name, and when they said they had to get a statement from the husband, a professor at UCLA, I figured it was the same one."

"What do you mean she was found dead? She's not dead. I just saw her." Marcus's voice choked on the last few words.

"I don't know any details. She was shot. That's all I know."

Marcus was silent. His mouth felt dry, he couldn't speak, and his mind raced over the time he had spent with Elizabeth. He heard the white noise of Jack's car through the cell phone.

"Hey, you alright?" Jack asked.

"What?" Marcus responded, no longer paying attention to Jack's questions.

"Did anything out of the ordinary happen between you two? Did you fight?"

Marcus could feel his breath moving in and out of his open mouth, and tightness took hold in his chest. He tried to think of each detail of her visit in chronological order, the things she said, and how she was feeling.

Finally, after a long pause, he replied, "Everything was fine. She fought with her husband before coming over."

"What time did she leave your house?" Jack asked.

"I'm not sure, maybe around 9:30 or so. She was here when you dropped me off, and she stayed for about an hour. Jack, what is going on here? Am I in danger?" His jaw clenched as he looked quickly around the room.

"You're fine. I'll be there in five. Come out front," Jack said, then hung up.

Long after Jack had hung up, Marcus held the phone to his ear, and with flinty eyes, he stared into the distance. He looked at his half-written email about rescheduling a department meeting and was struck by how mundane his little daily routine had been. She was dead? It didn't seem real. It couldn't be real. There must be some mistake. What would happen now? He stood, then sat back down. She had just been there. He thought of her face, which was sad, but beautiful and vibrant. He looked around the room at the couch they had just been on and her glass of wine, still on the coffee table with one burgundy sip remaining at the bottom.

He slammed his laptop closed, then struggled to put on a pair of shoes with shaky hands. He made it to the front door just in time to see Jack pull up.

"Jesus, dude, this is terrible. I'm so sorry," Jack said as Marcus got into the front seat of the Crown Victoria. "Are you okay?"

"What happened?"

"I don't know."

Marcus didn't say anything. He sat in silence shaking his head while Jack pulled away from the curb. Finally, he asked, "Where are we headed?"

"The crime scene. It's just a few blocks from here. A couple of uniforms kept it blocked through the night. Zaragoza caught the case. She's the one who called me this morning when she found out that the husband was also a UCLA professor. She thought you might know him."

After a short drive, Jack pulled the car to the curb. They were five blocks north of Marcus's house, one street over. The sun was nothing more than an ambient, hazy glow to the east, struggling to burn off the fog.

Jack turned off the car. Marcus could see the yellow police line hastily strung between trees on the sidewalk a short distance ahead. His heart raced, and he put a hand on his chest.

"We don't have to do this if you don't want. You could stay here in the car, and I'll go talk to Zaragoza," Jack said.

Marcus took a long slow breath. "No, let's go."

Marcus shivered and buttoned up his blazer as he got out of the car.

Ana Zaragoza leaned out of the back of Elizabeth Shackleton's car, looked down the street to see Jack and Marcus coming, and snapped off her latex gloves. She was in her mid-thirties, fit and stocky, with long black hair pulled back and tied neatly into an impenetrable bun.

"Morning Jack," she said with a slight nod. Then with full, maroon lips and thin crow's feet lining her eyes, she smiled a rare sympathetic smile at Marcus and said, "Marcus, long time no see."

Marcus let his eyes drift over Zaragoza's shoulder toward the shattered driver's side window of Elizabeth's car.

"I'm so sorry about this mess. Just learned from Jack this morning that you may know the victim."

Marcus was silent and made brief eye contact with Jack. He felt nauseous. His morning bowl of cereal was heavy in his stomach and he fought the urge to retreat back to Jack's car.

"Can you identify her for me?"

During the preceding night, 94,568 people had died around the world, but numbers can be cold and cruel. Each of those deaths was consequential in some way to someone who remained living. Notwithstanding the genocidal attacks taking place on the Bantu ethnic people in southern Somalia, 587 of those people died brutally at the hand of another human. In the early hours of the morning, while Marcus slept, fourteen people died who were three degrees separated from him, two who were two degrees separated, and only one whom he knew personally. Had he been asked to guess these numbers, he probably would have got them right, within an order of magnitude; but knowing that people die and are killed, that it happens all the time, and sometimes to people we know, didn't help nor prepare him for what he saw inside Elizabeth Shackleton's car.

Zaragoza brought Marcus and Jack around to the driver's side, where the door was open and the window was broken. The break looked like a white spider's web with concentric rings of shattered glass around two holes. Marcus bent down to look through the open door. Elizabeth was sitting upright, seatbelt still on, leaning to her right. The first thing Marcus noticed was the blue tank top, which he had watched her painstakingly put back on just hours earlier. In the manner she was seated, it was bunched up around her mid-section and exposed a patch of skin just above her hip. The skin looked dry, cold, and colorless, nothing like it had the night before with her youthful blood pumping through it. He wanted to reach out and touch her, to comfort her, but couldn't.

There was a dark red hole, large enough to put a pinky finger in, just above her left cheekbone with dried blood below it. The entire right side of her face, where the bullet had exited, was mostly missing and could be seen as small chunks and splattered blood on the passenger side of the car.

Marcus lifted his hand to his mouth and spoke through it to Zaragoza, not looking at her. "That's her." His mouth began to water.

"I'm so sorry," she said and put her hand on Marcus's back as he stood and turned away from the car. Marcus breathed slowly and squinted into the distance. Zaragoza was silent.

"What happened here?" asked Jack.

"She was shot at close range, probably sometime around ten last night," Zaragoza answered. "We found two casings on the ground underneath the car. Both bullets were on the passenger side floor of the car. From the looks of her injuries, the perp came to the side of the car, shot once through the window, missing her; then the second shot caught her in the front part of her head."

"Do you have any prints? Anything to go off of here?" Jack asked.

"We'll get the car printed, but it looks like the shooter never touched the car nor went through it in any way. Her purse was still on the passenger seat, closed, undisturbed, with blood sprayed on it. The bullets were from a .40 caliber handgun, potentially with a silencer on it, based on the lack of smoke powder on the window, no burns on her face, and the fact that no neighbors heard the shots. Whoever it was, he wasn't interested in anything except shooting her."

"Does Richard, her husband, know about this?" Marcus asked Zaragoza.

"Yes, we sent an officer over to see him early this morning. I haven't got a chance to talk with him yet." Then Zaragoza paused. "Are you alright? You're looking a little pale."

The thought of Richard made Marcus's skin tighten and crawl.

"Why don't we go back and sit down in my car," Jack said.

"No, I'm fine," Marcus said, gaining control of himself.

"When did you see her last?" Zaragoza asked Marcus.

"Last night. This must have happened shortly after she left my house," Marcus said.

"Was there anything abnormal about her visit? Did she seem scared or tell you she had fought with anyone?"

"She fought with her husband before coming over. It happened pretty regularly. I think a car may have been parked on the street outside my house the whole time Elizabeth was there." Marcus could feel himself start to get angry. "I couldn't tell when I first saw the car, but there may have been someone waiting for her in it."

"Does her husband know where you live?"

"I don't think so, but he's my department chair and would have access to my address."

"Can you remember the make and model of the car?" Zaragoza asked.

"No, it was too dark. I couldn't make it out. A dark-colored sedan of some type," Marcus answered, disappointed in himself. "I didn't think much of it at the time, or I would have paid closer attention."

"No problem," Zaragoza said, trying to be comforting. "It may not have been anything anyway. Jack, why don't you take Marcus home, or to work, or wherever he's going. I have your contact information, and I'll get back in touch with you if I have any other questions. Marcus, I'm really sorry." With that Zaragoza turned back to the car to resume her search of the backseat, leaving Jack and Marcus to walk back to Jack's car.

Marcus shook his head and whispered to himself. Then finally he said out loud to Jack, "This isn't right. She wasn't mixed up in anything that would get her killed like this."

While he spoke, Jack's phone was ringing. He waited for Marcus to stop talking, then answered it. "Yeah. Yeah. When? Sounds good. I can do that. Alright, give me twenty. Okay, see you later."

"What was that?" Marcus asked.

"Vargas. He wants me to go to the EPA headquarters downtown with him, look into what the dead guy in Reseda was working on," Jack answered.

"I'll come with you."

"I don't think that's a good idea. I'll drop you off. If I hear anything about Elizabeth, I'll call you right away," Jack said.

"The dead EPA guy, what's his name, Lindster, the unidentified guy in the chipper, now Elizabeth. I think her murder may be connected." Marcus continued, "Let me help."

"It won't be alright with Vargas if you tag along with us. I'll drop you off. I'll call you immediately if I hear anything. I'll come by when I get done with Vargas."

Marcus could feel a knot forming again in his throat. "Someone shot Elizabeth. Right here, probably someone who staked us out at my house. I can't just go about my day. I have to do something." Marcus said with uncharacteristic emotion in his voice.

"Dude, I understand. This is a fucked up situation. I am so sorry about this." Jack fell silent, looking into the distance at Elizabeth's car. "You have to let Vargas and me go through the procedure. Zaragoza is following up on any leads she can with Elizabeth. We're on this the best we can be."

"Is Zaragoza going to tell Richard that Elizabeth was at my house?" Marcus asked.

"She might have to as part of the investigation, but she might not if she considers him a suspect."

"Alright. Shit. Just drop me off on campus then."

In the distance, two coroners tried with difficulty to get Elizabeth Shackleton's stiff body out of the seated position and onto the ground where the unzipped body bag waited to receive her.

37

No fewer than three times. Three times! That's the number of occasions that the Earth has vaporized. Praise be to those massive chunks of ice that pummeled our little revolving ball of sticky magma as it swept on its curve through the early solar system. Without them, we wouldn't have our seas, our rivers, or our lemonades. Gradual accretion around planetary embryos was punctuated by cataclysmic events. Collisions of heavenly bodies took their toll. Some impacts were so substantial that our ball of molten rock, our planetesimal, momentarily flew apart, minuscule particles diffused and suspended in the vacuum of space, eventually coalescing, rearranging, and reorganizing, but with miraculous water, and perhaps the organic building blocks of life, on the surface. These violent events left their signatures on the primordial planet—our rotation speed, the tilt on our axis, our seasons, the number of hours in a day. The moon was created by one of these devastating impacts, at just the right speed and angle required to liberate a splash of liquid mantle, which coalesced, but didn't return to the surface. Now, the Earth drags the moon around its rotation, and the moon slows us down. Each subsequent day is slightly longer than the previous; each year has fewer and fewer days. Just as the Earth pulls on the moon, the moon exerts its force on us.

In the mid-summer days of 1936, above the dense fog of the California coast, its full-bellied mass receded to a safe distance, the moon gently tugged on the Pacific, pulling its waters on a rising tide up onto the land.

38
Weedpatch Camp, California
1936

Car tires crunch along a gravel road, then roll to a stop on the freshly wetted dirt. The door swings open, and a beautiful woman's shoe with a slight heel, an unlikely shoe for a labor camp, steps out of the back seat and softly breaks the thin crust of hardened mud.

It's only been a short while, but she is changed completely. As she walks from the car to the camp, a man in a blue suit and dark glasses closes the door behind her. Her youngest siblings don't recognize her at first. They stare and begin to circle, whispering to each other. Her older sister recognizes her instantly, but the look on her face is foreign. A little boy pulls on the fine material of her blue dress.

"Oh my goodness. Look at you. We had no idea you were coming. Mom and dad found work, so they ain't goin' to be back for an hour or more. They'll be happy to see you."

Her lame sister clears a box crate at a table in the shade of an overhead tarp. "Can I get you something to drink? Come sit down. Talk, tell me all about it." With the wave of her one good hand, "You children go on now. Give your sister some space and let us talk in private. And don't you wake that baby. Who's your friend in the car? Are you staying long?"

"No, we ain't stayin' long."

"He's handsome."

"He's just a driver, paid to take me around sometimes. I brought you some things and some money for mom and dad."

"We'll get to that later. You look so beautiful in your dress."

"Thank you."

"Tell me what happened. Tell me how you like what you've been doin'."

"It's better than any alternative. Right? Gettin' bent over and wrinkled up like a raisin pickin' fruit in the fields. It's quadruple the money for one-third the work. I was a little girl, sis, when the doctor came to get me. I didn't know nothin'. Now it seems as if I've seen the world. I've seen how it works."

"Where did they take you?"

"To a place called a ringer house, one that's part of a chain of houses. Girls get moved around. Don't worry, ringers are safe places, respectable even in some parts. They're sanitary, and the men are screened, and I got a room to share with another girl. The doctor has other doctors who take good care of us. You get to keep all of your tips. Sometimes with ten or more customers a day, you can collect twenty-five extra dollars."

"Twenty-five dollars?"

"Yup, and if you don't go out on the town too much, you can save up money really quickly. But I like to go out. Oh, you should see it, the lights on Sunset Strip, Hollywood, the movie stars. I once saw Mae West right on the street. Her and I were like two normal people just passin' each other on the sidewalk. Some of the girls talk about becomin' movie actresses. Maybe I'll do that someday. Anything is possible in Los Angeles."

"Here, have a sip of some of this fancy tea. Pa got it at the general store in Arvin."

"Thank you. I feel good. You can stay healthy working in a ringer, and earn a lot until you get another job that pays better or get married. Someday I'll find the right man and get married. You'll see. Everyone will be there."

"That'll be somethin'. How much work is it?"

"All the girls share the different shifts. The second shift has the riff-raffs and those who drink too much, and the girls rotate on the weekend late shifts. Mostly the drunks are fine. They don't knock you around or nothin'. Usually they just can't get it up, and that slows down the works in the house. Most customers have had a little to drink, enough to do the deed. I never drink on the job unless a customer demands it. Maybe when I'm out on the town, I'll have one drink, but not when I'm working."

"Where is it?"

"A neighborhood in Los Angeles. Nothin' too conspicuous, an innocent looking house with a negress landlady who answers the door. She works for the doctor, too. She invites the right types in, has them wait in the front sitting room. Asks them who'd they like to see. If they tell her to show them what she's got, then she'll let the madame know, and she sends out all the girls who ain't working at the time. Then we come in wearing evening dresses or sometimes even lounging pajamas, depending on how busy we've been. Some of the men have us parade around a bit. Most know who they want soon as they see her. Some kind of connection, hard to say, but I can tell right away when a man is going to choose me. From there, he's brought back to a girl's room, inspected for disease, and cleaned up. So many men act all big and important in the sitting room, but soon as you get them into your room, they change from a lion into a lamb. I seen plenty of men who get all touchy when something sets them off and they're like little boys."

"Do you like doin' it?"

"If you're good at what you're doin', like any profession, you can be a real necessity in someone's life. Like a policeman or a doctor. I don't know how many crimes could be prevented just by havin' a man visit a ringer before he intends to commit that crime. The madame tells us we're providing a necessary service, an important service."

"Do you get picked often?"

"I get picked just as much or more than most of the other girls. Obviously being pretty helps, but sexy is even more important."

"If the doctor would've chose me, I bet I could've been sexy," says her sister, glancing down at her shrunken, claw-like hand.

"I bet you could. Not all pretty girls are sexy, and a lot of sexy girls ain't perfect. They say men like all types, but they usually go back to the same type of girl over and over. If you work hard and put a lot of interest into doing a good job, the customers notice. You gotta work on having a pleasant personality, be generous and gentle, do what the customers ask of you. That's the best way to get them to repeat and leave large tips. Pretty girls in the middle that ain't too fat or skinny get most of the repeat customers. The rails and the fatties take the leavin's. You gotta visit with a man a little, smile a little, ask him if he's been in town long, don't ask him about his business. You gotta be friendly, but not too friendly, especially to the repeats. You don't want men asking to take you home after work or gettin' too sweet on you. Most girls have boyfriends, and you don't want them gettin' sore."

"Boyfriends?"

"Yes, most have boyfriends. Some of their boyfriends help the girls get customers. Sometimes they's just some guy you meet out on the town, who you see on nights off, doesn't know nothin' about your profession. Probably wouldn't approve, though, especially with all the hubbub that comes and goes in the newspapers. All this tommyrot about white slavery. The doctor may have brought me and some of the other girls into it, but knowin' what I know now, I would have gone willingly." Looking around, she says, "It's the only way out of this place for the whole family."

"Pa found some good work, so we've been eatin' pretty good. Ma says it's honest work."

"They got a huge garment factory over in East LA that hires hundreds of women. You think they're virtuous? They wouldn't sell their bodies? They're sellin' their bodies, to be broken down by hours on a sewin' machine. Look at their faces and figures and you'll see why they wouldn't make it ten minutes in a ringer. The doctor wouldn't have chosen them, even if they wanted to go. They sit around whispering about us, condemnin' what we do. Most of them are homely, flat-chested box cars, prattlin' on about Jesus and their virtue, when they'd starve to death in a two-bit house."

"What kinds of men have you met?"

"I've had all kinds. One that never wants to touch me, just sits there and looks at me, then eventually gets up the courage to touch himself. One wants me to pray with him. So I sit there on my knees, elbows up on the bed, eyes closed, pretendin' to talk to his god while he mutters on about Jesus. Then he gets all worked up and takes me from behind, tellin' me the whole time to keep prayin'. After he finishes, he goes on about how I'm a goddess and that he just made a goddess out of me. I like that, like I'm part of some type of ancient religion."

"You get to go to church?"

"Not anymore. Them Christian reformers, with their sad little peckers and prudish wives, ravin' on about how evil it is what we do, probably just want to be with us. Turn us into goddesses. After workin' this job for a while, you learn that there ain't no shame in it. Life isn't what people tell you it is. There ain't nothin' wrong with enjoying yourself. There's value in it, you're paid what you're worth, and people are paid a lot less for much worse jobs. Just look around at this camp."

Both sisters sip their tea and look out across the sun-bleached camp.

"Most men I see are nice enough. They want to think you're interested and enjoying yourself more with them than anyone else. It helps them. A banker customer of mine keeps my money safe and helps me plan the right way to save it. I got plenty for Ma and Pa and the whole family to move out of this camp. If I can keep workin' like I am, I can keep the whole family in a nice apartment near downtown."

"Sounds nice."

"I know, we'll see what Pa says. I have enough money saved away for us to use until Pa can get a good payin' job. They say there's good schools in our area, too, for the little ones. They could go to school and not be pickin' up walnuts all day. If I'da stayed here, if the doctor wouldn't have picked me, who knows what future we'd have."

The two girls look up from their table.

"Look at this family rollin' in here now. What is that? Ten, maybe eleven of them up on that trailer? They better hope they got some pretty girls with them, or they ain't goin' to make it."

"You goin' back today?"

"I can't wait to get out of here again, to get us all out of here. This place ain't right. I remember Pa always tellin' us, virtue is its own reward, and I never understood that until now."

39

We are all caught in currents that begin to swirl and drain in unknown directions years before we become aware of them. We ride on the strange and mysterious tides of time. What shore we wash up on is not for us to know. A pebble dropped into a calm creek can change the course of a raging river many miles downstream.

Six months prior to their arrival at the Weedpatch labor camp, cold water had welled up off the West Coast of California. That cold water was partially responsible for determining the remaining course of Levi's life.

The current in question surged upward from the ocean depths on December 13th, 1935, and rubbed up against the West Coast, pushing its way under the partially constructed Golden Gate Bridge and into the San Francisco Bay. All that would have been fine; cold water comes and goes, except that this specific current ran head-on into unusually warm December air sweeping westward from the interior of the state. The collision that ensued caused two days of abnormally dense fog to settle in the bay; fog so thick that a murderous man could hide in it and not be found.

40
North Point, San Francisco, California
6:22 PM, December 17th, 1935

Out in the bay, the cold current had settled in for the third day. The days were short, and the night had already fully come. Joe and Dean Callahan sat smoking cigarettes at a small wire table on the edge of the bulkhead building of Pier 42. A slow-moving breeze from the east was flowing over the pier, finally thinning the dense fog and bringing the distant ringing of buoy bells. As the sky cleared, a quarter moon above the eastern bay glistened and reflected off the ripples of the silky black bay waters. A hazy, salt-laden, golden-brown halo sat a few hundred feet over the two men, where smoke curled up from their little table.

Joe Callahan could taste salt where his mustache dove aggressively into the corners of his mouth. He massaged the corners with his tongue as he sat wiping his brow with a white, smoke-stained handkerchief. He had just completed the loading of thirty cases of Cartan & McCarthy Irish Whiskey and was still sweating from the exertion.

"You get 'em all unloaded?" his older brother asked him.

"Yeah, it's all up on the trailer. That shit ain't light." Joe said as he caught his breath and released a plume of smoke into the wet air.

"Good, cuz the egg man gunna be here early in the morning to drag that thing away," Dean said, then looking up over Joe's shoulder said, "What the fuck is that?"

Both men stood and turned around to watch a large figure pull itself up out of the dark waters onto the metal railing above the dock. It was a heavy-browed man with a stocky neck, an oversized head, and thick black hair that looked like a helmet. He was wearing a blue jumpsuit, stained black and glistening in the dimness. With unusual grace and speed, he jumped down from the railing onto the wooden dock. His feet were bare and looked like those of a corpse. Without hesitation, he moved unhurriedly toward the two brothers.

Pointing a sturdy, disturbingly long finger at Joe, he said, "Give me your clothes and your boots. All of them, now. "

"You can go fuck yourself. I'm not givin' you..."

Joe didn't get to finish his sentence. The man moved quickly to grab Joe with one hand by the neck and forced him effortlessly to the ground. Joe feebly tried to swing a fist at him and missed entirely. With his free hand, the man buried his thumb, the diameter of a banana, into Joe's right eye socket. Joe screamed a scream much too high pitched for a person of his size, then went limp and unconscious as the man smashed the back of his head onto the dock. Dean was paralyzed by fear. Everything had happened too quickly. He stepped back against the bulkhead building and was standing with his cigarette in his hand, mouth gaping.

"Which one of you has larger feet?" said the man cooly while unbuttoning Joe's jacket.

He had to repeat his question before Dean came to his senses and answered, "I do."

"Take off your shoes and socks. Remove your billfold and set them all over here."

In the 108 years in which the water temperature in the San Francisco Bay has been accurately and consistently recorded, it averaged just over fifty degrees Fahrenheit, a temperature cold enough to paralyze even the most experienced swimmers. The water is churned and pushed by the surface winds and extreme tidal currents, which range between ten and thirty knots per hour, making swimming nearly impossible and often deadly. For half the day, an ebbing tide swiftly and unsympathetically sweeps deluded swimmers out beyond the bay to the deadly waters of the open Pacific.

Across the unforgiving mile due north of Pier 42, in the middle of those fatally cold waters, sits a graywacke sandstone hilltop island called Alcatraz. During the last ice age, Alcatraz peaked a small mountain, then the ice melted, the surrounding valleys filled with water, and the San Francisco Bay formed. Since that melting 15,000 years ago, Alcatraz has been variously occupied by different groups of Native Americans, proud to come ashore on the island, but not knowing what to do once they got there.

In 1850, President Millard Fillmore took the island from the natives by executive order and commanded the building of the Western United States' first lighthouse. A poorly built fortress followed, which was quickly turned into a military prison to house Confederate soldiers and the very same Native Americans who, in an earlier time, had braved the bay to come to the island. In 1933 the U.S. Justice Department took control of the island, converting it to a federal penitentiary for particularly incorrigible prisoners who attempted escape at other prisons.

In the twenty-nine years that Alcatraz was active, there were fourteen attempted escapes involving thirty-six men, all but five of whom were shot to death, drowned, or returned to their cells after failed attempts. The remaining five, whose bodies were never recovered, were presumed drowned in the frigid waters of the bay as they were swept out by the swift currents under the Golden Gate Bridge. Four of those five men did actually die during their escape attempts; their bodies consumed nearly to completion by marine life in the Kirby Cove area under the northern portion of the bridge. The one man who didn't die, Ralph Roe, came ashore on Dean Callahan's pier on that foggy December evening in 1935.

Ralph Roe was serving 99 years for having robbed the Farmers' National Bank of Sulphur, Oklahoma on September 10th, 1932. He was sent to the Oklahoma State Penitentiary, from which he quickly escaped. During the gun battle that precipitated his original capture at a rented cottage outside Norman, Oklahoma, Roe's girlfriend, Olivia Ann Nichols, was shot and killed by Frank Smith, an FBI special agent stationed in Oklahoma City. Roe made a silent but determined vow to himself while watching Smith testify against him in court, that he would avenge Olivia Ann's death. Roe was detained outside Frank Smith's house two weeks after his escape, transferred to Leavenworth, then on to Alcatraz.

For months, Roe planned his Alcatraz escape with an accomplice named Ted Cole. Cole was a convicted kidnapper with a psychological disorder. He was unable to shit in anything but a sink. His condition expedited his transfer to Alcatraz, where he was cured of his affliction in solitary confinement.

The unusually dense fog on the morning of December 16th, 1935 provided a long-awaited opportunity for Roe and Cole. At 12:48 PM, they crawled out of a window in the mat-making shop on the north end of the island. Once outside, they collected three empty metal oil cans, made their way down to the water's edge, and hid in a rock cave. When they were discovered missing, the dense fog made the search for them nearly impossible. Roe and Cole sat silently in that cave as the tide rose and a thick black darkness fell over the island. When the next day was dawning, the fog still heavy, Ralph Roe used a large wrench he had kept from the shop to beat Ted Cole to death. Roe undressed Cole, slipped his naked body into the bay, and tore his jumpsuit into strips to lash the three empty cans together into a raft, then he waited, watched for the tide to swing, and for darkness to come once more.

41

Dean Callahan had the obnoxious habit of keeping a large roll of cash in his front pocket. It made him feel rich, and he thought it made his dick look bigger. He liked to peel off ten-dollar bills while paying for something expensive, with everyone watching. So as he stood shoeless, his brother lying beside him unconscious on the dock with dark blood oozing from his right eye, Dean knew that he had just given the man who came out of the water a beautiful pair of size 11 handmade cap-toe Oxfords and a roll of tens worth over four hundred dollars.

Ralph Roe walked away calmly into the night and was never seen in San Francisco again. A short distance from where he came off the dock, he found a Chevy coupe with the keys in the ignition and three-quarters of a tank of gas. He drove south on Highway 101 through the night, arriving in Paso Robles before sun up. After sleeping in the car, he was awoken by the late-rising December sun on his face. He filled up the Chevy and spent the morning in a diner enjoying his first real breakfast in several years. After eating, he visited Dick Bruhn's apparel shop for a new suit, and Ollie's Barber Shop, where he had his head shaved clean. He explained to the old barber that he was a traveling salesman looking to stay in the Paso Robles area for the holidays. He offered the barber two week's worth of rent for the apartment above the shop, where he stayed quietly during the holidays while any investigations into his and Ted Cole's disappearance from Alcatraz would dissipate.

It was late morning on January 2nd, 1936 when Ralph Roe got back into his stolen Chevy. His plan was to drive south on the 101 to Los Angeles then on to Mexico, where he would cross the border and never return. He considered the risk of scoring one more bank robbery somewhere in Southern California and decided it was too great. Besides, the money that he collected from the Callahan brothers would last him quite a while. No doubt the federal penitentiary system and the newly formed Federal Bureau of Investigation were circulating posters with his likeness on them. Bureau; who uses a word like bureau? Roe thought. Have those Frenchy sissies in Washington never heard of the word agency?

Where a conscience or sense of duty resides in a normal person, there was emptiness in Roe; emptiness and burning self-preservation. He had a dull ache, though, a memory he couldn't let go. He had made a vow to himself to avenge the death of his beloved sweetheart Olivia Ann. She died in his arms, with the metal from Frank Smith's bullet still warm in her chest. He knew she was innocent, and he knew he was almost entirely responsible for her death. Yet it was the vow he made to himself to punish Smith that kept Ralph Roe from driving toward the border on that day. Instead, he did the only other thing he could think to do; drive east toward Oklahoma and Frank Smith. Smith would have already learned about his disappearance from Alcatraz, as he had during his first escape from McAlester Penitentiary, and would likely be on guard. He'd have to be more patient this time.

It was early afternoon when Roe reached Bakersfield from Paso Robles. He would never make it to Oklahoma, nor much farther east of Bakersfield for that matter, but didn't know that as he sat in a booth near the window in a small roadside diner reading an abandoned newspaper. He saw a gray-haired man with a goatee looking at him from the counter. He thought little of it and went back to his food and newspaper. Moments later, the man casually sat in the booth across from him. He was holding a mug of coffee and placed a folded piece of paper on the table across from Roe.

"It's my lucky day running into you," said the man as he slid the paper, folded in half, across the table to Roe.

Without saying anything, Roe picked up the paper and unfolded it. It was an FBI wanted poster with Roe's photograph on it. He quickly refolded the paper and scanned the diner, looking for a way out.

"Now, now," said the man, "no need to get too excited. You're not in trouble, at least not yet."

Roe gained control of himself once he saw that the diner wasn't filled with cops, and no new cars had pulled up in the gravel lot outside. Roe had a low, hoarse voice that surprised the man. He said, "I don't know who that is. Now why don't you get up and walk away."

"I don't think I will. I'm nothing, if not good at recognizing people. Son, you're going to have to do better than just cutting off your hair," the man said calmly.

"I ain't your son, and I ain't the man in your poster," Roe said.

"It's a figure of speech. You did an amazing thing, and there are a lot of people looking for you. Most don't even believe you made it. They think you're at the bottom of the San Francisco Bay, head nibbled off by fish."

Roe was silent.

"What I can't figure out is why you're here in Bakersfield," the man continued. "Smart guy like you, seems like you'd be halfway down to Columbia by now."

Roe pushed his plate of food away from him at the table and began readying himself to stand.

"You best stay seated," said the gray-haired man as he reached his arm to the side to open his herringbone sport coat just far enough so that Roe could see the dark brown leather holster that housed a Colt double-action revolver. "I'm not with law enforcement, but I can still cause you a great deal of trouble."

"What do you want?" asked Roe, sliding back into the booth seat.

"I want to talk, like two civilized men. I want to know your plan. I may be able to help you. My name is Dan Collins, Dr. Dan Collins," he said, extending his hand across the table, awkwardly asking for a handshake.

Roe looked at his hand briefly, considered his options, and said, "Why would you want to help me?" while briefly shaking Collins's soft little hand.

"I run several operations in this valley, and I could use a man with your particular skills. A man with some discretion. I don't know about you, Mr. Roe, but I believe in fate. I believe in serendipity. You and I ran into each other in this diner on this particular day for a reason. We need one another now."

"I don't need you," said Roe with a look of disdain and distrust on his face.

"I wouldn't be so sure of that if I were you. Wherever you're headed, you're likely to get caught again. I can provide you with a new identity, new papers, and a place to stay. I'd be willing to wager you're still driving a stolen car. I can fix that. Right now, you get stopped by a traffic cop and you're headed back to Alcatraz, or worse." Collins said all this like a protective father figure to Roe. "You're going to need money soon, too. And besides all that, I found you, I recognized you, and now you don't have much choice."

Roe sat silently looking around the diner for a long time. Finally, he answered Collins. "I have business I need to attend to in Oklahoma. I can come back after two weeks."

"Son, do you think I'm dumb?" Collins asked with irritation. "You think you're going to drive out of here and I'll just wait for you to return? You think I'm going to let this opportunity pass?" He shook his head and looked down at the table. After a long moment, he looked up at Roe and said, "I'm not sure what your business is in Oklahoma, but I think I can guess. You be patient with that business and it'll happen. I'll help you make it happen. Right now, you need to lay low, and you do need my help."

Ralph Roe was smart. He was also a heartless sociopath driven entirely by self-preservation. Just that morning he had stopped for gas on his way from Paso Robles to Bakersfield. The only reason he actually paid for the gas instead of following the skinny teenage attendant back to the station office to break his neck, which he could have done as easily and with as little remorse as untwisting a bottle cap, was that Roe was concerned that there still may be a manhunt out for him. He wasn't interested in drawing any attention. While Collins spoke, he weighed his options. He decided to reach across the table and crush his windpipe, then he thought better of it. Collins may actually be valuable to him.

"Alright," Roe said, "I'll hear your proposal."

"For now, I'm going to follow you out to your car, get in with you, and we'll drive to a quieter location."

That was January 2nd, 1936, when the accidental meeting between Dr. Dan Collins and Ralph Roe took place. It wasn't until mid-January when Roe ceased to regularly think of ways to kill Collins, escape Bakersfield, and move on with the business of avenging Olivia Ann. He was staying at Collins's farmhouse south of Bakersfield while waiting for the new identification papers that Collins had promised. On January 18th, just two weeks after their first meeting, Collins slid an unsealed manila envelope across the dining room table at the farmhouse. Inside was a new California driver's license with a picture of Roe, head shaved, with a new name. Also in the envelope was a newspaper article from The Daily Oklahoman reporting the apparent hanging suicide of FBI Special Agent Frank Smith.

After Roe finished reading the short article about Smith, he looked up at Collins, who nodded and said, "Go on, there's more."

At the bottom of the envelope he found a grainy, recently taken, black and white photograph of Frank Smith with a noose around his neck. He was alive and about to be hanged, his two hands were outstretched in front of him, holding a framed photograph of Olivia Ann Nichols.

"I had that one commissioned for you personally," Collins said with a look of smug satisfaction.

A week later, when Collins provided Roe with a new vehicle and the option of leaving the farmhouse, he decided to stay. It wasn't long before the gray-haired doctor began to employ him for odd jobs and explain to him the details of his various operations.

42
Downtown Los Angeles
Present Day

"Who'd you make the appointment with?" Jack asked Vargas as they got out of the car in the noise and heat of the midday mayhem of downtown Los Angeles.

"We're looking for Steve Duarte, the director of the EPA Region 9, Southern California Office."

While the rhythm of a jackhammer beat in the background, a bus played the high whining notes of its brakes in harmony with the horn section of angry humans in their cars. The two detectives crossed the wide sidewalk and went through the glass doors facing the street. Jack looked up before entering the building. Since he was a child, tall buildings made him uncomfortable. The doors hissed as they sucked closed behind them, holding in the cool, conditioned air, which smelled of cleaning products from the first-floor bathroom. On the fourth-floor, they exited the elevator, crossed the hallway to the wooden reception desk with stenciled letters that said Environmental Protection Agency Southern California Office. Vargas slid his card across the desk to a handsome young man who smiled and greeted them.

"Detectives Jorge Vargas and Jack Bratton here to see Steve Duarte."

"Just a moment please," he said before picking up the phone. "Okay, Mr. Duarte can see you now. Just head back along there, and he'll be out to meet you."

Jack and Vargas passed the reception desk and walked along the edge of a spacious room full of cubicles with more than thirty people at work. Steve Duarte came out of an office in the corner. He was an effeminate man in his mid-forties with a clean-shaven boyish face and beautiful features. He looked scrubbed and tidy, as if he'd just gotten out of a shower. He wore a tight-fitting white Oxford shirt with the sleeves rolled up, bright blue skinny tie, and light khaki chinos that tapered along the leg. Everything about his appearance was purposeful; no detail had been left unconsidered. As he moved gracefully down the hallway with a smile, he looked more like a salesperson at a department store than an EPA director.

"Mr. Duarte," Vargas said as he held out his hand. "I'm Jorge Vargas, this is Jack Bratton. LAPD detectives. I believe you're expecting us."

"Yes, nice to meet you. Let's head back to my office, and please call me Steve."

As Jack followed the two men along the edge of the room, he made eye contact with a red-headed woman who stood looking at him over the wall of her cubicle. She stared at him, raised her eyebrows, and made a slight nod. There was something intriguing about her, something beautiful and not quite right. Jack slowed. He was sure in that moment that he had never seen anyone like her, yet she was familiar. Jack smiled at her, but she didn't smile back, just nodded again as if trying to get his attention, then looked away quickly and sat back down. Jack wondered if he knew her.

The three men sat across an olive green metal desk. Vargas took out his notepad while Jack leaned back in his chair, bracing himself for another session of his least favorite part of his job.

"How can I help you gentlemen? I'm assuming this is about James," Duarte asked with an unmistakable gay affectation. As Duarte went on, he strained his voice, a naturally smooth baritone, a few registers up. "It was sooooo tragic for us all to hear what happened to him," he continued. "We were close around the office. Have you found out anything about his disappearance?"

"We're actually here to try to learn a little more about what Mr. Lindster was working on in the weeks or months before his disappearance," Vargas said.

"Sure, I understand. James's job was to designate areas where federal money would be spent on cleanup and to investigate responsible parties to recover incurred costs during a cleanup process. Basic investigation for future enforcement of the Compensation and Liability Act. Sexy stuff," Duarte said sarcastically, trying to glance back and forth between detectives. "There were several cases that he was working on over the last six months. Nothing unusual."

"What were those cases?" Vargas asked.

"Let's see. Hold on a minute." Duarte stood, opened a metal drawer in a filing cabinet behind his desk and rubbed his hand along the top of the files, eventually coming to one that he pulled out. He studied the file. "He was working on the reports for site stabilization from the Pemaco chemical mixing site down in Maywood. It burned back in the mid-nineties, and we've been working with the county and owner ever since." Duarte placed the file on the desk in front of Vargas. "Here you go, Jorge. Take your time with it."

Vargas held back the automatic cringe that would have come from hearing his first name roll out of someone's mouth in that manner. When Duarte said Jorge, he purposefully over-pronounced the Spanish vowels and pronounced the J with an H sound that someone would make when trying to free something deeply lodged in the back of the throat. Possibly he did it to impress Vargas or maybe because he just reveled in the opportunity to speak with a little flare of a foreign language. Duarte was prone to the pretentious and irritating habit of hyperforeignism in his speech. Any word from outside the English language, even those that had long ago been successfully assimilated, he pronounced in a foreign and excessively awkward manner, and most often incorrectly. After a week-long visit to Cuba, his friends and colleagues at the EPA had to suffer the puckered lip pronunciation of that country's name as Cooooba.

"Oh, it's okay, you don't need to do that," Vargas said as he took the file.

"Do what?" Duarte asked.

"Pronounce my name that way."

Jack was smiling to himself, knowing that from then on, he was going to imitate Duarte when saying Jorge.

They sat in silence as the awkward moment passed, then Vargas continued, "Were there any other cases?"

Duarte went back to the cabinet. "Looks like he was following up on paperwork from the old Del Amo rubber plant in Torrence, the Montrose wastewater ocean discharge issue in Palos Verdes, and he just finished the five-year review of the San Gabriel Basin Aquifer for dioxane contamination." He placed three more files on the desk. "Sorry I don't know more about what he was working on. There are a lot of people in our office, and we cover all of Southern California. James's work was mostly concentrated in areas around Los Angeles."

"No problem," Vargas said. "Would you mind if we received copies of these files?"

"Not at all, it's all public information," Duarte said. "What's this about? Are you trying to establish a motive for James's disappearance?"

"We're just trying to get more information."

"I don't think you'll find anybody wanted to kill him because of the work he was doing. It's all pretty boring paperwork around here. Not exciting stuff like what you two do," Duarte said while looking straight at Jack, then gave him a little wink.

"Alright," Vargas said, standing. "I think we have what we need. Thank you for your time."

"Oh honey, anytime." The word honey wasn't forced in any way; it just seemed to slip out. "You two come back if you need anything else from me. Anything."

Vargas awkwardly stuck out his hand for a shake and, while Duarte held it, he said, "I'll let you two see yourselves out. Copies of these files will be sent over to the address you left at the reception desk."

Jack and Vargas walked back by the cubicles, past the reception desk, and into the hallway. As they waited for the elevator, the red-headed woman Jack had seen on his way into Duarte's office exited the bathroom near the elevator and walked by Jack. While he stood dumbfounded, she made brief eye contact, slipped him a folded piece of white paper, and without saying a word, walked back into the EPA office as if she hadn't seen them at all.

43
Weedpatch Camp, California
June 13th, 1936

Tom and Ella Mae White were laboriously unloading their trailer when Dr. Dan Collins and Ralph Roe left Collins's office in the Weedpatch camp administration building and walked along the dirt road in their direction. The sun was blazing over the San Fernando Valley, the air was hazy, and the temperature in the camp was beginning to peak.

Between loads, Tom rubbed the point of his shirt collar. It was a nervous tic he carried from childhood. He was comforted by the feeling of the material between his rough fingers. Somewhere deep in his subconscious, the softness of the collar was equated with the softness of his mother's left nipple, which she allowed him to pinch, rub, and flick while breast-feeding from the right, the only breast that yielded milk.

The White children were scattered about while Patsy used a wash-basin in the nearby sanitary building with great satisfaction. An hour earlier, Levi had unhitched the trailer and drove out of the camp with the intention of scouting nearby service stations for potential work.

Tom saw the two men approaching and didn't recognize Ralph Roe from the passenger seat of the forest-green truck the night before. "Good afternoon gentlemen," he said as they reached the partially unloaded trailer.

"Afternoon," replied Collins with a smile. Roe hung back a few paces from Collins and didn't say anything. "My name's Dan Collins, Dr. Dan Collins. I'm the camp administrator and member of the Kern County Board of Supervisors."

Tom thought it strange that Collins didn't introduce his associate. He looked briefly over the doctor's shoulder at the hulking bald man behind him who was looking away disinterestedly. Tom took off his hat and wiped a bit of perspiration off his forehead with his shirt all in the same motion. He then held the hat to his chest and stretched out his other arm to shake Collins's hand.

"Pleasure to meet you, Doctor," he said while looking down on Collins, who was much shorter than he. Stepping back, like a graceful matador, Tom swept his hand in Ella Mae's direction and said, "This is my daughter Ella Mae."

"Ella Mae," Collins repeated, turning his interest away from Tom, making no effort to conceal the fact that he was looking his daughter up and down, as if he were about to purchase a farm animal. "Ella Mae," he said again. "Look at you." Collins reached out a limp, downward turned hand, as if he were going to try to grab the upper sides of her fingers or as a King would present his ringed fingers to a subject.

"Afternoon, Doctor," she said while awkwardly trying to firmly shake his hand.

"How can we help you, Doctor?" Tom interrupted.

Collins turned back to Tom. "I like to meet our new guests, welcome them to my camp, and find out a bit about them. The man you met at the gate as you came in will be by later for you to fill out the needed paperwork for your stay."

"Ah, I see. We appreciate your hospitality. In our very brief time on the premises, we've found the camp's facilities to be far more than acceptable. Just now my wife Patsy is taking advantage of the sanitary building, or she would be here to sing its praises. The luxury of warm running water isn't one that we've had bestowed upon us for some time now," Tom said.

"Where are you arriving from?" asked Collins.

"We've traveled west from the center of our beautiful country. Shawnee, Oklahoma, where we owned a home and a modest piece of land whose arability all but deceased over a good portion of the preceding decade, a story no doubt familiar to you. However, by the looks of the land here, not a story with which you're personally acquainted." Tom put his hat back on and started to grind his shirt collar between his thumb and forefinger.

"We've all seen our fair share of hard times. How many children do you have?" Collins asked, looking around the camp.

"Ten children in total, ranging in age from Ella Mae here to our baby Thomas, who's still shy of a full year. They sure are glad to settle for a bit, as are Patsy and I. Our traveling hasn't been the most comfortable," said Tom.

While Tom talked, he watched Roe in his peripheral vision, who was moving around the White camp, surveying it, looking for something.

"How many daughters?" Collins asked.

"Ella Mae has three younger sisters," Tom replied, a bit surprised by the question.

"What are their ages?" Collins continued in the tone of a medical examination.

Tom saw Roe lift a tarp on the trailer and peer underneath it.

"Can I help your associate locate something?" Tom asked Collins.

"Don't worry about him sir. What are your daughter's ages?" Collins said sternly. Roe continued to reconnoiter the White camp, completely ignoring Tom.

"Ella Mae will be nineteen soon, Jesse is sixteen, Anna nine, and Lily is six," said Tom.

"Seven," Ella Mae said under her breath.

"Yes, apologies; our youngest daughter is seven now," said Tom. "May I ask why you inquire?"

"Just trying to get to know our new guests as they arrive. Who was the young man who drove out of camp an hour or so ago?" asked Collins.

"That was Levi Bratton, an acquaintance of ours from Arkansas."

Collins turned back to Ella Mae and asked with a smile, "Is that your husband? Maybe just a boyfriend?"

Ella Mae was silent and looked at her father.

"Pardon us, Dr. Collins. What business is that of yours?" Tom asked.

"Alas, Mr. White, it is my business. It's all my business. Now what about this Jesse girl. Is she around so I can take a look at her?"

Tom gave a surprised look to Collins, then he looked at Roe, who was finished surveying the camp. Roe stared at Tom, mildly interested in what his response would be. Tom ground on his collar vigorously, looked down at the ground, then said quietly, "Ella Mae, go get your sister."

"She went off with Billy and Sarah, past the vineyards to find the irrigation ditch," said Ella Mae.

Collins turned his head back to Roe and said, "We really must get that perimeter fence finished."

Roe's response was nothing but a slight, disinterested twitch of the eyebrows. Even though his eyes never seemed to open very wide, the whites on the undersides of his irises could always be seen. 'Sanpaku' is the Japanese word for this condition, meaning whites on three sides. In the west, where we don't have a name for this affliction, people affected by it are often called sickly or menacing. Roe was both. He stared at Ella Mae, who looked away quickly after they briefly made eye contact.

"You understand that this camp isn't free, Mr. White?" Collins asked, turning back to Tom.

"Yes, we were informed of that upon our arrival," replied Tom.

"I assume that like everyone else here, you don't have the money necessary to pay a non-subsidized rate for your stay," said Collins.

"The exact sum hasn't yet been made clear to me, but you would likely be assuming correctly. Until I'm able to gain employment, we're without the probable means necessary to stay anywhere with facilities such as those available to us here. I'm an accomplished mechanic and repairman and could earn a portion of our stay working in the camp. Would that be something of interest to you?"

Collins shook his head. "There are ways for your family to earn money while staying here," he said, looking at Ella Mae, "but they don't have to do with fixing machines."

All four of them stood silently for a moment, each gathering their own different meaning to Dr. Collins's comment. "Next Saturday evening, the camp is hosting a dance, and I hope you can all join us," Collins continued. "I'll have a look at your little sister then," he said, still staring at Ella Mae. "Well, have a good afternoon, and welcome to the Arvin Federal Government Labor Camp."

Without another word, Collins turned and headed back toward the administration building, with Ralph Roe following a short distance behind.

44

That afternoon Levi returned to the camp. He drove along the dirt roads between the lines of beige tents until he came to the mostly unloaded trailer. Tom approached the car as it stopped and waited for Levi to get out.

"Any luck? Have we any cause to be encouraged?" Tom asked.

"No. I went around to eleven service stations in the area. Each said they had more than twenty men just like me come by asking for work this week. Goddam waste of time and fuel," Levi said.

"Well, in your absence, we had quite the disquieting conversation with our new camp administrator and his associate," said Tom.

"What do you mean, disquieting?" asked Levi, confused.

"It became clear during the course of the conversation that the two gentlemen are interested in Ella Mae and Jesse," replied Tom

"What do you mean, interested?" asked Levi. He could feel his anger rising.

Tom said, "I'm not completely sure. Dr. Collins, the camp administrator, avoided any explicit language, but I have a bad feeling about this place, and I have an even worse feeling about those two men."

"What two men? Who else was here with the Collins guy?" asked Levi.

"A large, worrisome lad with a bald head was with him. Didn't say anything the whole time, just looked around the camp while Dr. Collins interviewed us."

"I knew it. That truck that was here earlier was the same one that came up to our camp last night, tellin' us Bakersfield was closed. Was the bald guy the one in the passenger seat from last night?" Levi asked.

A momentary look of shock came across Tom's face. "Could have been, I don't remember getting a good look at him in the truck. I don't mind saying this has all been rather rattling for me."

"Did either of them touch Ella Mae or Jesse?" asked Levi.

"No, but Collins certainly laid eyes on Ella Mae in a way that causes a father trepidation."

"What do you think he wants with them?" Levi continued his interview, while he turned toward the administration building.

"I can't reckon it completely. His curiosity extended only to those two, and he made a vague, yet troubling reference to them earning our keep here. I haven't shared this information with Patsy yet, but Ella Mae knows. She was standing here during his entire distasteful interrogation. It was his supposed entrance interview."

"Tell me the truth, Tom, did they touch Ella Mae?" Levi asked, no longer looking at Tom. He was focused on the administration building across the camp. The forest-green truck wasn't parked out front.

"No they didn't. There's no need for alarm. We can't yet be confident about the meaning of this interaction, and we have to be careful here. We just arrived to what is ostensibly a nice facility. Jesse wasn't here when Dr. Collins and his colleague visited us. He mentioned that the camp is holding a dance next Saturday evening, and that he would be interested in seeing Jesse then." Tom paused and was almost speaking to himself when he said, "Disconcerting, no doubt."

"How much money did he want from us?" Levi asked.

"He didn't say exactly, but referenced the likely fact that we lack the means to pay an unsubsidized rate," answered Tom.

"I'm going to talk to this so-called administrator right now," said Levi, walking toward the administration building.

Tom followed him, saying, "You be careful, son. That man's associate didn't look like the negotiating type."

Levi walked quickly through the camp, climbed the wooden steps up onto the porch of the white building, and knocked loudly on the screen door with the knuckles of a fist. He didn't unclench his fist after knocking. He waited for a few moments, then knocked again. Nothing happened. Levi peered into the window next to the door, but couldn't see anyone on the inside.

"Can I help you, sir?"

Levi turned around and looked down from the porch to see the man in the bright white shirt who had greeted them from the small guard building when they arrived at the camp. He was still holding his clipboard, looking cautiously at Levi.

"I'm looking to speak with the camp administrator. Collins," Levi replied.

"He's gone home for the evening. Is there anything I can help you with?" asked the man, falling into his usual tone of mock hospitality.

"No, I need to speak with this Collins fella," Levi said angrily.

"Dr. Collins may or may not be back in the morning, but you're free to come by and make an appointment with his assistant to speak with him."

"An appointment?" Levi asked with confusion and disdain in his voice.

"Yes sir. Dr. Collins is a busy man. He runs this camp and three others like it in the area. He's also a member of the Kern County Board of Supervisors."

"Alright," Levi said, coming down off the porch. "I'll be back tomorrow." He stared at the man as he passed him and rejoined Tom. The two of them walked in silence back to the camp.

45

Dan Collins nor the large bald man in the forest-green truck were at the camp the next day, nor the day after that. Levi's anger with Collins was quickly replaced by his frustration with his failed attempts to find work. The guardhouse man in the brilliant white shirt came by with papers to sign, but both Tom and Levi were out looking for jobs, and he never discussed payment with Patsy.

They arrived at the camp on Thursday, June 13th, and by Wednesday the 19th neither Tom nor Levi had found work. They'd wake up early in the morning to drive the surrounding farms asking if they needed labor. Most farms had freshly posted signs reading "No Workers Needed" outside their gate, so Tom and Levi moved on. At the end of a long morning of rejections, they came upon a farmhouse outside Greenfield surrounded by beautiful vineyards with a sign nailed to the wooden fence by the road that read "No axin for werk." Tom laughed out loud, a sad and defeated laugh. He thought that the luck of land ownership isn't correlated in any way with intelligence.

Turning Tom White and Levi Bratton away as farm laborers would eventually ruin several of the farms from which they were denied. Tom was a man of understanding, experience, and uncanny knowledge, and Levi was capable of great feats of endurance and work. The opportunity presented by these two men was never realized by the farmers, service stations, and landowners, whom they begged for work and whom themselves lacked the innovation and intelligence to survive the economic hardships of the late 1930s. Due to circumstance and unfortunate luck, Tom and Levi found themselves without means, growing more desperate, on the outside of a gate, laughing at the sign written by an illiterate with money, food, and security.

Tom had outfitted the trailer for the twelve-person White family for two weeks, which at the time of his planning didn't include Levi. When Tom and Levi returned from their sixth day of unsuccessfully trying to acquire work, the gas gauge on Levi's Chrysler was nearing empty. They visited a store to buy a piece of meat on their way back to the camp. Tom's money was gone, and Levi's was running low.

Patsy and Ella Mae sat waiting for them in the camp. Patsy was sitting on a wooden box while the baby nursed on her, and Ella Mae was stacking dishes on the table under the large tent. Most of the children were milling around the camp bored and hungry, waiting for their father to return, waiting for something, but they didn't know what.

"Any luck?" asked Patsy.

"We covered every farm and business within a wide radius of this camp, and there's still nothing."

"We have to do something. All these children can't go on much longer eatin' just bars and seedlings."

Patsy was referring to two of Tom's culinary innovations that had come to him at the farm in Shawnee, which would eventually become trendy, others claiming to have invented them, more than forty years later.

On the farm, they had come into possession of a large quantity of rolled oats from a neighbor. Oats in the years leading up to their departure from Oklahoma were inexpensive. They also happened to be calorically and nutritionally dense. Tom and Patsy pressed the rolled oats with rice syrup and a small amount of molasses, then briefly baked them. The resulting cake was cooled and cut into rectangular bars. These bars, which many years later would be reinvented as granola bars, could be stored easily for long periods of time. A child could eat one as a meal and be relatively satisfied, and now the Whites had hundreds of them stacked in a box on their trailer.

Tom stumbled upon the second innovation three years before they left Shawnee. While planting a spring hayfield he decided to soak some alfalfa seeds in a jar overnight. After dumping out the water in the morning, he set the jar on the windowsill next to his desk for several days.

Upon returning to the jar, Tom noticed a dark green lawn of germinated alfalfa seedlings filling the bottom of the open jar. He reached down into the jar, pulled out a pinch of the tiny plants, inspected their green kidney-shaped leaves, and put some into his mouth. The sprouts were tangy, earthy, sweet, and crunchy. Tom was smart enough to know that the acidic, tart, yet sweet taste of the seedlings meant they were full of vitamin C.

He sat back at his desk, still chewing, pinched the collar point of his old denim shirt, and rubbed it as the realization of this discovery washed over him. He could buy a large bag of alfalfa seeds for next to nothing, the seeds could be stored indefinitely, and with a little fresh water and light, were magically transformed into a green carpet of tasty vitamin factories.

Tom contemplated his discovery for days. Before he was a farmer, he was in the U.S. Navy, and before that, he was a scholar. He reckoned that alfalfa seeds, which looked like termite droppings, could have changed the course of human history. Had Europeans in the fifteenth and sixteenth centuries, with their brutal drive to explore, conquer, and pillage the world, made the same discovery, their countries and kingdoms would have been vastly more powerful. Instead, their explorers and naval armies spent long days at sea, all their fresh food having run out, living on cured meats and dried grains. As their vitamin C deficiency led to a plague of scurvy, they lost battles, left whole continents unexplored, and kingdoms failed. The alfalfa sprout could have changed all that.

A bag of alfalfa seeds in the dry hull of a ship could have produced enough vitamin C, with only light and the wastewater from their cooking, for all the sailors in Europe. Instead, these brave men, their crews ravaged by a disease they didn't understand, melted down in a mental malaise of festering sores and bleeding gums while fighting over the remnants of a lime. Maybe it was better that so many of them failed, Tom thought. The alfalfa sprout was too powerful, too dangerous, for men of that age to have discovered.

While others in Weedpatch camp suffered their thin stews and tried for potatoes and a bit of meat, the Whites fended off hunger with granola bars and alfalfa sprouts. This diet was a monotony that was quietly perceived by the children as a type of suffering, but they weren't malnourished, just bored.

"We'll find something. The quality and comfort of these facilities demand that we stay long enough to exhaust all our employment options," Tom said. "We'll move on in a few days if we can't find anything soon."

"It's true, we haven't been this clean in a long time," said Patsy, "and lots of folks have been talking about how nice this dance is going to be on Saturday. Guess it's worth staying for that."

46

At any given time in human history, 1.3% of the human population has red hair, a condition caused by a recessive mutation, almost invariably inherited from a red-headed parent or a parent who is a silent carrier. Because it is inherited, and so rarely occurs completely de novo, certain human bloodlines harbor red-heads, whereas others do not; but human bloodlines are precarious things, each requiring sustained survival through reproductive age from every successive generation. Over 99% of all human bloodlines have gone extinct, yet red-heads remain.

The female red-head, who had handed Jack a piece of paper with a meeting place and time, was spawned from a long line of red-heads, some famous, some infamous, others obscure. She had avoided a near-death experience that very morning. A bolt slipped from a construction worker's hand thirty-five stories above the downtown Los Angeles street, bounced past the safety net, and landed like a bullet, cratering the sidewalk mere feet from where she walked to her job as an assistant inspector at the EPA. Her particular genealogy, reverberating with the echoes of extraordinary individuals and contaminated by a mutation that leads to fair skin, freckles, and an orange head, had nearly been terminated many times. It traced back nine generations, to Europe in the mid-1700s, when maybe not the first, but definitely the most famous of her red-headed relatives was born. That man, Nicolas Baudin, with his fiery and commanding presence, proclivity toward promiscuity, and position as a commander in the French naval fleet, was ultimately responsible for nineteen independent bloodlines throughout the world from which many current-day red-heads came.

Baudin's long and mostly ignoble life was filled with near misses, close calls, and brushes with death. Like the EPA woman that morning, Baudin avoided an untimely demise countless times, eight of which he told stories about in his later years. The most pivotal, and frankly the most interesting, involved lime trees and a terrifyingly calm night in the dark and salt-laden air above the Indian Ocean.

On that night in May of 1792, a slow and heavy nighttime breeze wafted across Baudin's ship, causing it to rock almost imperceptibly. The breeze was insufficient to fill the canvas sails that fluttered and slapped quietly in the darkness above. Were it not for that meager breeze, the discomfort caused by the heat and humidity of the equatorial Indian Ocean would have been too much for Captain Baudin to bear. He was seated on a chair above the wide wood planks of the ship's deck and not sleeping in his quarters, where he should have been, because his first mate, whose post he temporarily occupied, was violently ill. He bitterly sat watch over five lime trees. Sure, one could blame the ridiculousness of an experienced ship's captain needing to protect five small trees on bad luck or on the difficulties they had encountered in the preceding months, but really, it was because Baudin was scared. For six months they had been floating in the Indian Ocean en route from Mauritius to Bombay. The whole journey should have taken only two and a half months, but in the abnormal spring of 1792 the trade winds had died early and completely.

As Baudin rocked back in his wooden chair, it creaked under his weight, and he pulled on a loose piece of skin on the edge of a sore that wouldn't heal on the back of his freckled hand. Baudin knew nothing of vitamins nor the mechanisms of sicknesses caused in the human body when they're absent in the diet, but what he did know was that his crew of thirty-three men, the bodies of twelve dumped overboard in the preceding week, was suffering from a lack of fresh food.

It wouldn't be for another sixty-nine years that Frederick Gowland Hopkins was born. Hopkins, a sickly child from Southern England, would go on to win the Nobel Prize in the latter part of his medical career for the discovery of what he called "accessory nutrient factors" in food. One of those accessory nutrient factors particularly abundant in certain fresh foods is vitamin C. Its absence in the diet for over a month causes scurvy, a disease characterized by open sores, bleeding gums, muscle pain, malaise, anger, jaundice, fever, and eventual death. Scurvy first presented itself to the sailors on Baudin's ship forty-three days out of Cape Town. By the fifty-fourth day, it was raging through the crew, and the weaker men were dying.

The lime trees, which they had brought on board in Cape Town as an afterthought, were all that remained of freshness on the ship. Everything else, including the humans, was salted, dried, cured, and partially rotten. Those fourteen oblong green globes each needed to be guarded and rationed properly if the remaining crew were going to make it to shore alive. The hull could have been filled with gold, the deck studded with diamonds, and it wouldn't have mattered. The only currency at that point was sour fruit.

Captain Baudin's gums ached, and he could taste the iron of his own blood as they leaked. His skin, like most of the men on board, had grown crepe paper-thin, with bruises and sores forming at the slightest bump. Three limes had disappeared the night before, enough for the whole crew for the week, and now he could trust only himself and his first mate to ration the fruit properly to keep the men alive.

Nicolas Baudin was an experienced captain and brutal when he needed to be. He had sailed under the flag of five different nations, from Europe to the Caribbean and back three times, around the Cape of Good Hope to India and China four times. He survived a brief skirmish with a Spanish man-of-war, sinking the ship, killing everyone on board in the process, and earning himself the nickname El Canela Frances or French cinnamon throughout the Spanish navy. All those adventures, yet he had never been in as dire a situation as the one he currently found himself. By his count, he had fathered over twenty children, all over the world. He cared deeply about his legacy. He didn't want to go to a watery grave in the middle of the Indian Ocean with news of his death reaching his loved ones years later, if at all.

He loved the ocean. Since he was a boy working in the salt ponds on Ile de Ré, it was all he ever knew, but he wanted a hero's burial in solid ground in Western France where he was born. If the wind didn't rise for another week, maybe two, many of the remaining men would perish, the fight over the limes would intensify, and who knew how long it would be until they were slipping his body over the deck rail. He needed to recover the three limes and get slices passed out to the remaining men.

Just then, Baudin heard the noise of footsteps in the distance on the wood planks of the deck. He rocked his chair down onto all four legs, stood, and listened again intently, peering off into the darkness. The noise came again, this time closer, but its source was still not clear to him. Baudin picked up a hatchet next to his chair.

"Who's there? Come closer," he yelled into the darkness in the direction of the noise.

Out of the darkness into the area where light from the stars was gathered and reflected down from the sails stepped a group of four men, each carrying a heavy wooden belaying pin like a club. They were sickly, angry men with sunken eyes.

"Evening, Captain," said one of the men in the center. "We'll be needing some more of those limes."

"I can't allow that. You'll get your ration in the morning like everyone else."

"You see Captain, that just isn't enough. We're going to die out here, each man eating only a little wedge of lime each day. We've decided it's better that a few men get them all and stay strong to get all the others to shore."

"Did you take the three limes last night? Step closer into the light so I can see you," Baudin commanded. "Is that you, Stanislas? Anselm? Andre? In honesty, I'm not surprised by René, but the three of you joining him is unexpected. You're going to return those pins to the rails and bring me the stolen limes."

"We'll do no such thing," said René incredulously. "Those limes are ours, and you men are going nowhere. I'm the captain of the ship now."

Without hesitation, Baudin took a long step forward with his left foot and swung the hatchet with all his weight squarely down onto the center of René's forehead. For the rest of his life, when Nicolas Baudin would remember those few moments when he took René Ledru's life, two obscure details would always haunt him. The first was the sound the hatchet made as it entered René's head, and the second was the effort required to extract the hatchet after René had fallen to the deck. He heard the sound of a walnut cracking, a crab leg breaking—a sharp snap muffled by softer material embedded inside. As he fell backward onto the deck, blood sprayed out of René's head where the skin burst open, landing and mixing imperceptibly with Baudin's freckled face and orange hair. Baudin let go of the hatchet, allowing it to fall with his victim, and it stayed firmly and deeply embedded in René's brain. The three other men around him recoiled in fear and shock.

Baudin stood with wide blue eyes, watching in the starlight as the last trembles of life shook through René's body. He turned to the men and said, "Put those pins back in the rail and bring me those limes."

"Yes, yes sir," one of the men stuttered.

"We ate one of them," said another.

"Bring me what remains, and do it now."

As the men rushed off, Baudin looked down at his hand, which was shaking. He stepped forward, grabbed the hatchet handle, and pulled. It didn't release from his victim's head. He placed the heel of his boot on the dead man's chest and pulled with all his force, and the hatchet came free with a jolt, as Baudin stumbled backward.

The men brought back a whole lime and one that had been cut in half. "This is all that remains," said Stanislas as he handed Baudin the fruit.

"Get his body overboard, and the three of you return to your chambers," Baudin commanded.

The next morning, Baudin awoke in his chair on the deck where he had no memory of having fallen asleep. He looked over his shoulder to notice the low angle of the sun rising out of the calmness of the eastern sea, casting long shadows over the blood-stained boards and out into the sea to the west. He cut a slice off the remaining half lime and placed it into his mouth. He squinted when the tiny fish egg-like cells burst under the pressure of his bleeding gums and released their acidic sweetness. As the burning juice spread out in a thin film over the sores in his mouth and throat, Baudin heard the sails above him flutter and slap from a stiff breeze rising with the sun. Moments later, the sails were full, a brisk wind was blowing, and they were moving once again, for the first time in many weeks.

Baudin eventually did make it back to western France, after a long recovery in Bombay and another harrowing voyage around The Cape involving the particularly tempestuous summer of 1794. Four years later, while acquiring a new ship and a handsome commission to carry spices from Martinique across the Pacific to Kenitra, Morocco and back up to Amsterdam, Baudin met Maria van Rensselaer, the daughter of an aging Dutch merchant. On the night before Baudin was leaving once more for another long sail westward, he and Maria van Rensselaer brought about the bloodline that weaved and twisted its way through Europe, to New Amsterdam on the eastern coast of North America, and eventually, many years later, to California where a young red-headed woman sat in a cafe waiting for Jack Bratton to arrive.

47
Downtown Los Angeles
Present Day

The young red-head in question, the indifferent descendent of some murderous French sailor, as she knew the story, had handed Jack a piece of paper on which was written in considered handwriting, Arda's Cafe on 6th at 6:45 PM. She had decided to use the @ instead of the word at, then crossed it out, thinking it might confuse him.

When Jack received the note and was asked about it by Vargas, he was surprised that she had been so forward as to ask him on a date in that manner, but acted as if that type of thing was a regular occurrence in his life. In actuality, even though he had heard of such things happening, they never did to him, and he entered the cafe suspiciously, clean-shaven and showered. Just before their meeting time, he had stood in the darkness across the street, trying to make out if she was in the cafe, but couldn't see all the tables well enough to know.

The image of her face was trapped in his mind since his visit to the EPA, and he was excited and a little nervous to see her again. When he came through the door, Jack saw her seated in the back, facing him. She nodded at him much in the same way she had from across the cubicles earlier that day. Jack approached the table.

"Is it only you, or is the other detective coming as well?" she asked, looking up at him and making only a half-hearted attempt to conceal her disappointment.

In the few seconds after she asked the question, the true nature of their meeting became clear to Jack. He didn't know if she registered the momentary flash of embarrassment that moved across his face, which he immediately tried to conceal with irritation. "Sorry to disappoint," he said, seeing that the table was set for three.

"Not at all. Please sit down," she said politely, still looking over Jack's shoulders to see if anyone else was joining them. "Thanks for coming."

"Is someone else coming?" Jack asked.

"No, I'm just making sure no one I know comes in or that you weren't followed."

"Followed?" Jack asked as he sat down.

"I don't know why I'm even involving myself in this, but I loved James. He was an amazing man. Just doing his job. He should never have got involved in all this either."

"Whoa, whoa, wait a minute. Slow down and back up a bit. My name is Jack, Jack Bratton, and you are?"

"Do you need to know my name?" she asked. She had a way about her that made everyone around her uncomfortable, especially men. She inadvertently made them feel as if they had offended her. Her resting face was beautiful, skeptical, and bored, which made Jack feel that she may get up and walk away if he weakened or wavered momentarily. Jack stared, possibly a little too long, at the rust-colored freckles that spread out like a constellation across the ridge of her nose to the upper runs of her high cheekbones. As he looked closely, he thought he saw that the freckles were oriented just right along the right side of her nose to spell out the word "halt." Her eyes were startling, light green, almost chartreuse in the tinted dim light of the cafe.

"Yes, I need to know your name. Why did you ask me here?" Jack asked, looking down at the folded cloth napkin on the table.

"James Lindster's murder and his work at the EPA," she said in an almost angry whisper.

"Okay, and your name?" Jack asked calmly.

"Bridge Gardinier. My full name is Bridgette, but everyone calls me Bridge."

"Alright, Bridge, catch me up. Do you work at the EPA?" Jack asked.

Before she could answer, she was interrupted.

"Would you two like something to drink?" asked a waitress in her mid-twenties with dark bangs and the rimmed glasses to match.

"I'll have a glass of red wine," Bridge said, looking at Jack.

"Same for me," he said, thinking that this may become a date after all.

"Yes, I've worked for the EPA for three years. I'm an assistant inspector there. I prepare cases for potential investigation, and I worked closely with James. He was responsible for getting cases ready for EPA action. We'd investigate sites and present those to the director,

Steve Duarte, who would make decisions about how to proceed."

"Yeah, we met Duarte this morning. So how did that work go with James?"

"James would always be upset when we put a lot of work into investigating a site that he thought deserved more attention and Duarte wouldn't want anymore follow up on it. Mostly these were benign cases that didn't really matter or weren't big priorities, and it's always about resource allocation. If there wasn't enough money to fully investigate and deal with property owners and attorneys, then Duarte would shy away from it. James was a dreamer, an optimist, an idealist. He thought it was the EPA's job to fight. He had certain cases he thought were important, and when Duarte would ignore them or deprioritize them, then James would be upset."

"Did they ever fight?"

"Fights between James and Steve were pretty regular occurrences. James thought Steve should never have gotten his job as director, and that he was brought in only to protect the public image of the EPA. James accused him regularly of not actually caring about environmental cleanup. Their bickering was normal, and it all stayed in-house until about a month or so ago."

"What happened?"

"Here you go. Two glasses of Merlot. Can I get you something to eat?" asked the waitress with a smile.

"We'll just have the wine for now," Bridge said.

"Okay, I'll give you some time with the menu," replied the waitress and headed back toward the cafe bar.

"Anyway, James and I had prepared a long report about a San Fernando Valley groundwater contamination issue. We worked on it for the last six months. I bet Duarte didn't even tell you a thing about that case did he?" Bridge paused and took a sip of her wine.

"He didn't," Jack replied, lifting his glass and making eye contact with Bridge over the rim of it. "Cheers," he said awkwardly and touched his glass to hers, neither of them knowing what they were toasting. "What was your case about?"

"Cities throughout northern LA and the San Fernando Valley have groundwater test wells. Someone from the EPA tests the water every year in the wells, looking for groundwater contamination. Since the eighties, the wells in the eastern part of the valley have come up dirty."

Bridge took another sip of wine and Jack followed.

"All the groundwater in those parts of the valley is completely contaminated, undrinkable, pretty much unusable for anything, and has been for years. And James had been looking into this for a while. Based on geological maps he was studying, the way the groundwater flows, and the level of contamination at the different test well sites, he was narrowing in on the source of the main contaminant. He was a genius."

Bridge paused to watch two men come into the front of the cafe, then continued, "Usually proving the sources of industrial contamination can be difficult, especially in places like the eastern valley, which was historically filled with manufacturing. But if anyone could do it, it was James."

"So what happened?"

"Well, James wanted to designate large parts of the eastern valley as a superfund site and name the responsible parties and have them pay for cleanup. James got more and more excited about it. Just before he disappeared, he went up there to take a bunch of pictures of a potential source site, which we usually never do. A while back, when we brought the initial report to Duarte, he said he'd get back to us on what we were going to do about it, but never did. Then James started pressing him. But when Duarte continued to bury our report, James threatened to go to the media. That was the last conversation I witnessed between them before James disappeared."

"Have you two decided on an order?" asked the waitress.

"Are you okay with us just having the wine?" Bridge asked Jack.

"Sure," Jack replied, then turning to the waitress he said, "No food for us then."

"Okay, let me know if you need anything."

"When was that last conversation you witnessed between James Lindster and Steve Duarte?" Jack asked Bridge.

"I remember it exactly. I've been thinking about it ever since. It was on a Friday a few weeks ago. The next Monday, James didn't come to work. I called his phone and there was no answer. The weird thing is, when I looked into the case files we'd been working, they were all gone."

"What do you mean, gone?"

"Completely missing. Like somebody had purposely erased everything they could find. I couldn't find any files in the cabinet where James kept all the photographs. Even stranger, his computer was gone off his desk. I thought maybe Duarte put him on forced leave, but he would have said something to me. Then when he didn't come in on Tuesday, I called his wife and found out she hadn't seen him in three days."

Bridge took a gulp of wine and stared motionlessly at the front of the restaurant. She winced as the heat of the alcohol coated her throat. The cafe was full and purred with activity—dishes clinked, people had to talk loudly to hear each other, and music played from a single speaker mounted in a corner. Jack looked over his shoulder at the front door. The two men who had come in were seated at a table near the windows that faced the street. Neither looked up at him. He looked back at Bridge. Her green eyes seemed to absorb the light of the cafe.

"Did you say anything to your co-workers about the case?" Jack asked.

"No, I was scared. Duarte knew that I had knowledge of what James was working on. It was the next day that he announced to the office that James was missing and that they had confiscated his files and computer, which he said was standard EPA procedure. So I continued to work on our other cases like I didn't suspect anything, but I knew that his files were missing before Duarte found out that James was gone. Then we all found out that he was found in Reseda. It was devastating. He was a personal hero to so many of the people who worked in the office, including me. When I overheard the receptionist making an appointment for the LAPD to see Duarte, I didn't want to miss my chance to talk to you guys."

"Why would Duarte cover up something that James had been working on? What makes you think that this groundwater contamination in the valley has anything to do with Lindster's disappearance?" Jack asked, looking at her wine glass in an effort to pace his drinking with hers.

"I don't know," Bridge replied, shrugging. "This is a case that should have been pursued. It doesn't make sense."

"Did you keep any of the files or photographs he took?"

"I didn't. James was careful that we kept all the records and reports straight and on the computer on his desk. He thought it was best that way, so we weren't involved personally. Now I think he was just protecting me." She took her last sip of wine, then stared at the empty glass with a surprised look. "I miss him. He was such a passionate man. He used to always say about environmental destruction that once great wrongs are done, it's rarely possible to undo them, but that doesn't mean we shouldn't try. I think about that all the time. I couldn't let the information I have about what he was working on get covered up."

Bridge held her empty glass in both hands, silent and fretful, then after a pause asked Jack, "What are you going to do now? What happens?"

"Well." Jack finished the last of his drink. "You've given me enough to revisit Duarte and ask him some other questions."

"You'll make sure not to mention me or our meeting, right?"

"Of course not. When can I see you again?" The question was only partly about police work, and both of them knew it. Jack's eye contact faltered momentarily. "I'll probably need to ask you more questions about the case."

Bridge handed him a card. Written on the back, in the same tidy handwriting from the note he received earlier that day was her phone number. "Just call me, and we'll work out another meeting place. I should get up and leave before you do."

"Can I give you a ride home?" Jack asked.

"No, my car is just down the block," Bridge said.

"Okay, you go out before me, but go slow, and I'll make sure you make it to your car."

"Sounds good," Bridge said, standing.

"Oh yeah, I keep meaning to ask you, what was the source of the main contamination that you and James discovered? Did you ever figure it out?" Jack asked.

"James may have just before he disappeared, but he never told me, and I didn't see the case file before Duarte got to it."

48
Weedpatch Camp, California
June 1936

Levi and Ella Mae had taken to walking in the late afternoon, crisscrossing the camp, so they could enjoy each other's company and have some time alone. Some days Ella Mae hopped alongside Levi, on others, she carried her jumping stick while holding his hand. On this particularly warm evening, Levi carried her pogo stick and lumbered along, tired from the long and disappointing day. His heavy work boots made impressions in the freshly wetted dirt road. Ella Mae, who seemed to be half his size, glided along next to him, her bare feet silent as they kissed the ground, leaving only the slightest pockmarks in the dust.

"You didn't see either of those two men again today did you?" asked Levi.

"No, neither come round the camp," replied Ella Mae.

"You know to stay away from them, right?"

"I know."

"I don't know what I'd do if I found out that man touched you," Levi said.

"It's alright, we ain't seen either of them."

"I've got a bad feeling about this place," said Levi.

"Yeah." Ella Mae paused, and both of them stopped walking and turned to face each other.

Ella Mae looked down at the ground. "I talked with a woman down on the other side of the camp this morning. Says Doctor Collins come round inquirin' about her oldest daughters and lookin' em over a few months back."

"What happened?"

"She said he sent that large bald man to come collect them for some work a few days later. Dropped them back off at the camp after a week. She claimed everything was fine. The old woman said they come back with money and new clothes and she'd been eatin' well since."

"It ain't right," Levi said, looking into the distance.

Ella Mae continued, "When I asked her if she knew what they had done, she got a look in her eye like she was gonna wail on me. She knew very well what they done, she said, but they didn't have no choice. Anyway, she said it weren't no different than the men goin' out sellin' themselves, diggin' in the ditches for next to nuthin'. Ain't no dignity in any of it."

"Well, if he comes round lookin' for you or Jesse he's got another thing comin'."

"She made it sound like it weren't no problem. Just needed to cooperate with Collins, and life in this camp got a lot better for them."

Levi was silent and Ella Mae continued, "I've been thinking a lot while you and Pa are out lookin' for work all day, 'bout ways I can help. We need to do somethin'."

Levi squinted into the distance. A plume of white smoke rose a few miles to the north. The afternoon was dry and hot, and the valley exhaled a low hum. Each time a plow or shovel broke into the rich San Joaquin soil, it belched a little of its primordial moisture, dust, and microorganisms into the atmosphere. The ancient marsh that had once filled the valley lived on in the air, and the inhabitants felt the oppressive weight of it above them.

Levi lifted Ella Mae's chin up, and they looked into each other's eyes. "You stop worryin'. I'll think of somethin'. Somethin's gunna happen soon."

49

Levi didn't sleep well that night. The restlessness and desperation of their situation had bothered him during dinner when he watched Patsy cut the roast into impossibly little pieces, so everyone could have one. Shortly after falling asleep, some distant reverberation woke him. Upon becoming fully awake, he was unsure if it was real or if he had dreamed it. It was a low, growling alarm, dim and far off, that aroused an undercurrent of anxiety in him. In the darkness and heat, he could hear Ella Mae breathing softly.

As he lay there he rewound the reel of time in his head from that moment, back to Arkansas and the McAlester lot. His mind returned to the familiar landscape of many of his nightmares: the scene of his father's death. He hadn't been there in many years, but in his dreams, current day events, apprehensions, and images were often superimposed over that dimly lit cabin room.

On that night many years ago, he could see the black blood running in the moonlight from Obediah Bratton's mouth for several minutes after he had stopped moving. His father's eyes were wide open long after he was dead. Minnie had gone out of Uncle John's bedroom and left Levi standing in the corner, making eye contact with his dead father. He was so scared that Obediah would rise, and he would hear the terrifying growl of his voice again. Now he saw Obediah's angry face speaking in his gravelly snarl "No axin for werk, let em' whore themselves" repeatedly as the blood from his mouth sprayed on the cabin floorboards in front of him.

Levi watched the darkness change to sepia in the early morning and fell asleep as the sun was rising. When he awoke, and Ella Mae was gone, he held his breath. He stumbled from the tent in the morning sun and saw her and the whole family packed tightly around the camp's wooden picnic table.

"There he is. Nice of you to decide to join us this morning," said Tom, smiling at Levi from the head of the table. "Jesse, pull that box over and make room for Levi."

"We're celebrating Timmy's birthday." Ella Mae said, standing next to the stove. "Buckwheat pancakes, honey, and hot milk with chocolate powder. Come sit down."

Levi didn't feel like sitting, but he did anyway. Seeing them all happy renewed him. Seeing Ella Mae smiling, caring for her younger siblings, reminded him of his purpose. Tom's proud face, his love for his family, these things wore off on Levi. He finished breakfast and packed his lunch for a day of hunting for work with Tom.

As they drove out of camp, Levi saw the forest-green truck parked at the camp's administration building. Ralph Roe sat lounging in the morning sun on the steps leading up to the building's porch. Levi pulled the Chrysler to the side of the dirt road. He glanced at Tom, who said nothing, then got out to approach the building.

"Is Collins in there? I'd like to speak with him," Levi said as he approached the steps.

Ralph Roe was sitting on the stairs, leaning back on his elbows. His massive frame nearly blocked the entire entrance to the building. He stood and stepped down off the stairs in front of Levi. He was taller than Levi and much wider. He tilted his head down as he spoke, and his sanpaku eyeballs moved up in the sockets, accentuating the bloodshot whites under the irises.

"Who you lookin' for?" Roe's voice came out like a low hiss, as if every word were spoken at the end of a long exhale.

"Man named Collins. Runs this camp. He in there?" said Levi.

"Don't know, maybe," Roe said in a mocking, seemingly disinterested way.

"Well, stand aside so I can check. I need to speak with him," said Levi.

"Nope. Administration's closed. We ain't takin' no visitors," Roe said calmly.

"Move outta my way," Levi said, looking straight at Roe.

That was the moment that defines so many similar interactions, the same pivotal moment that has been shared between men countless times in history, the point of inevitable confrontation when each man has to make split-second decisions about how to proceed, the level of threat posed by the other, and how to best achieve his outcome; evaluate and assess. Evaluate and assess, then act, and all in milliseconds.

Levi didn't hesitate, nor was he afraid of Roe, although he should have been. A long moment passed, then another. Adrenaline coursed through their veins. Each man waited for the other to capitulate. Finally, Roe took a step back to the side of the little path in front of the stairs. "Fine," he said, "take a look for yourself."

Levi proceeded up the stairs, watching Roe through his peripheral vision the whole time. His fists were clenched so tightly he could feel his fingernails digging into the palms of his hand. He swung the screen door open, knocked loudly on the door, waited briefly, then tried the handle. It was locked. He turned, looked at Roe, and walked back down the stairs, watching him closely. Like a gunshot, the screen door slammed shut and each man flinched.

"I guess he's not in there," Roe said mockingly as Levi passed him.

"I guess not," replied Levi, on his way back to the Chrysler where Tom stood by the passenger side door.

"Lookin' forward to seeing y'all tomorrow night. Especially those two daughters of yours," Roe called after them as Levi reached the car.

"You keep your eyes off them," Levi said as he turned around to face Roe.

"Oh, yeah, or what?" Roe said with a smile as he sat back down in the sun on the stairs.

Levi didn't reply. His heart raced with anger. He and Tom got back into the Chrysler. Tom could hear Levi's loud breaths as he fumbled for the ignition with a shaky hand. They drove over the big hump at the entrance to the camp and down the road in silence. Ralph Roe smiled to himself for a few moments, then proceeded to fall into a deep, undisturbed sleep on the sunny steps.

50
Westwood, California
Present Day

"Groundwater contamination?" Marcus asked.

"Yup, that was her story," Jack replied. "Now we'll have to go back and question Duarte again." He was looking tired and beyond his years, sitting slumped over on a wooden chair across from the couch where Marcus sat in his living room. Marcus glanced down at a barely perceptible glistening smear that he and Elizabeth Shackleton had left from the night before.

"Have you heard anything from Zaragoza?" Marcus asked.

"No, nothing new. She talked to Elizabeth's husband. He was distraught. Didn't report anything out of the ordinary. Hadn't seen a car parked with anybody in it around their house."

"Interesting."

"When Zaragoza told him that Elizabeth was over here, she said it seemed like he wasn't surprised, almost like he knew."

"Oh man, I'm in deep trouble," Marcus said with a sigh.

Marcus got up and looked out the window across and down the street, in the same way he had when Elizabeth visited him for the last time. He saw nothing out of the ordinary, which reinforced his suspicion that someone had been watching them the night before. He turned to look at Jack, but his eyes wandered off to the rest of the room and all the things Elizabeth had touched the night before. It was an outrage to Marcus that the world would just move on after her death. All these objects just sat there, as if she hadn't ever touched them. He didn't want to move on without her.

"Hey, man, are you doing alright?" Jack asked.

Marcus was distracted and barely heard Jack's question.

"What's going on here?" Marcus asked. "Why would Duarte not tell you about Lindster's case?"

"I don't know. There's something wrong with that office."

"Did Vargas get all this information too?" Marcus asked.

"No, he thought I was on a date with her."

"Apparently so did you. Do you trust what she told you?"

"Either way, we need to find out more about Hoerburger and his little henchman Remmy," Jack said. "I think we need to visit Hoerburger again, this time at his house. I'll see Vargas in the morning and let him know about Steve Duarte. He needs to be revisited for some actual answers about what was going on with Lindster."

"Sounds good to me. Pick me up here after you meet with Vargas in the morning."

"Alright. Don't you have a lecture to give tomorrow or anything?" Jack asked.

"It can wait."

51
Weedpatch Camp, California
June 1936

On Saturday morning, the camp swirled with excitement. The sanitary units were crowded. Clothes needed to be washed and dried, and offspring tracked down, caught, and cleaned. Men who hadn't shaved in weeks considered the possibility. Women who were, in general, much younger than they looked mended, patched, repaired, and cleaned clothing with great skill. The first of many Weedpatch Camp dances was in the making.

A large wooden stage had been constructed in an open area near the back sanitary unit in the week leading up to the dance. A mess of wires and lights loomed overhead like an electrified octopus. As the hot afternoon subsided, the men returned from work, or looking for work, the musicians began to populate the stage, and the camp buzzed. The campers prepared themselves for their invited guests, knowing they were about to don clothes and smiles they hadn't worn in weeks. They emerged from tents, awkward in their best dresses and jackets, bashful but proud, and walked around the camp for no good reason other than to be seen by other campers.

The sun had gone down when Levi finished changing the oil on the Chrysler and made his way to a sanitary unit. He carried a razor, a small bar of soap, a clean brown shirt, and freshly washed pants folded in his arms. He was careful to not touch anything with his darkly stained hands. He stood at the sink, scrubbing the oil and dirt from his hands, surgical white light bathing him from above, accentuating his hooded eyes and sharp features. The water was barely warm. All the primping campers had used up the hot water long ago, but what remained was warm enough for a shave.

As Levi shaved, he looked closely into the sanitary unit mirror. It is in a well-lit bathroom mirror where the vulnerabilities, age, and degradation of human skin are most apparent. He pondered the peg-like hairs projecting from his cheek. How long does hair continue to grow after death? Why do men have beards and women don't? Although he doubted that question as soon as he thought it, having seen some of the migrant campers down from Oregon. He remembered the old black man at the gas station, his dark, oily skin reflecting the sun, white stubble emerging in discrete patches. A lifetime of daily abuse with a razor had taken its toll on the old man's skin. There were whole collections of follicles too weary, too broken, to push out hair.

Women like a closely shaved man. Is it possible that they didn't sometime in the distant past? At one time, men with robust beards reproduced more frequently, and now women, with their fickle preferences, have changed their fondness for facial hair at a rate unmatched by evolution in men. Is this seemingly unnatural daily routine the result of the volatile whims of women? No matter. Ella Mae was waiting, and he would bend down toward her as they danced and twirled, and he would lift her soft, light frame gently to her toes, their cheeks would touch, and she wouldn't flinch at the sandpaper texture of his face. He moved the razor over the curves of his proud, beautiful chin, then, wiping his face with a hand towel, he looked down on himself in the harsh sanitary light of the mirror and smiled a private smile.

Cleaned, shaven, and changed, Levi emerged into the warmth of the pink, late afternoon, walked back to the Chrysler, and returned the towel, soap, and work clothes neatly to the front seat. As he put on his overshirt, he turned from the car to see Ella Mae standing behind him. She was smiling, a radiant vision, flushed with youth and health. She wore a grayish-blue dress that covered her body like morning fog laying on a coastal mountain range. It hugged tightly to the plains of her torso and hips, fell loosely over the rolling hills of her thighs, then flared out and dissipated just below the buttes that were her knees. Up from the valley of her torso, the blanket of fog projected forward abruptly over the soft mountains of her breasts, then sloped back gently to wrap her neck in a short V with a frilly, windswept collar. The small sleeves exposed her tan upper arms, and her hair fell onto her shoulders in shiny, relaxed curls.

Levi paused to take her in, to permanently and purposely set in his mind what he was seeing. This pause made her nervous. "What?" she asked.

"Look at you, you're wonderful," Levi replied as he reached out to grab her. He bent to smell the sweet loam of her scalp, kissed the top of her head, and moved his hands up and down the stiff material of her dress. In the distance, the musicians were warming up. The shrill call of the fiddle was faint over the pumping bass. Neither Levi nor Ella Mae had ever danced with the other, at least never standing up, in front of people, and with their clothes on, and they were excited and nervous.

Ella Mae wrapped her arms around Levi's waist and felt a bulge tucked into the back of his belt, under his jacket.

"What's that?" she asked.

Without answering, Levi bent forward, lifted his overshirt, and extracted a Smith and Wesson .22 revolver from his belt.

"Where'd you get that?" she asked.

"I got it the night I went down into Bakersfield without you. I don't want any trouble with Collins and his man, but if it comes, I want to be ready."

"Levi, you have to be careful," she said, looking up at him with worry in her eyes.

"Don't worry. Everything will be fine."

"I don't like that thing. Never liked 'em."

"I'm not going to let anything bad happen to you or anyone in your family," Levi replied while tucking the gun back into his belt.

The sun was finally down, and now darkness was quickly coming on. They stood together in the dirt road of the camp, Ella Mae in front of Levi, pressed tightly against him, his arms folded around her from behind with his hands on her stomach. They looked to the west as the dying light of the day cast a maroon hue over the tractor smog and dust of the western San Joaquin Valley sky. An ugly little moon was on the rise behind them, but they didn't turn around to see it. As it crept up over the foothills of the Sierra Nevada to the east, it formed a brown, half-circle halo in the dusty sky.

52
Westwood, California
Present Day

After Jack left, Marcus returned to the couch. He was exhausted, distraught, and entertained thoughts of not getting up, just closing his eyes and drifting off for the night. His bed, which was twenty feet away, might as well have been across town. Each time he closed his eyes, he saw Elizabeth, and each time her image was changed. He tried to keep his eyes open to retain the integrity of her image.

Then he noticed Jack's wallet on the coffee table, which Jack had removed to show Marcus the note from the red-headed woman. He stared at the wallet blankly, blinking slowly, his eyelids were like thick sheets of vinyl. Ten minutes passed, maybe it was fifteen. His eyes were shut for a long time, but he wasn't fully sleeping. Marcus wondered how long it would take Jack to discover the wallet missing and return for it, then he closed his eyes again.

A loud knock came at the door. It's about time, Marcus thought, as he dragged himself off the couch, grabbed Jack's wallet from the coffee table, and went to the door.

"I thought you wouldn't figure it out 'til morning," Marcus said while opening the door.

Jack wasn't standing on his porch. Instead it was Rem. His bulk blocked the opening, and he was backlit by the porch light. He seemed stooped over, like he would hit his head on something if he didn't bend down. Marcus stumbled backward in surprise, and Rem ducked into the house behind him and closed the door.

As darkness falls on the human world and our endogenous circadian clocks predict the oncoming of night and the necessity of sleep, a small gland at the brain's core squeezes out a few drips of concentrated melatonin. As cells are bathed in this hormone, the body's processes slow, and sleep comes quickly. The melatonin in Marcus's body, which increased in concentration and made him ever more groggy as he lay on the couch, was cleared from his body in an instant at the sight of Rem. Adrenaline, melatonin's nemesis, ran over his muscles as a bolt of fear and shock went through him.

"Mr. Hoerburger would like to see you," Rem said in his booming low accent.

Marcus stood stunned with his mouth open. "Now?" Marcus asked, still awkwardly holding Jack's wallet.

"Yes, you will come with me. I hope you don't make our trip forceful," Rem said, trying to enunciate each word as clearly as possible.

Marcus turned to look back at the couch where his phone was sitting on the coffee table. Rem followed his eyes and said, "You can leave your phone."

"What does Hoerburger need to see me about? I don't know anything. I can come by his office tomorrow. Why can't it wait 'til tomorrow?" Marcus pleaded while slipping Jack's wallet into his back pocket.

Rem didn't answer. He made a slight shrugging gesture and tossed his head toward the door. "Let's go."

When Marcus didn't move, either out of stubbornness or fear, Rem moved closer to him and placed a hand on his shoulder. The weight of the large hand and the intense pressure it exerted as Rem squeezed was enough to wake Marcus from his stupor.

"I'll follow you out," Rem said.

53

Marcus's mind raced and his breaths were short. He considered running, but didn't. On the sidewalk in front of Marcus's house, Rem pointed to a black sedan parked across the street and said, "Get into the driver's seat of that car." Marcus recognized it as the same car that was outside his house during his meeting with Elizabeth. He thought of her and wondered if he would soon meet her fate.

Once they were in the car, Rem extracted an oversized, black handgun from the back of his belt and placed it on his lap. With one hand as large as a small octopus draped over the gun, Rem handed Marcus the keys with the other.

"Drive," was the first of a string of short commands as Rem pointed in the directions that he wanted the car to go.

Marcus drove slowly, watching silhouetted canopies and high palms gliding past, backlit by the orange, high-pressure sodium-vapor night sky of the city. He tried to pay close attention to each turn, to recount where he was being taken. They seemed to wander for twenty minutes, Rem commanding each new direction, avoiding main thoroughfares, from Westwood into the tight curving streets of the dark canyons above Beverly Hills.

"This one up here on the right," Rem said, pointing to an all-white monstrosity of modern architecture, as if a titanic sugar cube, all lit up from within, floating in the darkness had crashed and was now embedded halfway into the chaparral-covered hillside next to the narrow canyon road. "Pull into the garage."

Marcus considered speeding forward and crashing the car into the dark hillside beyond the house, but Rem seemed to recognize this and lifted the gun from his lap and pointed it in Marcus's direction. "Don't try anything crazy," he said.

An unnecessarily large, bright white garage door rolled up in front of the car, and Marcus turned down a sloping driveway into the building. The garage had the cool blue fluorescent glow of a surgery chamber. Rem reached over, turned the engine off, and the car rolled to a stop.

Then the two men were sitting in silence, listening to the garage door finish its long descent, slicing through the thin, dry air like an unhurried yet determined guillotine, closing Marcus off from the safety of the public space outside. The door locked into place with a thud. Marcus could hear Rem's deep, steady breaths as he seemed to consider what to do next.

Rem looked at his watch, then turned to Marcus and said, "Mr. Hoerburger is waiting upstairs. Get out."

Rem followed Marcus up narrow white stairs that led from the buried garage to the ground floor of the house. He prodded Marcus up another flight of stairs to a spacious, fully carpeted room, with exposed concrete walls, devoid of furniture except for a seating area around a white leather chaise lounge in the corner. On one wall of the room was another set of stairs leading up one more story. Each concrete step appeared to grow out of the wall behind it and float in space. The room looked like an art gallery that had recently been robbed. The concrete walls were bare except for one remaining oversized painting on the side opposite the stairs.

There it hung; *The Death of Socrates* by the early nineteenth century French neoclassic painter Jacques-Louis David, depicting a bare-chested Socrates on a white chaise lounge of his own, his tight lily-white skin stretched over bulging muscles, ranting on, a finger turned to the heavens, while baby-faced, curly-headed boys wept around him, one with a gingerly placed hand on Socrates's thick upper thigh.

The floor to ceiling windows on one whole side of the room flaunted the Los Angeles night skyline in the distance; a gridded sea of yellow lights interrupted abruptly by square-topped skyscrapers protruding like the remaining teeth of an unfortunate old man's foul-smelling mouth.

"Sit down," Rem commanded, pointing to one of two molded plywood chairs in the seating area, then he left the room up the flight of stairs.

Marcus scanned the room frantically for exits, and there were only two; the stairs that led up to Rem and the one down to the garage. He heard nothing from the room above him. He stared at Socrates, then at Los Angeles, then back at Socrates. The founder of Western thought looked to Marcus like an aged chimpanzee with a fake silver beard. Marcus stood, considering going back downstairs to look for an exit.

"That's the original. The thing on the wall in the Met is a fake," said Jeff Hoerburger as he descended the concrete steps into the room. "It cost me a pretty penny, as you can imagine."

He was holding some kind of pink drink and being cautious not to spill any on the carpet as he came down the steps toward Marcus. He was wearing a white turtleneck, a black vest, brand new jeans with a crease down the front, and white New Balance sneakers. He looked as equally ridiculous as the first time Marcus had seen him in his office.

"I think it's the gayest painting ever," said a second man following Hoerburger down the stairs. "But in Athens, everyone was gay." He was a younger man than Hoerburger, dressed in a light blue seersucker suit and white loafers, as if he were just returning from an evening stroll in 1920s Charleston. He was coddling a drink of his own.

"Dr. Melter," said Hoerburger, taking a seat across from Marcus on the chaise lounge, "please, sit back down. Thank you for joining us."

"Joining you? I'm not joining you. It's not like I had a choice."

"Yes, perhaps. Rem can be quite persuasive. Can I get you something to drink? We're having maraschino martinis."

While Hoerburger spoke, the second man stood facing away from them, rocking back and forth, looking out over Los Angeles.

"What am I doing here?" Marcus asked.

"Where were you last night?" asked the man in the seersucker, still not facing Marcus.

"I was at my house. What's this about?"

The man turned away from the window and faced Marcus with a friendly, unforced smile. He set his drink down on the table next to them and sat by Hoerburger's side. His smile disappeared as he stared at Marcus. Speaking to Hoerburger, but continuing to stare at Marcus, he said, "He's beautiful, isn't he? It's such a shame."

"Just answer our questions, Dr. Melter," Hoerburger said. "We can bring Rem back in to ask them again, if you'd like."

"I was at my house."

"During what hours?"

"From about 9:00 PM on."

"Did anyone visit you?"

"Yes, a friend came by."

Hoerburger took a slow sip of his drink, and Marcus could hear the glass clink against his falsely whitened teeth. He licked the remains of the thin pink fluid from his mustache with his lower lip.

"Okay, go on," Hoerburger said. "Who visited you? Give us the full name."

"Elizabeth, Elizabeth Shackleton." The name didn't escape Marcus's throat easily. He hadn't said it since learning of her death.

"Elizabeth Shackleton," Hoerburger repeated the name, looking at the man in the seersucker suit, who responded by shaking his head.

"Rem, come join us," yelled Hoerburger in the direction of the stairs.

Marcus could hear movement one story above. Rem came down the stairs gradually, each stair step straining under his weight. All three of them watched in silent amazement. His movements were smooth and agile. His grace was in the effortlessness with which he carried his mass. Even though he was larger than most large men, he moved as if at any moment he could jump into a pirouette, followed by a few fouettes, and finish off with soaring grand jeté. He restrained from doing any of those moves and instead stood at the bottom of the stairs, wondering why he had been disturbed.

"Rem, we asked you to check on Dr. Melter last night," Hoerburger said to Rem.

"Yes, I did," Rem replied.

"Yeah, well, you royally fucked this up," said the man in the seersucker suit in a high-pitched whine.

"It can be fixed," Hoerburger said calmly.

"What would you like me to do with him?" Rem asked, his voice so low it cracked. The juxtaposition of his voice with that of the man in the seersucker was extraordinary.

"We're going to have to clean this up," Hoerburger said, looking at Marcus.

"Did you think Elizabeth was someone else?" Marcus asked Rem. He felt the violation and anger rising in him, as it had when he first learned of her death. His cheeks grew reddish-brown and hot.

Rem looked at Hoerburger, then back at Marcus.

"I don't know," Rem responded with a shrug.

Marcus shook his head in disbelief and disgust. "Are you fucking kidding me?" Marcus yelled at Rem while standing to face him. "You killed her because you thought she was someone else?"

"It doesn't matter now," Rem said, approaching Marcus, who foolishly stood his ground.

Rem was standing so close to him; too close. Marcus didn't expect what happened next. He looked up at Rem's face and saw his nostrils flare, like a hard breathing thoroughbred halfway down the track. Rem punched him solidly in the gut. The fist came up from below and landed firmly in his intestines. A hot flash of pain coursed through Marcus's guts as they slammed against his solar plexus, then he crumpled onto the carpet, yearning for breath to come back, but it wouldn't. He moved his mouth like a goldfish on the floor below the water bowl from which it had just escaped. Rem looked down on him disinterestedly while Marcus's silent, involuntary yawning movements continued, the face muscles contorting and contracting to help pull air into his unresponsive lungs. Eventually, the spasms of his diaphragm ended, and he took his first breath, a long hissing wheeze.

Rem lifted the heel of his boot and prepared to bring it down on Marcus's head.

"Hey. Stop," Hoerburger commanded. "That's enough. Take him downstairs and keep him there until we discuss what to do next. And don't hit him again up here. I don't want blood on this carpet."

Rem pulled Marcus from the floor and down the stairs they went. Once they were back in the blue surgical light of the garage, Rem threw Marcus onto the cold concrete floor. Marcus pushed himself up onto his knees and turned around just in time to see Rem winding up for another punch. This one landed squarely on his nose. Constellations formed and light danced in Marcus's field of vision. He lost focus on the visible world and fell uncontrollably back, hitting the back of his head with a hollow thud on the concrete floor. An arc of white light came into view as his head met the floor, then there was darkness. The sound of running water came to Marcus, then that of material tearing, then darkness once again.

54
Weedpatch Camp, California
1936

The actual events surrounding the inaugural Weedpatch Camp community dance would only be pieced together much later, based on eyewitness accounts taken in statements by the Kern County Sheriff's Office during the investigation of incidents leading to two deaths and one disappearance.

At approximately 9:15 PM on Saturday, June 22nd, 1936, Dr. Dan Collins stood on the low bandstand erected above the wooden dancing platform to speak to the Weedpatch campers and their guests. When questioned later, the man in the entrance guardhouse placed Dr. Collins's arrival at the camp, along with his bald associate, at around 8:15 PM. During his brief speech, Collins spoke eloquently of hospitality in hard times, of creating an island of joy in a sea of despair, his role as county supervisor, and of doing what needed to be done in desperate times to get by, then, over the sound of a forced, peppered applause, he yielded the stage, and the band began to play. Campers and their guests streamed onto the dance floor through a surrounding wall of children who watched in awe as they saw their parents move in ways completely foreign to them.

After his speech, Collins sat on one of the wooden benches lining the dance floor, pulling on his goatee, watching the band and dancers. According to witnesses, he socialized with the seated campers around him, then at approximately 9:45 PM he left the dance with the intention of returning briefly to the administration building, but was never seen again. Minutes after Collins's departure from the dancing platform, the tall bald associate of Dr. Collins's was seen standing motionless near the musicians, watching the campers dance. During the sheriff's interviews, days later, several campers would remark that the tall bald man seemed to be looking for someone.

Meanwhile, Levi and the Whites danced with joy and abandon,

Patsy, first with Tom, then with Levi, Ella Mae with Levi, then with her father, Jesse with Timmy, then whomever else would ask them. Round and round they went, laughing and smiling, swinging and twirling, clapping and stomping. The fiddle was relentless. Levi and Patsy were dancing on the far edge of the platform when Levi looked across the crowd of dancers to see Ralph Roe holding Jesse and Ella Mae by the arms, escorting them off the dance floor into the darkness beyond as they struggled against his strength.

Coils formed in Levi's intestines, cinching them into a tight knot, and all his heat rose instantly to his face. "Patsy, get Tom and have him follow me," he said sternly, looking to the other end of the dance floor where Tom was swinging two children in his arms. Levi crossed the dance floor in Roe's direction. He was moving quickly along the dark dirt road, pistol in hand, two hundred yards from the dancing platform when he caught up with them.

"Hey," he yelled as he approached. "Let them go."

Ralph Roe swirled the two girls around to face Levi, still gripping tightly to the back of their arms.

"Dr. Collins has an appointment with these two," Roe said with his typical disinterested hiss.

Levi repeated his command, "Let them go," this time lifting the pistol directly in Roe's direction. As it turns out, it wasn't the first incident in which Ralph Roe had a gun pointed in his direction and, in Levi's perception, he was terrifyingly unaffected.

"I don't think I will," he said calmly to Levi. "You have no idea what you're doing. Why don't you head on back to the dance. These girls will be back around in no time."

Levi stood his ground. The fiddle squawked Cripple Creek in the distance. The moon had risen, and there was enough light for him to see Jesse and Ella Mae's shocked faces. He looked at them, then at Roe, then back at Ella Mae again. He stepped forward and lifted the pistol directly to Roe's face. The end of the barrel was three feet from his nose.

As calmly as possible he said, "Go on now, let them girls loose. Don't want to, but I'll pull this trigger if I have to."

Now it was Roe's turn to decide. With all his unnatural strength, he stepped back and turned to the left, pushing Jesse away from him. At the same time he pulled Ella Mae between him and Levi, shoving her in Levi's direction. Roe followed Ella Mae, grabbing the outstretched gun and pushing it upward. That was when the campers witnessed the first of two gunshots. The second would come less than thirty seconds later. In subsequent sheriff's interviews, most of the campers would place the first shot around 10 PM, saying that it wasn't easily heard above the music, and most thought it little more than a jalopy backfiring in the distance. Half of the interviewees didn't hear the muffled second shot at all.

In those intervening thirty seconds between shots, Ralph Roe and Levi Bratton rolled in the dirt struggling to gain control of the weapon. Roe's strength was matched by Levi's anger. Levi rolled on top of Roe with his hands around his neck. While Levi choked him, Roe fumbled for the antler-handled knife in the leather scabbard he wore on his hip. He swung the long blade up and stabbed Levi under his outstretched arm, piercing his left lung. Levi's arms gave way, and he fell onto Roe. Both men rolled to one side, where the gun sat in the dirt. Levi grabbed the gun and turned it in Roe's direction, and the second shot rang out in the night. A bullet, traveling at over five times the speed of sound, left Levi's .22 on a course upward through Roe's neck and out the back of his head, killing him instantly. He was gone before he heard the shot. Both men lay motionless, side-by-side, on the ground when Tom arrived. Roe's knife was still in Levi's side.

Each of us is born with several little lights burning on the inside, and we keep them glowing as long as we can. They represent our health, hope, our optimism, and our life force. Levi Bratton came into the world bathed in his mother's lukewarm blood at the bottom of a back porch bathtub, illuminated by three. The first was soon extinguished at the sight of his mother murdering his father. The second dimmed and sputtered nearly to darkness as he was forced to leave Arkansas and Armer's Service Station. That second light, brought back to a full warm glow by Ella Mae and the Whites, was blown out in a shot of white pain as Roe's dirty knife entered his lung. Ella Mae and Tom struggled to keep his remaining light burning as they laid him on his bedroll in the tent next to his Chrysler.

Ella Mae lit the candles next to the bed, and Tom gently rolled Levi onto his back. She held the sides of his head, looked into his eyes, and whispered to him. Levi let out a painful gurgling moan as Tom pulled the knife from his side. In the flickering canary wax light, they could see the dark blood filling his open mouth. Levi's breathing was difficult, and his eyes were open. He stared at Ella Mae. She let go of his head and clutched his outstretched hand, refusing to cry; then, placing his hand on her belly, she nodded. A smile came across his face. Levi wheezed, coughed up blood, and cringed in pain. His breathing stopped at 10:18 PM on Saturday, June 22nd, 1936. He was three months shy of his 26th birthday.

Minutes after Levi's death, Tom left the tent and his weeping daughter and walked in the direction of the camp administration building. He wasn't seen again until the early morning hours of Sunday the 23rd when Patsy discovered him sitting in the front seat of Levi's Chrysler, staring off into the distance and rubbing his shirt collar. Police officers from the Kern County Sheriff's office arrived at the camp entrance at 11:30 PM the previous night, following a report of gunshots heard at the camp dance. They discovered a man lying motionless on the dirt road with a small group gathered around him. The police officers were surprised to find the camp administrator missing. The next day they looked for the county supervisor at his farmhouse, but were told that he never returned from Weedpatch the previous night. Dan Collins was never seen again after leaving the dancers the evening of Levi Bratton's death.

55
Northwestern Los Angeles
2015

The western scrub-jay is a wicked smart, mean, and thieving little bird. *Aphelocoma californica.* Named for its sleek head: *aphelos*, meaning without, and *coma*, the tuft of feathers or crest, found on the larger, more docile crowns of its close relatives. Like most successful animals, the scrub-jay is opportunistic, omnivorous, and ruthless. In the spring and early summer, they kill and eat insects, lizards, and other small animals. They also quietly pursue unsuspecting adult birds of other species who eventually expose the localities of their nests, then the scrub-jay patiently waits and watches until helpless young hatchlings are left alone.

In the fall and winter, when hatchlings are too big to attack, jays eat the abundant live oak acorns, with which, by no coincidence, they share a native range. Always scheming, and too smart for their own good, the jays hide more acorns than they eat, thereby inadvertently planting the lost nuts. Then the spring rains come, and the golden west greens up and the jays once again substitute a constipating diet of acorns for the more varied and delicious diet of bugs and other unsuspecting little animals.

In late October of 1663, a western scrub-jay in the fourth year of her life buried an acorn in a tight pocket of dark and fertile soil in a canyon ravine a few hundred feet below the spot where she and her partner were constructing their winter nest. Distracted by the tribulations of her own offspring and the abundance brought on by the late spring rains, she never returned to consume that acorn, and the long life of an oak began.

Through the hard shell and up out of the soil above, the first leaves emerged, unfurling in the glowing Southern California sun. The days blinked by and the mesic seasons revolved in anticipated succession. In its first one hundred years, the oak raged in the battle for light, then from up above the willows and sycamore with which it shared the wet canyon, it witnessed over centuries, the shifting of vegetation, the battle for resources, disturbance regimes, and the occasional fire, by which everything was reset. Waves of vegetation pulsed and flowed on the hillsides above the canyon.

The occasional human visited, looking up in awe, sensing the sly haughtiness of a superior organism, then scurrying about the trunk in an almost imperceptible blur, stealing the oak's progeny to be ground into crude holes in local rocks and eaten in hot baskets. Then the humans came in full force, different humans, and many more of them, and with them a road that stretched out through the canyon floor, and square wooden structures surged over the vegetation on the rolling hills beyond. At first a dirt path, widening with each season, inched its way toward the trunk of the old oak. As time passed, the path flowed with increasing numbers of humans with their livestock and carts, widening all the while, and large oaks and sycamores all around disappeared in its wake. The path was paved, and the canyon roared in a daily blur of exhaust, noise, and rolling metal boxes.

On an afternoon in early June, three hundred and forty-eight seasons after that devious little western scrub-jay had inadvertently given this immense tree its life, it witnessed a strange human interaction below its heavy branches.

A car arrived with a cloud of dust, and a man got out of the passenger side and hurried to the base of the old oak tree, while a second man waited in the parked car. The first man hid quietly behind the oak's trunk as a second car arrived. A man with a square-jawed confident face, blemished by a large mole on his cheek, stepped out and looked cautiously around. The man waiting in the first car got out. He was much larger than all the other humans the oak tree had seen in its many years. The two men approached each other, exchanged a few words, then walked to the back of the second car where the trunk was opened. From its outstretched limbs, the oak was witness to the two men standing silently staring at a dead man in the truck, curled in a fetal position.

The man hiding behind the old oak's trunk stepped out where he could be seen. While the man with the mole was momentarily distracted, the giant struck him over the head from behind, dragged him behind the first car, and shot him in the back of the head. The shot rang out and was absorbed and muffled by the oak's dense canopy. The weak sound that remained blended with the roar of the traffic beyond. The two men then lifted the man with the mole and dropped him on top of the other man in the trunk of the second car. Each man got behind the wheel of a car, pulled onto the freeway, and accelerated into the flock of cars, never to be witnessed by the old oak again.

As the dust settled, a distant descendent of the western scrub-jay who planted the old tree sat silhouetted in the high branches, watching the action. Curious and irreverent by its very nature, the bird didn't wait long to come down from its perch to investigate the remains of the scene. There in the dust, drying quickly, was a maroon pile of human debris, skull bone, brains, and blood, left on the dirt where the man had been shot. The jay picked vigorously at the nutritious bits of human organ meat. In a year of drought and unfortunate luck, that scrawny scrub-jay, who would have otherwise fallen victim to its harsh environment, received the crucial nourishment needed to make an egg. As a result of that warm meal, the lineage of the original tree planter would go on another generation. Other giant oaks would be inadvertently planted, a lucky few of which would witness the coming of the wet times, the greening and changing of all vegetation, and the human world as it raged through its last centuries.

56
Los Angeles, California
Present Day

In the same moment that Marcus moved in and out of consciousness on the cold concrete floor in the garage of Jeff Hoerburger's Beverly Hills mansion, tied up with duct tape, gelatinous blood drying on his nose, Jack Bratton sat at his desk at the West Bureau police station 4.3 miles away. Although he would soon be derailed, Jack had planned to sit there for thirty more minutes, struggling to fill out a report on his part of the investigations into the death of James Lindster, then he would drive home and pass out for a long night of righteous sleep as he thought about his conversation with Bridge Gardinier.

The chain of events leading up to the moment when Jack Bratton got up from his desk to leave the police station is probably more accurately described as a web of events. A web has neither a beginning nor an end. A web in time is a matrix of unfurling occurrences; each can be traced to several others, bound by the unyielding lines of cause and effect; an exquisite web with ridges and valleys, joined hand and hand. Push on any point of the web and it pulls on every other.

In the rainy days of September 1965, a baby girl was born prematurely in a grass hut under the shade of an ancient kapok tree in a riverside village in the central highlands of Vietnam. She was born in the midst of the largest U.S. military deployment to South Vietnam. Even though her mother didn't survive the labor and her father, an American helicopter mechanic named Terry, lay rotting at the bottom of a casket in the Arlington National Cemetery, she was unusually vigorous for such a small child. She would live the first eight years of her life before she was given a name.

Thirty-two years later, on a hot night in late May of 1997, cars hurried by out on the interstate between Plainview and Lubbock, Texas, but in the sweet, smoky tranquility of room twenty-eight, a man drew the vinyl curtains for the last time. Instead of going for help, he dragged his wife's body from the carpet to the bed and listened to the hums and gurgles of the air conditioner. He thought of the love note written on the inside of a ring in a pawnshop in Amarillo and how it would eventually be found. They would only be names etched in gold, no history, no meaning, no failure, just beautiful golden cursive, and he was comforted. He put the cold steel inside his mouth and took his last deep breath.

Three days later, Zephyrbury Rosenbaum, the largest boy in his class of 165 seniors, was getting his first hand job in the back of a school bus as it meandered down the road on an end-of-the-school-year field trip. He had finally talked her into it, and it was worth all that effort. Melissa's skinny brown hand, like a delicate sculpture, slid the foreskin of his uncircumcised penis up and down with unskilled, sporadic jerking motions until clear droplets of pre-cum swelled and emerged from Zephyrbury's urethra. For once, he stopped talking. Moments later, Melissa looked up from her cramping wrist and screamed as the bus lurched down a dirt embankment and flipped over in the river. The droplets of Zephyrbury's pre-cum swirled and mixed with cold brown water as he fought for his last breaths in a pocket of oxygen trapped under the seat of the sinking, upside-down bus.

Seventeen years earlier, in the first morning light of Tuesday, December 9th, 1980, Zephyrbury's mother bore down on her birth canal, struggling to push him out. Her labor pains began the night before when she learned of John Lennon's death by multiple gunshot wounds while she sat watching Monday Night Football. She was a petite woman who carried the large child with great difficulty, and during Zephyrbury's birth, his head was crushed in several locations by her narrow pelvis. Upon learning from the doctor about the unlikely survival of a baby with such injuries, Zephyrbury's father abandoned the planned name for the child and wrote on the birth certificate Zephyrbury Rosenbaum. Perhaps it was because Led Zeppelin's "In Through the Out Door" was all he had listened to since its release the previous year, or perhaps he was having a distraught moment devoid of creativity. Either way, Zephyrbury was all he could come up with.

In an effort to spare the mother from seeing her firstborn's monstrously deformed face in the small coffin, the doctor decided to manually reshape the barely breathing baby boy's head. By squeezing each semi-solidified skull plate into its approximate location under the loose skin, molding the tiny head in his hands like a clay ball, the doctor inadvertently and miraculously saved Zephyrbury's life. Other than the normal trials and tribulations that come with having an unusual name, he would go on to live out seventeen full and imaginative years.

Four years after the tragic drowning of Zephyrbury Rosenbaum and sixteen of his classmates, in a nearby town, a woman sat at her desk in an empty house distractedly studying a form. Her only son was dead, the victim of careless friendly fire in the cold desert in northern Afghanistan, but her principal concern at the moment was choosing which of several checkboxes to mark. All of them seemed appropriate, and at the same time, completely unsatisfactory—Irreconcilable Differences or Incurable Insanity or Irretrievable Breakdown or Incompatibility. She looked up for a moment and listened to the sound of machines in the basement, then forced out a long, steady fart, which the seat cushion accepted with grace. What was the difference? Did it really matter which box she checked?

As it turned out, it did. Had she chosen to place her wavering blue ink on any checkbox other than Irreconcilable Differences, things would have gone differently for both Jack Bratton and Marcus Melter on that night fourteen years later, when Marcus was stranded in the Beverly Hills basement, struggling feebly against his duct tape shackles, while Jack grew tired of filling out his report.

The vigorous yet nameless Vietnamese girl was taken in by an aged prostitute in Ho Chi Min City, where she developed a nasty heroin addiction with an American POW who was released without ceremony from Chí Hòa Prison eighteen years after the end of the war. They traveled together to his hometown of Amarillo, Texas, where they lived the tumultuous early years of a wild and loving marriage between two heroin-addicted misfits before both dying in a hotel room outside Lubbock from apparent overdose and suicide. Distracted by the news of his brother's suicide, a bus driver in Henry, Illinois, didn't see the stopped car on the bridge in time, swerved around it, and flipped the bus into Shaw Creek, killing a teacher and seventeen students. The driver, who was also the coach of the high school football team, was haunted by his role in the death of the students, particularly that of Zephyrbury Rosenbaum, one of his favorite players, whom he pulled from the wreckage of the bus with his pants down around his knees, his little bluish-white semi-erect dick flopping to one side as he laid the boy on the bank. The driver never recovered from the incident and was eventually divorced by his wife for irreconcilable differences, the only no-fault grounds for divorce allowable in the State of Illinois. Her successful divorce allowed her to move near her sister in California, where she found work as a receptionist for a chemical company in Glendale. She was eventually remarried to Lee Pike, the grandson of Eddie Pike, a hobo who had hitched rides and rode the tracks west to California shortly after World War II. Like his grandfather, Lee Pike loved to sing quietly to himself and did so continually throughout the day.

At 11:02 PM on a Wednesday night, Lee Pike and his new wife left the parking lot of the West Los Angeles School of Dance, where they had just completed what they both considered to be a triumphant ballroom dancing lesson. As they rolled along, Pike was singing to his wife, raving about the different moves and how gracefully she had gone through them. His hips swayed in the driver's seat, and his wife smiled and laughed, her arms stretched out, jazz hands flaring. At 11:14 PM, with a tune escaping his lips at high volume, Lee Pike proceeded through the intersection of Beverly and Pico Boulevards traveling at forty-two miles per hour, headed south on Beverly, not noticing the red light he was running.

Eleven minutes earlier, Jack Bratton had pulled out of the parking lot of the West Bureau police station on Venice and San Vincent Boulevards in his black, unmarked Crown Victoria and headed west on Pico toward a long night of sleep. Jack drove slowly, as he always did, tapping out a beat on the steering wheel with his finger, and was distracted by thoughts of the rusty freckles on Bridge Gardinier's face. Did they look the same in the morning light as they had in the cafe? Jack tried to think, but his mind was no longer clear. Ten minutes into his drive, he waited absentmindedly for twenty-three seconds at the traffic signal at Pico and Beverly before it turned green, and he accelerated out into the intersection. Halfway across it, Lee Pike and his wife slammed into the rear end passenger side of Jack's Crown Victoria, sending the vehicle spinning. A millisecond before the impact, Jack could hear the sound of Lee Pike's engine and what sounded like a man yelling the chorus to "All That Jazz" from Chicago.

It was when Jack reached for his wallet forty minutes later, that he realized it was missing. He hadn't noticed its absence after leaving Marcus's house, nor while driving to the station, sitting at his desk, or getting back into his car. Only after the accident, after talking with the Pikes, after dealing with the traffic cops, when the tow truck asked to see Lee Pike's auto club card, did Jack place his right hand on his back pocket and realize the comforting bulge of the wallet was gone. By searching his car and rewinding the story of his evening in his mind, he remembered showing Marcus Bridge's note, which he had pulled out of his wallet. Jack reached down and yanked on a portion of the Crown Victoria's fender that was bent in by the accident. He freed it from where it rubbed on the tire, jumped in the car, and was at Marcus's door eight minutes later.

57
San Joaquin Valley, California
June 23rd, 1936

Two men walk along a tree line at the back of a field in the mercury morning light of the San Joaquin Valley. This is the end, the time awaiting each of us. It's two days past the summer solstice and the light in the five o'clock hour is sufficient for them to find their way along a narrow path in the tall summer grass. A pair of geese fly low overhead, and the man in front stops to look up at the graceful line they cut through the morning sky. A tall gaunt man pushes the stopped man from behind with an outstretched shovel. Limping and wounded, the man in front takes his time.

"You needn't do this, sir," he says, not turning back and speaking the words quietly.

He gets no response. All the pleading, all the threats, all the explanations are done. The tall man in back is usually longwinded and wants to respond, but doesn't.

Out past the grassy field into the side ditch and through another line of trees into the next field they go. The heat of the valley from the previous day has dissipated, and in the coolest part of this new day, white sheets of valley fog hang just overhead. At the edge of the fourth field, they push down under the silvery sandbar willows. This is the spot. Down on your knees, don't look back. Standing behind him, the tall man stares for a moment, squinting into the distance, then takes a long look around him. The deep crevices in his cheeks are relaxed into shallow valleys as the skin on his face is swollen from lack of sleep. He listens to the whimpering man while studying the back of his silver-haired head. One hand rests on the shovel handle, and the other rubs vigorously on his shirt collar. Once he's satisfied and calm, a swift swing of the shovel followed by a sturdy strangling grip does the deed.

In the near darkness under the willows, in the black soil just above the sand, he begins to dig a hole. The sun rises above the fog and the morning remains cool. His work goes quickly, and soon he's rolling the limp body into the dark pocket of earth. He pushes the clods back in, covers the mound with old leaves and a few branches, then sets off with wet boots back through the fields. Numbness begins to overtake him. He lays the shovel with the others against the back of the administration building and washes his hands, not in the clean washbasins of the sanitary building, but in the faucet around back. Kneeling, the last bit of soil now cleared from his hands, he takes a long drink of water.

58
Beverly Hills, California
Present Day

The throbbing pain of his broken nose woke Marcus from a stupor. Like an impaired worm, he rolled onto his side and tried to sit up. His stomach muscles burned as he tightened them. He was breathing hard through his open mouth, pushing himself against the wall. The garage was immaculate in the bright blue light of the fluorescent tubes. Marcus laid his back against the unfinished drywall and surveyed the cavernous garage. A cardboard box, the size of a child's coffin, was propped against the wall on the far end. Marcus's eyesight blurred, and the walls seemed to bulge and sway. Heavy white sails made of desert gypsum will get you nowhere, he thought, then he opened his eyes, and the walls were plumb once again. Marcus studied the raw concrete floor where he'd been knocked out by Rem's swift and effortless punch. Dread and panic welled inside him as he saw the maroon puddle of his own gelatinous blood where he had laid. He struggled feebly against his restraints and, breathing hard, he tried to listen to muffled sounds from above. As he listened, he heard a boot land heavily on the upper portion of the flight of stairs leading down to the garage.

59
San Joaquin Valley, California
1937

Willie Bratton convulsed and rolled in Ella Mae White's expanded womb, deciding it was time to trade the rich nourishment of her placenta for the comfort and sweet milk of her breasts. Ella Mae had wished he'd made up his mind sooner. Late-stage pregnancy made her constantly uncomfortable and had turned her once slender, sleek, deer-like ankles into swollen doughy trunks. For some time, she thought herself ready for the trade; the chronic discomfort of pregnancy for the brief, acute pain of labor. She wanted him out, but it wasn't her choice. Even before he was born, she didn't understand him as well as she would have liked. After the thirtieth week of her pregnancy she wasn't able to bounce on her pogo stick, an activity that was comforting for her but disturbing for Willie. He would respond by kicking the upper portion of her uterus repeatedly until she had to lie down, rub her belly, and softly apologize again and again.

Her labor took place in the same tent, on the same makeshift bed where Levi Bratton had been laid in his last dying moments seven months earlier. Her blood and amniotic fluid soaked the blankets as she screamed at Patsy. Although Patsy had birthed ten of her own children, she wasn't experienced on the receiving end of the bed. Tom, however, was. Except for Ella Mae, who was born to a lesbian midwife who came down from McLoud to help Patsy through what was by far her most difficult labor, Tom caught each of his children with composure and patience in the upstairs room of the farmhouse in Shawnee.

With a chrome Rayovac flashlight in his mouth, Tom White calmly massaged his wet fingers around his daughter's swollen and dilated birth canal, coaxing Willie into the world. As the decision to enter the world had been his, Willie didn't wait long to appear. In the sixth hour of Ella Mae's labor, with an excruciating push, he slid, eyes open, into Tom's hands, let out a long moan, and took several deep breaths. Like a scowling little Buddha, with precociously large hands folded across his chest, he waited patiently to be fed.

Ella Mae White and Willie Bratton—she insisted on giving him Levi's last name—passed the cold, dry San Joaquin Valley winter in the guy-wired lean-to that Tom rigged next to the geodesic dome. Ella Mae quickly regained her slender natural shape as Willie sucked any remaining fat out of her.

Shortly after Willie's fourth birthday, the family moved, against Tom's mild protest, to a poorly built house in Burbank, along the eastern floor of the San Fernando Valley. All the houses in the neighborhood were hastily built to accommodate workers employed in war effort aircraft fabrication at the nearby Lockheed Air Terminal. Tom's experience with experimental tent construction in the Weedpatch labor camp was noticed by the US Army Air Forces Western Technical Training Command during a test flight of the new B17 bomber over the San Joaquin. Tom had fashioned several large community meeting tents on the outskirts of the encampment. He had assumed the role of camp maintenance director after the disappearance of Dan Collins, which allowed the Whites to remain in the camp rent-free.

In late May of 1942, with another long San Joaquin summer on the horizon, Tom was approached by a manager at Lockheed with an offer to hire him to construct elaborate camouflage tents over several of their new aircraft factories and parking lots in northern Los Angeles. The offer of a house and car, even though they had never seen either, and a decent wage was one that Patsy refused to let Tom refuse.

On the day that the White family left Weedpatch camp, after having resided there for nearly five years, Tom didn't turn around nor look back. He had grown attached to Weedpatch. Much of what the camp had become, including many of the comforts of its residents, was a result of Tom's ingenuity.

"Here we go again," he said to Patsy once Levi's old Chrysler had been loaded and hitched to a much smaller trailer than the one on which they had arrived.

Patsy pulled Tom's hand down from where it vigorously rubbed his shirt collar, held it tightly, and said, "We'll be fine. We had to leave eventually and now we'll have a house."

"Yes, I do believe we will," Tom said with a crooked smile that bent the deep impressions of his hollow cheeks. He squinted and his smile faded. "We always seem to be fine."

60

Events define a life. Willie Bratton's life was framed by six. We are who we are because of what happens to us, the choices we make, and the things we do. History casts its long, ugly shadow on the present. We have inescapable ghosts in our pasts, from whence each of us has come—road signs seen from the backside, cracks in the plaster, desensitized and discolored scars, shallow creekside graves, little greasy stains, grainy photographs, or voices in the head that can't be silenced. Willie Bratton's journey through life was influenced by six events, and even though each one touched many lives, these incidents would also come to shape the path of his only son.

61
Event One of Six

On the day that Willie was born, out beneath the trees of the Arvin cemetery, beneath the hidden roots of those trees, the murderous relics of bygone eras accumulated and stratified in the dark loam. A Colt Special Model musket ball, shot in 1861, and a Kawaiisu chert arrowhead, shot eighty-one years earlier, were buried two feet below his father, who lay shrunken on the floor of a pine casket. Under his deflated body was a perfectly good Smith and Wesson .22 handgun, shot only twice on a summer night seven months earlier.

His father's murder, an event that he had no hand in, would shape the way Willie related to the world. The curse of the Bratton bloodline was the broken father-son relationship. Willie's great-grandfather grew up fatherless, and each successive generation's father died too early to raise his son.

62
Westwood, California
Present Day

There was no answer when Jack called Marcus on the way to his house, so he figured Marcus would be asleep. Upon his arrival, though, Jack saw all the lights on, so knocked loudly. When Marcus didn't answer, he turned the handle of the unlocked door.

"Anybody here?" Jack called loudly into the empty house.

He saw Marcus's phone on the coffee table and picked it up to see his recent missed call. After a quick search of the house, finding neither his wallet nor Marcus, Jack stood on the porch with a puzzled look. The same cold fog from two nights earlier was blowing in from the west and settling into the Los Angeles basin, but the additional two days had made the moon fatter and brighter. It showed through the high fog above the orange glow of two million street lights and four million souls as the center of a luminous ring with a diameter as wide as the entire city. Jack looked up at the halo as he walked from the porch to his car, and the moon remained at its center, moving with him.

Think, Jack. Think. Focus. He sat silently in the Crown Victoria, cradling Marcus's phone in his sweaty palm. He could see that a long crease formed by the accident was distorting the reflection of the moon on the shiny black hood. On a hunch, he picked up the radio, called dispatch, and asked for Jeff Hoerburger's address. Five minutes later he was crossing Santa Monica Boulevard headed north toward Beverly Hills.

63
Beverly Hills, California
Present Day

Marcus was relieved to see that what he had perceived as the heavy boot of Rem descending the stairway to the garage was actually the suede loafer of the man in the seersucker suit. He walked confidently with a pleased look across the garage toward the cardboard box leaning against the wall. Like a child on Christmas morning, he tore open the box to reveal a pogo stick with pink plastic handles. He picked up the toy with great care and reverence, and as he returned to the stairs, seemed to notice Marcus for the first time.

"Oh, you're still here?" he said, approaching Marcus with a fake look of concern.

He squatted in front of Marcus, who was sitting with his back against the wall, taped legs outstretched in front of him. He studied Marcus with an intensely inquisitive look, first his body, then his face. He drew in close and said, "I guess it won't be long now before you're gone."

With an unnaturally long and skinny hand, he reached out and swiped a finger along Marcus's cheek, then stared at his finger where it had touched Marcus's face, closed his eyes, and smelled it with a deep inhalation. He shook his head as he exhaled. Without a word he got up and walked toward the stairs, carrying the pink-handled pogo stick.

"Hey, come on. Come back, let me out of here," Marcus pleaded. "I didn't see anything. Please, let me out of here. People are going to be looking for me," Marcus yelled at the man, who let out a forced, high-pitched chuckle and continued toward the stairs.

64
Event Two of Six

"You can make it. I've done it three times. Come on, Tommy, don't puss out again." Willie was ten years old when he spoke those stinging words to his uncle. He hadn't done it three times, he hadn't even done it once, but he was insecure and manipulative enough to try to convince Thomas White, who was eleven at the time, to jump from the cliff into the river below.

Thomas was kind and easy going and didn't want to disappoint Willie. He looked down at his dusty bare feet, then to the water thirty feet below. His legs felt weak and he stepped back from the edge. He instinctively put his hand deep into the right pocket of his shorts, feeling for something that wasn't there.

"Come on, Thomas, I'm not going to wait all day. Are you jumping or not?" Willie asked with clear disappointment in his voice.

"Are you sure you've done this?" Thomas asked.

"Yeah, you just jump to that pool right there. No problem." Willie pointed to a bit of swirling green water no larger than a bathtub.

"It seems too shallow and too small," Thomas said. There was a slight shake in his voice.

"It isn't at all. You go and I'll come in after you."

"Alright," Thomas said and stepped back to the edge. He stood silently for a moment, clenched his fists, took his last unobstructed breath, and leaped into the air.

The headwaters of the Los Angeles River are in the western San Fernando Valley; Dayton Creek, Caballero Creek, Calabasas Creek, Bull Creek, Bell Creek, Pacoima Wash, Verdugo Wash, the names go on and on. All these meager little trickles, most running only after a storm, converge along the valley floor and run east before making a sharp turn south to pass through the Los Angeles Basin and down into the Pacific at Long Beach. At the south end of the valley, past the highway and the trains, the Los Angeles River runs dry for a good part of most years, but in a wet year nobody forgets that it is a river just the same. In the hard, long winter of 1948, the rain was unrelenting, and the river rose and ran angrily over rocks that had been dry for decades. As the spring came and the current subsided, gravelly pools were formed, the rocks were heated by the sun, and old sycamores cast their dappled shade on perfect swimming holes.

Once school was out, Willie and Thomas spent the early summer exploring the remaining pools and swimming wherever they could in the quickly drying river. Thomas had a nascent curiosity about the world and how all its parts worked. He was just a baby when Willie was born, and both were mostly raised by Thomas's older siblings in the post-war chaos of Patsy and Tom's house in San Fernando. The boys slept on a wide cot in the corner of a tent in the backyard. The Whites stretched the small house and the various tents that Tom had erected to their capacity.

On the afternoon of May 28th, 1948, Willie and Thomas left the house for the long journey on foot, through the suburban streets and continuous front lawns, along the railroad tracks, through a culvert under the highway, and down into the waiting river. As they walked along the tracks, Thomas kept his hand in his pocket where he rubbed his lucky nickel, which he had found several weeks earlier on the sidewalk near the house. Fearing that someone would claim it as their lost coin, he kept it hidden deep in his pocket and shared the secret knowledge of its existence with no one.

"What do you have in your pocket?" Willie asked Thomas, noticing that he was walking with his right hand buried deep in his shorts.

"Nothing," Thomas said.

"Let me see then," Willie said, approaching him from behind.

"No, it's nothing."

"Come on, what's in your pocket? Show me."

Thomas pulled out the dull nickel. "It's mine, I found it by the house."

"Let me see it."

"You have to give it back."

"I will, let me see it."

Thomas reluctantly handed the nickel to Willie.

Willie studied the coin and looked around. "You know what we should do? We should leave it here on the tracks and get it on our way back to the house. A train will come by and smash it."

"No, I want to just keep it," Thomas said, stretching out his hand for the coin.

"I want to see what it looks like smashed and spread out. Let's leave it up on the track," Willie said.

"Come on, give it back," Thomas pleaded.

"Let's flip it. If it comes up heads, it stays on the track, tails and you get to keep it," Willie said.

"Alright, but I get to toss the coin," Thomas replied, realizing the deal was his only chance of getting the coin back.

Off the thumb of a child, flung into the air end over end, the nickel made a vigorous ascent, slowed gradually to a stop at the top of its arch, then returned to the earth with a dull clink. Both boys rushed to see what side had landed up; heads. As he placed the coin onto the track, Thomas felt a knot in his throat that couldn't be swallowed.

"Come on, let's go. We'll be back to get it after swimming," Willie commanded.

There the coin lay. For two hours and thirteen minutes it sat undisturbed on the Southern Pacific valley branch line track until a cargo train rolled by carrying sugar beets from the Oxnard Brothers processing factory. It was a lucky coin indeed. The first six wheels to pass over it didn't touch the coin at all. Each had a hollow defect, and Thomas had unknowingly placed the coin in the exact location for it to lay momentarily unblemished, but the good fortune of even the luckiest nickels eventually runs out, and the seventh wheel flattened it completely.

That particular nickel had been struck in the San Francisco Mint on January 14th of 1931. The head of a Native American graced the coin's front, and on its backside was depicted the majestic American bison. When the Southern Pacific flattened the buffalo's massive hunched back, stout beard, and protruding foreleg, the images and delicate shapes on the nickel immediately took the shape of Procellarum, Imbrium, Serinitatas, and Fecunditatas, the dry lunar oceans that stretch across the upper face on the nearside of the moon. These dry seas can be seen with the naked eye as darkness against the light gray cratered and pocked surface. If one stares at the full moon from anywhere in the northern hemisphere, even the most unimaginative can see the shape of the buffalo across its face, with the white shot crater of Copernicus shattering the magnificent animal right through its heart.

Forty-two minutes after the train had passed, Willie was running back to the house to get help for Thomas, who lay on the dried rocks, not breathing. As he came up over the tracks the nickel caught his eye. He paused briefly, and breathing hard, he bent to pick up the distorted, oval nickel, now as thin as the sides of a soda can. With the nickel moon gone, the grease from Thomas's fingers and the sweaty palms of the countless others who had touched the coin in its seventeen-year life spread out into a thin film on the warm steel track, forming an iridescent rainbow halo of human oil.

65
Beverly Hills, California
Present Day

Jack saw Hoerburger's glowing cube from a distance as he approached. The Crown Victoria let out a knocking sound from the rear tire as Jack rolled it to a stop fifty yards down the street. He sat looking at the house for several minutes, calculating his next move. Why was he there? Where was Marcus? Was Rem there? Think, Jack.

The night was cooling as the air drained through the canyon, and Jack smelled the faint rotten sweet tea scent of sycamore and sage on the air. He shivered and zipped his black fleece as he stepped out of the car. Instinctively, he reached for his back pocket, which was flat, still missing the wallet.

Hoerburger's residence was tucked into the hillside and, except for a pair of closed garage doors, wasn't accessible in any way from the street. This wasn't a mansion meant for unannounced visitors. Jack walked up the opposite side of the street, past the house, casually looking at the large windows on the second floor, but couldn't determine if anyone was home. Farther along the street, Jack crossed and turned uphill looking back to the third floor of the cube. He stepped over a low fence and was out in the chaparral on the edge of the canyon road. A narrow deer path took him back toward the house. By the light of the waxing moon, its high and wide halo still lingering, he pushed his way through woody shrubs to a sloped clearing where he was on the same level with the upper windows and could peer into the house.

Jack sat silently, listening to his own breath, smelling the warm sting of sage all around him. The spice of the chaparral sage reminded him of the foul body odor of the three half-naked homeless men he'd helped pull from a culvert along the 110 freeway during his first few months as a rookie police officer. While Jack worked, his senior partner talked on the phone in the car. The third man to emerge from the culvert was intently clutching something in his right hand. Upon peeling his palm open, Jack discovered that the man was holding the ring finger from his left hand, which had been severed the day before.

"This man needs medical attention," Jack said to his partner, returning to the car.

"Hold on, babe," the man said into the phone. "What?"

"One of these men lost a finger. We need to get him to the hospital, it can still probably be sewn back on."

"One of those nasty ditch dwellers? Hell no. Hold on. Babe, I have to go. I'll call you back later." While hanging up, he got up from the passenger seat of the car and approached Jack. "Bratton, what are you doing?"

"We could save this guy's finger," Jack said, holding the severed digit out.

"Let me see that." He took the finger and threw it into the shrubbery beyond the culvert.

"No," Jack yelled.

"We're not taking some shit-stink pipe rat to the hospital for a missing finger."

"I'm so sorry," Jack said to the shirtless man from the culvert as he went to look for the finger.

"When you're done looking for that thing, Bratton. Let's get going."

After ten minutes of fruitless searching, Jack returned to the car.

"You have a lot to learn about this job, partner."

Jack put the car in gear and drove away silently.

Jack looked up at Hoerburger's mansion as a man in a suit carrying some kind of metal stick came to the wide upper window. Jack instinctively crouched down into the shrubs before realizing there was no way he could be seen. He recognized the man at the window as Steve Duarte, the EPA director whom he and Vargas had visited that very morning.

Jack's mouth involuntarily fell open as he sat stunned, watching Duarte at the window. Duarte was rocking back and forth and talking angrily to someone who Jack couldn't see. Duarte turned from the window, excitedly waved the hand that wasn't carrying the metal stick, then moved away. Jack saw nothing happening in the house for several long minutes.

He slid down the slope of the clearing, pushed through another stand of toyon, sumac, and sage, and emerged on the outside of a white plastered wall a short distance from the upper backside of the house. He held onto the top of the wall and pulled himself up to see over. On the other side was a strip of manicured lawn lined on each side with blooming birds of paradise. Even in the low-light of the moon they glowed with gaudy orange extravagance. Past the lawn was the monolithic whitewashed back wall of the house, its plastered surface interrupted only by several small rectangular windows and a glass door leading into an upper story. As Jack looked over the wall, a light from the house flooded the lawn area. He dropped back down along the backside of the wall and landed on a dried stick, which cracked loudly under his weight. While he crouched and listened, he thought he heard a door open.

Jack waited for what seemed like an eternity, five minutes, maybe ten. The light on the back of the house didn't go off, and he heard nothing more. Carefully and quietly, Jack pulled himself up onto the wall for a second time. He saw that the door was closed and the area was clear, so he jumped down onto the spongy lawn. Jack stood quietly listening, then cautiously crossed the lawn toward the house. As he moved to the door, he looked up and the floodlight left a metallic blue streak across his field of vision. He saw a slight but quick movement of a brown figure, like the trunk of a tree, to his left and behind him. In the split second that he turned to look, he heard a loud clicking sound and felt a slap on the back of his neck, then all the muscles in his body contracted at once. The floodlight seemed to enter him, fill, and consume him. Red spots appeared in the white light as randomly distributed as the freckles on Bridge Gardinier's cheeks. Jack felt the cold, wet lawn on his face and thought, at least I can rest here for a bit, then there was blackness.

66
Event Three of Six

Mary Louise Miller, the pride of the Northern San Fernando Valley, let out an abbreviated scream, a manic giggle, as the car left the blacktop. It all happened so quickly that Willie's smirk remained on his face even though fear and doubt had registered in his mind several seconds earlier. The car was five feet in the air, its wheels spinning freely. They sailed over the second set of tracks.

Four hours earlier, Willie lit a cigarette and waved the smoke out of his face. He smiled, looked into the setting sun, then back at the house. His black hair was browned at its tips from the relentless summer light, and his blue eyes were squinted. Ella Mae watched him from the kitchen window as he struggled to roll the pack into the shoulder of his tight white T-shirt.

"With little doubt, that boy could never help but become his father."

Ella Mae turned to where Tom was hunched over, seated at the kitchen table behind her, also looking out the window, shaking his head.

"Yeah," she replied with a mixture of pride and trepidation.

"So many years have passed, I remember the details with more and more difficulty. Willie is near the age his father was when he died. We'll never know how a boy grows up differently without a father. We've done the best we can to try to guide him. I reckon every man becomes who he's going to become, no matter what they're a witness to and what events transpire around them."

"I suppose so."

"I wonder if anyone has a choice about who they become. Growing up without a father, I reckon the world can have its way with you if you're not careful," Tom said, still looking out the window.

"He seems so much like Levi, sometimes, in certain moments, it's hard for me to look at him," Ella Mae said. She stared silently out the window, got lost in a brief reverie, then turned to the table where she cleared the empty plate in front of Tom. While picking up the plate, she gently pulled his hand down from his collar.

Willie leaned back against his blue Dodge and waited for the sun to slide behind the horizon while finishing his cigarette. He grabbed his tongue with his thumb and forefinger and doused the cigarette butt with the wetness, then flicked it into the street. He nodded at Tom through the kitchen window and got into the car under whose hood he spent the preceding two months of summer after graduating high school. Like his father, he was seduced by the machine, by his own ability to make it run well, and the feelings of self-worth that flowed from under the hood. He was two months past his eighteenth birthday, and he wanted badly to feel alive.

The warm evening air flowed over his face as he raced through the dusky suburban streets of Van Nuys toward Northridge where Mary waited for him. She wore a tight-fitting dark blue blouse tucked into a black poodle skirt under a wide white belt and stood timidly hiding behind the post of a streetlamp resisting the urge to bite her fingernails. Willie pulled up, leaned over, and flung open the passenger door with a wide grin. Mary looked around and quickly hopped in. They drove in silent anticipation along the winding road through the Granada Hills until Willie brought the car to a stop on a wide turnout overlooking the valley. Below them were the black chaparral-covered hills and orange street lights that stretched out in lines along the valley floor. The western sky was purple with the last remaining light, and the moon hadn't yet risen from the east.

"Where does your daddy think you are?" Willie asked as he turned off the car and took her by the hand.

"Josie came and got me and we said we were headed over to her house for the night."

"That man doesn't think I'm fit to sit in the same room as you. Someday I'll show him he's wrong."

"Don't worry about him. I love you so much."

"I know." Willie looked down and studied a black grease spot on the edge of his thumb that he'd failed to clean after changing the oil on the Dodge hours earlier. "When we're apart and I close my eyes all I can see is your face," he leaned in for a kiss, pulling her tight to him.

Mary grabbed Willie with both hands on the side of his head and pushed him away from her. "I want you to touch me like you did the other night," she said with an excited smile. She took one of his hands and brought it up underneath her skirt. Touching Mary, Willie was reminded of earlier that day when he had taken a drip of slippery motor oil and rubbed his finger back and forth to lubricate the soft rubber gasket on the oil filter. Mary breathed hard and shaky, and Willie smelled the onions she had eaten for dinner on her breath.

"Harder," she whispered and made a high-pitched, breathy giggle when he exerted pressure on her again. Her eyes were closed, and Willie watched her as she involuntarily arched her back and looked as if she was in the early stages of a yawn.

While Mary's body fluid dissolved and washed away all the remaining spots of grease on Willie's hand, the moon came over the low hills on the eastern edge of the valley. After several minutes, Mary left the car to urinate and spit out the salty pearls of Willie's ejaculate onto the dry soil. He sat calmly in the front seat, watching the moon to his left. Like a sacred figure, with a gloriole made of a thousand stars, it sat perched on a throne of pillowy black hills. Countless stars, some of which Willie saw so clearly even though they had been dead and gone for centuries, spread out in a halo of light around the moon, each seeming to shine brighter than all the others, but only visible in his peripheral vision.

In those moments alone in the car, hearing Mary take her long, hissing pee, he gazed up through the windshield. The Milky Way tilted to the east over his head and showed through the reflection of the city lights below. Seeing, as if for the first time, all the upper spheres of heaven, imagining other galaxies, black holes, and exploding stars, he felt that he was a tiny void. Both Mary and Ella Mae loved him, and that, he thought, should be all he needed.

Willie and Mary didn't speak on their return drive down from the north edge of the valley into the crowded flatlands to the newly opened Dairy Queen in Studio City. Mary smiled a triumphant and satisfied smile and leaned her head out the window to let the evening air rush over her. She squinted as the wind blew her hair wildly. Willie drove more slowly than usual, smoking a cigarette in deep breaths, with one hand on the wheel, fingers tapping to the rhythm of a song inside his head.

At the Dairy Queen, Willie sat at a booth across from Mary watching her eat a sundae. She made a soft clucking sound as she ate and occasionally looked up at Willie to offer him a bite.

"What's up, Bratton? You still trying to fix up that piece of shit Dodge?" The voice came from behind them, and Willie turned to see three classmates at the counter. He didn't reply. "Looks like it's right there outside. I'm surprised it ran well enough to get you here."

"Yeah," Willie said casually and turned back to Mary with a forced smile.

"We're jumping the tracks later. Are you going to be there? We'll see how that piece of shit performs." One of the three boys approached the table. "Hey, Mary. How's it going?"

"Fine, Tim. How's it going with you?" Mary looked up at him with a smile that lit a fire in Willie's chest.

"Fine. Looking forward to seeing you out at the tracks. If your boyfriend's car can get you there," Tim said, turning to Willie with a smile.

"I've jumped those tracks so many times," Willie said. He had never jumped the tracks.

"Yeah, whatever, Bratton. We'll see. It should be no big deal then. We're headed out there now." Turning to Mary, Tim said, "See you out there, Mary," and walked out the front where the other two boys were waiting in the car.

"Alright, bye, Tim," Mary called after him.

After Tim left, Mary and Willie sat in silence, not looking at each other. The remnants of Mary's sundae softened and liquefied in the glass dish while beads of condensation grew on the outside.

Finally, Mary looked up at Willie. "Tim's a jerk. Baby, we don't have to go out there if you don't want to." She reached across and put her hand on his.

Willie pulled his hand away and said, "No, it's fine. I've jumped those tracks before. It's no big deal. It'll be fun."

"Come on. Forget about it. Let's just split. Go for another drive," Mary said.

"No. Let's do it." Willie stood and extended his hand to Mary, pulling her out of the booth. "We'll do it together."

When Willie awoke the next morning in a warm white bed at Mission Community Hospital, his neck and shoulder ached and he couldn't move his left arm. It would be explained to him later that he was in a car accident and that he had suffered a concussion, a broken clavicle, and a broken wrist.

Lying in the hospital bed, the crash from the night before seemed to take place years ago, and his head ached when searching for details in the dark fog of events that took place after leaving the Dairy Queen. Over several days his memory of the crash returned, but never fully. What Willie would always remember most was the roar of the engine when the car came off the ground, and the high-pitched screech of tire rubber landing on asphalt. Mary's original scream never registered in Willie's mind. Willie did recall a sound she made seconds later, after the wheels had come down at a terrible angle, and the car was rolling end over end. He heard a low, breathy groan involuntarily pushed forth from Mary's chest as she was smashed between the windshield and passenger door. That sound, the last Mary Louis Miller would ever make, he remembered so clearly, and would never forget.

67
Beverly Hills, California
Present Day

In a few short hours, the sun would cast its first light on the fractured city of Los Angeles as the day grew out of the eastern desert. The punch-drunk, hungover world, knocked out by the night before, would wake up hungry and ready to fight another day over the bones of inconsequential contention. Light would flow in, first over the inland empire, then eastern LA, then the beaches, illuminating the city streets and all the lingering meanness and hurt from the night before.

The slightest change in temperature would disrupt the stillness of the chemical-laden air, causing it to collect and roll out of the desperate concrete lowlands to higher ground in the dark perfumed canyons of the surrounding hills. Then the muffled wind song of the sycamore would hum in the ravines as the darkness over the hills subsided.

Outside Hoerburger's white monolith, the birds of paradise would gape, almost alarmingly, unfolding a soft cobalt blue landing pad draped in irreverent orange—colors on the opposite side of the wheel, and still fit for a prince. Sweet sticky nectar would begin to ooze, filling and lubricating moist crevices, preparing for even the earliest probings from curious avian comrades.

In a few short hours, the first light over the canyon would forecast the end of a night in which Jack and Marcus had experienced no true sleep. But for now, it was still dark, and the city below, for its part, was relatively calm. In the canyon, the night was as quiet as it was long.

When Jack woke, he involuntarily reached toward the pain on the back of his neck, but was restrained by duct tape around his wrists. As his senses returned, he felt his arms tied behind him and his feet tingled where the tape had been wrapped too tightly. He was lying on his side where the cold concrete stole the heat from his cheek.

"Pssst, dude, wake up," Marcus said in a loud, hurried whisper. "Jack, wake up."

Jack could hear the mechanical hum of the fluorescent lights, then the sound of muffled voices. His vision focused on Marcus, who was sitting up against the wall with a swollen right eye and dried blood on his upper lip. Jack's eyes were tired, and it hurt them to focus, but he made the effort.

"Looks like you took a serious hit," Jack said in a weak voice, struggling into a seated position. "What happened to me?"

"I have no idea. Probably Rem, the big guy we saw at Hoerburger's office. I saw him drag you in here and tie you up. I thought you were dead."

Jack moaned. As his vision cleared, he surveyed his surroundings. The mention of Rem's name caused a tinge of fear in his belly, and he pulled hard against his restraints.

"We have to get out of here," Marcus said. "Did you call for backup? Does anyone know you're here?"

It took Jack several seconds to remember what had happened. "No, I thought I was just going for a walk around the neighborhood to scope Hoerburger's place. I had no idea you were in here."

"We're fucked," Marcus said and touched his swollen eye with the back of his taped hands.

"You alright? How did you get here?" Jack asked.

"Rem came to my house."

They heard what sounded like muffled shouting upstairs, and both sat quietly listing.

"He took my gun, but before I left the car, I put my .38 in my ankle holster," Jack said in an excited whisper. "Help me get it out. Lift up my pant leg."

Jack rolled toward the wall and strained to put his leg up to where Marcus could reach it. He weakly gripped the pant leg and Jack scooted forward, pushing it up. The khaki material slid with difficulty over the neoprene holster, exposing an empty pocket where the gun should have sat.

"Damn. He must have grabbed it with the .45," Jack said.

"Roll over here and get your hands close to my mouth," Marcus said.

Like two inexperienced young lovers, they flopped around into an awkward backside sixty-nine while Marcus chewed on the tape around Jack's wrists.

"Hurry, I think I hear someone coming."

The sound of footsteps came on the raw concrete stairs. Jack rolled away from Marcus with his hands held tightly behind him just in time to see Rem gliding down the steps.

"Where do you think you're going?" Rem's booming accent brought back the insolence and anger in Jack. He was starting to feel like himself again.

"Remmy. Remmy. Remmy. Good to see you again. Come over here and pull off this tape and I'll let you see where I'm going. You can come with me."

Rem gave Jack a swift kick in the stomach, and he let out an involuntary groan and rolled away from him.

"That's fine. You can take the tape off later," Jack muttered.

"How does the back of your neck feel? A taser is supposed to knock out only the weakest humans. You went down pretty fast," Rem said with a smirk.

"Oh, I'll be alright," Jack said, cringing from the pain in his intestines.

"On your feet, Professor," Rem said, bending over to lift Marcus.

As Rem kneeled over Marcus, Jack pushed himself to his feet. Marcus had chewed through the tape enough to free his hands, and Rem didn't notice while kicking him. With his ankles still taped, he took two large hops and jumped onto Rem's back and held on like a rodeo cowboy with both arms locked around Rem's tree-trunk neck. As Rem fought to free himself, struggling to breathe, Jack squeezed with all his strength.

Rem backed into the wall, slamming Jack repeatedly into it. Marcus stumbled to his feet and awkwardly fell on them, trying to headbutt Rem in the chest, who kicked Marcus back to the ground. Rem's neck muscles were far too strong for Jack to compress his airway, but Jack had a free hand around the elbow of his other arm, making his sleeper hold strong enough to compress the carotid artery, cutting blood off to Rem's brain. The skin on Rem's face was like fine sandpaper on Jack's forearm, and he felt the wet spittle from Rem's mouth as he tried to bite his way out of the hold. After twenty long seconds, Rem weakened and came to his knees, then fell forward onto his chest, pulling Jack over with him.

Jack held on after Rem had stopped moving, then sat up and tore the tape off his ankles.

"Get his gun," Marcus said, panting heavily.

While still on his knees, Jack placed Rem's gun in the back of his belt. Jack could hear Rem breathing steadily.

"Check if he has a phone on him," Marcus said.

"No phone and no sign of either of my guns."

"Here, pull this off," Marcus said, with his taped wrists outstretched to Jack.

As soon as Jack had finished tearing the tape from Marcus's wrists, Marcus kicked Rem where he lay unconscious on the ground. "You stupid piece of shit," Marcus whispered under his breath as he kicked him a second time.

"Hey. Hey. Get ahold of yourself," Jack said, pulling Marcus off Rem.

"He killed Elizabeth."

"Piece of shit," Jack said, looking down at Rem in disgust. "He'll get his. But for now, we don't want to wake him up. Grab that tape from the shelf over there." They put Rem's hands behind him and taped both his ankles and wrists.

"We should tape his mouth. We don't want him yelling," Marcus said.

"Shhhh," Jack placed his forefinger over his mouth. They listened to muffled voices upstairs and what sounded like a woman laughing.

"How do these garage doors open? I don't see a switch."

"All the cars are locked. Come on, let's go upstairs."

Jack extracted Rem's gun from his belt and moved up the narrow white stairs with Marcus behind him. The ground floor of the house was quiet, and they could no longer hear any voices from above. They paused at the bottom of the second flight of stairs leading up to the third-floor room where Socrates sat dying on the wall.

At the top of the stairs, they paused and could hear the muffled sounds of a woman yelling from above.

"What's that?" Jack asked.

"I don't know, but it doesn't sound good. Should we call for backup?"

Jack was breathing hard. Beads of sweat oiled his cheeks just in front of his ears and turned his shirt into a patchwork of color. His forehead glistened like a pink glazed donut.

"No time. We need to check that out."

Jack held the gun pointed upward with both hands against his chest and listened intently for any more noises from above. There was only silence, punctuated by the sound of their breathing.

After a moment, Jack nodded to Marcus and took the first step onto the stairs leading up another floor.

"Stay close behind me."

The events that transpired in Jeff Hoerburger's mansion in the predawn hours would be recounted later in police reports, press conferences, and newspaper articles. As it turned out, none were accurate nor provided any of the gruesome details that transpired in the minutes after Jack and Marcus ascended those stairs.

68
Event Four of Six

Willie was shaken from a rare deep sleep. Some nights a sudden cloud burst and the crash of heavy rain on the tin roof would wake him, but tonight the sound was different. He lay in his cot listening. The heat and humidity of the jungle were oppressive, and Willie slept in nothing but a pair of olive-green boxer shorts. Another distant rumble came, followed immediately by a boom that shook the building. Willie sat up quickly, fumbling for his pants.

"Terry, did you hear that? Wake up."

"Yeah, I heard it. Get your boots on."

Seconds later, Willie and Terry stood at the door of their sleeping quarters. The black night sky turned orange with another loud boom, then came the unmistakable skipping bursts of gunfire.

"Grab your gun and helmet. Let's go," Terry yelled.

Willie's hand shook as he fumbled for his gun. Numbness and fear locked onto his legs as he turned to run after Terry in the direction of the machine gun fire. Nine months he had been in the central highlands of Vietnam, and this was the first time he'd been close to enemy fire. He thought, this is it; I'm going to die here tonight. Immediately following that thought, Willie's life review moment took place. Such a moment happens in everyone's life at least once. For some, it may happen as they draw their final dying breath; for others, a terrifying, near-death experience induces their moment, whereas in other rare circumstances, it is triggered by deep meditation, a drug-induced stupor, a particular splendid orgasm, or just plain, raw, unadulterated fear.

In less time than it took him to take a single running step, a deluge of chronological images washed over him, playing backward and forward the entire story of how he found himself in a Vietnamese jungle. Like a video in which he could see each consecutive still frame all at once, the images came, all the overwhelming vicissitudes of his time, observed simultaneously and in true order; his mother's unwavering love, Thomas' small casket, hidden remorse and paranoia, his coughing fit after his first cigarette, Mary Miller's sly smile, shattered glass, Tom's reluctance to get him a job in the mechanic's shop at Lockheed, the smell of motor oil on skin, the laid out parts of a dirty carburetor, learning the Lockheed helicopters from Terry, Terry's thick sideburns, late nights drinking at the Tonga Hut, signing the Army's papers with Terry, joining the 81st Transportation Company, arriving at Camp Holloway, lushness, frangipani, burning trash, diesel fuel, the smooth brown skin and white teeth of the Vietnamese women they visited, Terry's weakness for one of them, the rumble strip rib cage on the shirtless boy outside the camp, the high five he gave Terry when seeing last weeks shipment of thirty-five new Hueys, and his secret dread of having to fly in one. They were all there, all at the same time.

And then the scenes were gone, and he was running, and the noise was too loud for him to take the time to lament their instant absence. Another explosion lit up the night sky, and he saw Terry in front of him crouched behind a parked jeep. Running half-bent over, he joined him behind the vehicle.

Willie was breathing hard, and his mouth was so dry he had difficulty with the words. "What are we doing? Shouldn't we be going in the other direction?"

"They don't know we're here. They're all coming through that hole," Terry yelled over the crackle of machine gun fire, referring to an area fifty feet beyond the jeep where a ten-foot hole was cut and torn in the perimeter fence. "They're attacking the barracks and mortaring the Hueys."

While Willie, Terry, and the other technicians and pilots at Camp Holloway slept, a Viet Cong company of three hundred soldiers assembled outside the concertina wire fence surrounding the camp. At 10:48 PM on February 6th, 1965, they started cutting the fence and within minutes had created a hole large enough for the soldiers and the four mortars they carried to enter the camp and establish a position close enough to attack the sleeping quarters and parked helicopters. At 11:07 PM they fired the first mortar shot, destroying a helicopter completely, on which Willie and Terry had just reassembled the landing skids earlier that morning. Simultaneously, they fired on the camp buildings, killing eight soldiers and wounding hundreds of others while they slept, but Willie and Terry's sleeping quarters were behind the camp filling station, to the side of the main barracks.

"We have to stop them here or we'll take more casualties in the camp," Terry yelled in a loud whisper, which Willie barely heard over the explosions.

"But it's just us. We're fucked. We need to fall back to a safe position. If we fire from here, they'll kill us both," Willie said.

"If we don't defend this spot, the whole camp is gone. If we can hold this spot, others will come up from behind. Get your gun ready. How much ammo do you have?"

"Forget it, Terry, let 'em in. I'm falling back."

"Jesus, Bratton. People in the camp are dying. Don't be a coward," Terry said with an incredulous look.

As Willie started back in the direction of the mechanic's shop, Terry yelled, "Don't you fucking leave me here alone. Willie."

Willie turned to see Terry yelling his name. He saw Terry's lips make the movements, but heard no sound. A flash of white light surrounded them from the mortar explosion that destroyed the shop and filling station buildings. Willie was knocked unconscious.

By the time Willie regained consciousness, a reef of orange light stretched out over the low hills, and everything was silent. He touched his cheek and saw blood on his hand where it had leaked from his right ear, then he lifted his hot, stinging left hand and saw that he was missing the ends of three fingers, torn off in the explosion. He fell unconscious again.

When Willie awoke for the second time, light had flooded the sky from the east, casting a weak pewter glow over the open dirt and grass patches in the camp and the hills beyond. The smell of burning plastic stung in his nostrils. He pushed himself up to his knees with his one good hand, looked around, and crawled to where Terry lay slumped on the ground a few feet from him. The man who had been a loving friend and mentor to him for years, who had taught him nearly everything he knew about mechanics, the man whom he admired more than anyone else in the world, was dead on the ground, his face planted firmly in the damp orange soil. Terry's helmet had rolled to the side, and there were two purple volcanoes of dried blood and flesh where bullets had exited through the back of his upper neck and head. Willie rolled Terry over onto his lap and saw he was slumped over two machine guns. While he'd been unconscious, Terry dragged him behind the jeep and used both their guns to defend the camp.

"They're over here," Willie heard a voice yell from the direction of the camp. "Hurry, we got a man down."

A circle of soldiers formed around Willie and Terry. They watched, too tired to turn away, as Willie wept over his dead friend. Soon Terry's body was lifted onto a stretcher and Willie was helped to his feet. Men from all over the camp, some of whom he'd never spoken to before, were thanking Willie for what he had done. Willie was confused. His head throbbed, and he couldn't hear well over the ringing in his ears. The look of bewilderment on his face was met with half-hearted explanations, hearsay, and outright made up stories; "He's shell shocked." "Those two held them off singlehandedly." "They came in from over there and didn't know where they were taking fire from. They killed forty of them before they retreated." "Whole place would be gone if it weren't for them two." "You're a brave man, son. Dumb lucky, but brave. Guess there ain't no difference out here."

Later that day, after Willie had been evacuated to the 8th Field Hospital at Nha Trang, Presidential Advisor McGeorge Bundy visited to see the men wounded in the attack and met privately with Willie, thanking him for his courage during the raid.

"I'm no hero, sir. If it weren't for Terry Ogden I wouldn't have even been out there behind that jeep. I'd be dead now," Willie said, his voice choking out the words.

"I understand, son. Many of the men lying in this hospital are alive because of you. I thank you for your service."

"But sir, you don't," but by the time those words came out, Bundy was walking away. Twenty-four hours later, he would be in the pressroom of the White House explaining the need for further escalating the number of troops in Vietnam and telling stories of the bravery he'd witnessed while there on assignment.

Ninety-two medals of honor have been awarded to living soldiers for distinguished bravery in action during service in the Vietnam War. Willie's metal wasn't the first, nor the last, to be accepted graciously, but given mistakenly.

69
Beverly Hills, California
Present Day

Fifteen hours after the fact, on the evening news, a beautiful, yet just slightly off, Asian woman in her late thirties would read in a smooth, smoky voice, "While responding to an early morning call, the police found two people dead in the Beverly Hills mansion of chemical magnet Jeff Hoerburger. Both died from gunshot wounds, and the police suspect a botched robbery. The names of the two victims are not yet being released. Police are canvassing the neighborhood for potential eyewitnesses." Most of what she told viewers was either made up completely or meaningless due to factual omission. The actual events were much more complicated.

It was shortly before 2:00 AM when Jack and Marcus ascended the stairs onto the carpeted landing. Turning into the room, they saw Hoerburger and Duarte sitting calmly on the white chaise lounge, looking as if they were expecting them. Jack turned and pointed the gun in their direction. "Stay right there," he commanded.

"Mr. Bratton, you can put the gun down right there on the carpet," Hoerburger said calmly, pointing.

"I don't think so," Jack said with a confused look.

Hoerburger looked at Jack and shook his head, then up and to his right, and nodded. Lars Ostergard followed Bridge Gardinier down the stairs with a gun at her back and hand on her shoulder. She walked cautiously, concentrating on landing her foot on each step.

Her radiant orange hair was tossed loosely around her shoulders. She looked wild and luminescent. When they reached the last step, Bridge looked up with her yellow-green eyes directly at Jack. His heart raced with a combination of anger and excitement. Her face was flushed, obscuring the contrast between her reddish-brown freckles and fair skin, and Jack misinterpreted her look of concern with disappointment. He thought the flash of her eyes and the slight nod said, look what you've got me into. What are you going to do now?

Jack thought, watch this.

"Now, Mr. Bratton, put your gun down on the carpet over there, or Lars is going to make a mess of things in here, and none of us want that."

Jack turned back to Hoerburger and lowered the gun far enough to look at him directly over the barrel. He considered the situation, took a small step forward, and raised the gun again.

"Don't do anything rash," Hoerburger said, lifting his hands.

Lars pulled Bridge more tightly toward him, and a low, breathy groan involuntarily pushed forth from her chest. Upon hearing the sound, Jack looked away from Hoerburger and his eyes caught Bridge's once more. He could feel the knurled grip of the gun on the inside of his palm. The trigger was cool, smooth metal beneath his warm finger. He turned back toward Hoerburger and reluctantly bent to set the gun down onto the carpet in front of him.

"Kick it forward and step back from it," Duarte said in his high-pitched, angry voice. Jack obliged with a look of disgust.

"All three of you stand over there." Lars spoke with a deep Danish accent.

"The guy you chased over the fence at the house in Reseda?" Marcus whispered to Jack as they stood against the concrete wall.

"Yup."

Lars held his gun up to Bridge's back and shoved her over to where Jack and Marcus stood. With his gun still pointed at all three of them, he knelt to pick up the other gun and slid it into the front pocket of his hoodie sweatshirt.

Addressing Duarte, Jack asked, "You told Hoerburger about Lindster's work at the EPA and he had Rem kill him?"

"He knew about it all along. Anything I know, he knows." Duarte looked at Bridge and said, "and I also wasn't going to let that little bitch cost Jeff millions of dollars." Duarte and Hoerburger shared a loving glance and Hoerburger smiled.

"So who was in the chipper?" Marcus asked.

Hoerburger answered, "Not sure what his real name was, but he called himself Carver. He was supposed to make Lindster disappear, which he completely screwed up. So Rem and Lars took care of him too, sort of," he said, looking at Lars and shaking his head.

Duarte stood, pogo stick in hand, looking at Lars. "Took care of him? They didn't take care of shit. Halfway through the fucking chipper?" he yelled at Lars. "You were supposed to dispose of two bodies, not half of one. We wouldn't be here if you and your dumb ass brother hadn't fucked that up."

"The chipper was, kaput," Lars said, using the German word for lack of the English equivalent in his vocabulary. He shrugged, as if there was nothing that could be done.

"And what about Elizabeth Shackleton? Why her?" Jack asked.

"They thought Elizabeth was somebody else, probably her," Marcus said, nodding to Bridge. "Just plain stupidity and misinformation. They killed her trying to cover up something she knew nothing about."

Duarte approached Marcus, "See this pogo stick. It's a collector's item. First one ever made. Worth more than a month of your salary." Then with a weak swing, he tried to hit Marcus across the thighs with it. The intention was for the blow to punish Marcus and bend him over on the carpet.

"What the fuck? Why are you hitting me?" Marcus asked while mostly blocking the hit with an outstretched hand.

"Keep your mouth shut," Duarte said awkwardly with a crack in his voice.

"Steve, come sit back down," Hoerburger said, patting the chaise lounge beside him.

Steve Duarte was a collector who could only manage to collect one of everything before losing interest. He had little of the focus and persistence necessary to be a collector. His newest beloved addition wasn't actually the first-ever pogo stick, which was rusting nine feet down in the Bena Landfill fourteen miles north of Arvin. He had, however, bought on a whim an original Hansburg patent pogo stick from the 1930s. The rubber jumping pad had been broken off, leaving the jumping pipe sharp and jagged at the bottom, and the spring was jammed stiff with rust, rendering the stick unusable. Duarte bought it because he was attracted to the beautiful, pink glitter-embedded, Bakelite plastic handles.

"Go get your brother," Hoerburger commanded Lars with a flick of his wrist.

Lars lowered his gun, which he had kept pointed at Marcus, Jack, and Bridge. With the pistol held at his side and the other in the front pouch of his sweatshirt, he crossed the carpet toward the flight of stairs leading to the lower levels of the mansion. Just after he had passed, in one quick move Jack stepped forward, grabbed the Pogo stick out of Duarte's limp hand, and hit Lars over the back of the head. Lars stumbled forward, dropping his gun onto the carpet in front of him. Jack dropped the pogo stick and fell on top of him.

For a split second Hoerburger, Duarte, Marcus, and Bridge watched Jack, as if him landing on Lars and wrestling him for the fallen gun were taking place in slow motion. Marcus and Hoerburger moved at the same time, Hoerburger pushed himself off the chaise lounge and leaped in the direction of the two men on the floor. Simultaneously, Marcus went for the dropped pogo stick. While he grabbed it, he saw Duarte coming in his direction. As Duarte jumped angrily toward Marcus and his new prized possession, Bridge stuck her foot out and tripped him, causing him to fall hard on the sharp end of the broken steel jumping pipe. By chance alone, Marcus had propped it against the floor at just the right angle to impale the falling man. As the pipe exited the back of Duarte's neck, scraping his cervical spinal column and rupturing his carotid artery, the explosive clap of a gunshot pounded and reverberated off the raw concrete walls of the mostly empty room.

70
Glostrup, Denmark
1941

Although it was terribly unfortunate for Otto Gillot Hort and his gimp lover that he didn't see the untied shoelace responsible for his violent death, the circus incident allowed for Borg Ostergard to meet his wife. The show was delayed for three days on the outskirts of Copenhagen where the accident had taken place. While the performers grieved, the ringmaster changed the order of the acts to fill Otto's time, so that the show may go on. On the second night, Borg, a gargantuan Swede who played the "strong man" in several acts, met Camilla Eriksen in the only cafe in town. Camilla was also uncommonly large, and until seeing Borg smoking and laughing with his fellow performers across the cafe, she hadn't suspected that a man existed capable of satisfying her private size requirements. Three days after the flying midget's accident, the tent came down and the show went on to Jutland, en route to Borg's homeland, yet Borg was not with them. Two weeks later, he was married to Camilla, forming a union that would eventually spawn seven children, the youngest and largest of whom was Ole Ostergard, the father of Lars and his younger brother Rem.

71
Event Five of Six

When Willie turned from the counter to leave the shop, something caused him to look back. For years he would think of that gesture, but could never explain it. As he pulled the metal bar on the glass door he cranked his head around to take one more look at her. Why hadn't he just kept walking? Even then, after that first meeting, she didn't strike him as remarkable. Her face—with its high wattage smile and pink skin, the way her strawberry blond hair fell against her strong cheekbones, all things he would come to love later—didn't register with him, but one part of her body did.

She was hanging a set of clothes on an upper rack, and he noticed her ankles. They were slender, beautiful ankles, and the sight of them made him think of his mother when she was young. How beautiful she had been. How comforting she was. He remembered when she was much bigger than he, how she would hold him, humming quietly for hours. He remembered at elementary school events how different Ella Mae was from all the other mothers, who just looked like mothers, but she was young and radiant. He sensed their jealousy, how they all wanted to be like her and couldn't, so they watched her while bitterly whispering to each other.

As Willie left the shop onto the sidewalk, he thought of the long slow souring of Ella Mae's life, the men who came and went, the good ones who tried to stay whom he drove off. She always forgave him for his insecurity. These memories were shaded with regret, as most of his memories were.

It was May 4th, 1978, Willie's 14,563rd day on earth, and he had buried his mother the week prior, just shy of her sixtieth birthday. He was an independent, grown man, decorated war veteran, and mechanic shop owner, but when she died suddenly, a hole opened inside him that he didn't know she had been filling. He saw her once a week, sometimes twice a week, since returning from the war, and now that she was gone, he became painfully aware that he was empty and alone.

He had come to the dry cleaner that afternoon for a case of Hoerburger's TCE stain remover. There was nothing like it for cleaning engine parts, but it was only sold to the dry cleaning businesses around the valley, not the mechanic shops. Colfax Cleaners, the place near his shop where he usually went, was all out, so he crossed town in the direction of the Verdugo Hills Cemetery where Ella Mae lay under a freshly turned pile of loam. Jaimis Cleaners was a place he'd seen off Foothill Boulevard while returning from the funeral. He was struck by the spelling of the name and the lack of an apostrophe on the sign. At the time he made the decision to return to Jaimis, he thought he would visit Ella Mae's grave, but he never made it there.

The smell inside the cleaners only became apparent to him once he was back in the open air. The pleasant sting of the chemical scent left the surfaces of his nose and throat, and was replaced by the scent of hot dust and mock orange in bloom. He breathed deep and reached for a pack of cigarettes in his shirt pocket. There was no pack of cigarettes and hadn't been for years, but the habit stayed with him.

He took a few steps along the sidewalk in the direction of his truck, then stopped. And that was the moment. He had reached an intersection in time, a place where the web merged and branched. The case of stain remover was heavy under his arm, but he didn't notice it. He looked down at his feet, as if he were wondering why they were failing to move him to his truck, then his gaze moved from his feet to a cheese colored pebble no bigger than a marble embedded in the concrete, ground in half, polished and pitted, like a little moon surrounded by a halo of slaty cement.

He stared at the little stone for a full minute, refusing to cross it. He thought, maybe I'll go back in there again. Why not? I have nothing to lose. I have nothing but choice now.

He turned his head up and looked down the street at his truck, and squinted. He could imagine the passing of an opportunity, getting back into his truck with his case of stain remover, back across the valley to his shop, dinner alone, distracted by the television, finally falling asleep trying to ignore thoughts of his mother and his emptiness, then getting up to do it all again tomorrow.

Death was on the other side of that stone, and not a pleasant nor far-off one. He stepped on the pebble moon, turned on his heel, and the doorbell rang again as he reentered the shop.

Once he decided to ask her a question, her answer was always yes. Yes. Yes. It had become such a foreign word to her, but she wanted to say it again, and there he was, asking. She had said yes once before, and that led to a painful four years, two unknown soldiers at her door, a tightly folded flag, and a story with no details. Don't say yes again, she had told herself, it's too hard. Yes leads to pain; but yes was always there, always possible, always on her mind.

That morning as she had sat at her kitchen table with the love advice column, embarrassed to be reading it even though she knew she was alone, she read a piece of advice that made an impression on her. She read it four times, trying to make sense of it. Go through life regretting the things you've done, the things you've tried, the things you've agreed to, not the things you decided not to do, not the missed opportunities. Could I live like that? Could I forget the past and move on?

When she looked up from the freshly pressed shirt to see him coming back into the shop, the answer was already yes, and she knew it. He didn't, so it took him some time to stumble on to the question he actually wanted to ask, but he got there. She never said no to him. Yes, two people can forget their past. Yes, happiness is possible, and it can be chosen over guilt, insecurity, emptiness, and sorrow. One can become two, and yes, two can become three.

72
Laguna Beach, California
June 6th, 1962

To prolapse means to slip or fall out of place, and with regard to organs in animals, usually constitutes a severe injury or medical emergency. There are examples, however, where certain organs are purposely prolapsed, usually only for a short time and with a specific function.

In the tropical lowlands of eastern Borneo lives a medium-sized, yet ferocious Surilis monkey that, in addition to its typical diet of leaves and fruits, will eat the occasional rodent and other small animals. Its peculiar hunting ritual involves hanging utterly still in a tree and allowing its own rectum to prolapse over a period of several minutes. The sack-like orangish-red organ swells and pushes out the anal opening. Once completely prolapsed, the rectum mimics a brightly colored, delicious, tropical fruit, the size of an orange, and is conspicuously juxtaposed against the monkey's black fur. Then, while remaining completely still, the monkey waits to trap unsuspecting animals attracted by the curiously pungent smell and tasty appearance of the fruit-like organ.

The hooded seal, on the other hand, prolapses an organ at the opposite end of the body. During the long summer days in the northern Atlantic, these little fatsos flop their awkward bodies onto the ice sheets and black beaches of Danish and Norwegian islands. The males, which look like rotten sausages, grayed, spotted, and furry with fungal growth, are born with a grotesque sexual ornament adorning their heads, an inflatable bladder of pink skin on the inside of a nasal cavity capable of being prolapsed at will.

During their elaborate courting and mating ritual, males compete for female attention by inflating and flaunting this elastic, show-worthy skin. Engorged like a child's pink balloon, they wave it about to demonstrate its size to all the gawking females. The male with the largest flesh balloon wins the choicest females.

Alex Melter had learned both these natural history stories in the May 1952 issue of National Geographic, a gift from his drunkard American doctor friend in Mazatlán. He read the stories thoroughly and practiced saying parts of them out loud in English until he thought he spoke them well. While Audrey Thacker and Kate Bollinger waited for him in the adjacent bedroom, Alex mouthed the words of these stories in the shower. As the warm water melted away the miles, he debated which of his two memorized stories he should share. He wisely chose the latter, feeling that this wasn't the time to discuss hunting by rectal prolapse.

For many years Alex Melter stayed with those two women, whom he always thought loved each other much more than either loved him. He impregnated each of them twice, three of which were carried successfully to term, and on September 4th, 1980, Marcus Melter was born to Alex Melter, Audrey Thacker, and Kate Bollinger. Which of the two women was his biological mother never actually mattered to Marcus, though it would become obvious to him later in life.

73
Beverly Hills, California
Present Day

Since the evolution of anatomically modern humans in the jungles of East Africa 200,000 or so years ago, about 107 billion people have been born and lived out varied lives, scorning and defying the kingdom of entropy at every turn, each iteration manifesting the profound and often accidental reality of higher and higher complexity. This one ran upright through the jungle, then stood squinting into the distance, that one found a sharp stick, this one carried fire, that one honed a blade, this one felled trees, that one pulled a plow, this one built a lens that could look into a cell, that one built a lens that could study whole galaxies. This one took what that one had, this one killed with a pen, and that one with a keyboard; but they all died, and did so in surprisingly few ways.

Aside from disease and the complications of old age, most people have been impaled, shot, or torn apart by fixed or flying pieces of wood, steel, and other hard objects. As the twentieth and bloodiest of all centuries finally came to a close, the total number of violent deaths stood proudly just over forty million, and nearly two million have accrued in the first fifteen years of the twenty-first century. Of all those millions of deaths, Steve Duarte was only the third human ever to be killed by a pogo stick, and the other two involved misguided and ill-advised deviant sexual behavior leading to internal bleeding.

Unlike his brother, Lars was a smaller man than Jack, and not nearly as strong. As Jack landed on Lars's back, he could feel the absence of the bulk of muscle he had to contend with while strangling his brother. Lars had a quickness and determination that Jack wasn't fully prepared for. Lars arched his back forcefully to lift Jack and regain control of the gun he dropped. He grabbed the pistol from underneath him, rolled to the side, turned upward, and pulled the trigger just in time to shoot Hoerburger, who had landed on Jack's back, through the side of his face.

A mist of blood and small pieces of shattered jaw bone, each like a misshapen baby's tooth, rained down on Hoerburger's immaculate carpet as his body flopped to one side. Lars was lying on his back with the gun above him, surprised and confused at having shot the wrong person. Jack's ears rang from the explosion, and the room seemed to pulse around him. He brought his elbow down hard on Lars's neck, partially collapsing his windpipe and pushing it to one side, causing him to drop the gun. Shocked and panicked, Lars tried to draw breath as both his hands went involuntarily to his neck to survey the damage. He took short wheezing breaths as Jack picked up the gun, rolled him over, and kneeled on his back.

"Spread out your hands," Jack said. "Marcus pull the other gun out of his front pocket." Jack looked up at Bridge, who seemed to have a pleased look on her face, and they both nodded to each other.

Marcus was crouched over, still holding the pogo stick impaling Duarte, who was bleeding profusely, head down, arms limply hanging to his sides. When Marcus let go, a gurgling sound emanated from Duarte's throat and blood pulsed out of his neck with the remaining few feeble beats of his heart. Duarte was kneeling, propped up firmly by the pogo stick, like someone who had fallen asleep while praying at the altar. Marcus stared at his own bloody hands, still curled as if they were gripping the stick. The drips of Duarte's blood were surprisingly thick. Marcus watched them land on the carpet, pile on top of each other, and resist pooling or absorbing into the material.

"Hey," Jack said loudly. "Marcus. Grab the other gun out of his pocket."

Marcus hurried to Jack's side where he pulled the second gun from the front pocket of Lars's sweatshirt.

"We need to find a phone," Marcus said, still staring at the kneeling man as he continued to bleed out.

74
Burbank, California
May 4th, 1978

The receiver swung loose against the side of the phone booth, and the folding glass doors creaked closed as Noah Kirkwood stepped out into the fading afternoon sun. That was the last shot, the last hope, and his last chance. I'm totally fucked, he thought. The answer was a resounding, unequivocal no, and now he could join the ranks of his father and older brother as a completely failed businessman. He absentmindedly fumbled for a cigarette in his shirt pocket and leaned against the outer wall of the phone booth while contemplating his next move.

For several months, Mr. Kirkwood had failed to court Cormex with a business proposal to handle their nationwide sales and marketing of ethylene glycol. After leaving the University of Iowa School of Business, where he had enrolled ten years before to avoid the Vietnam War draft, he worked for a small chemical company in Dubuque. When IPE acquired the Dubuque company, he was offered a transfer to the IPE headquarters in Burbank, which he and his new wife gladly accepted. Shortly after arriving in Burbank, and with the strong encouragement of his mean and ambitious wife, he decided the only way to ever earn the kind of money she wanted was to break away from IPE's marketing and business division and start his own firm.

For three years, he traveled the Western U.S. and toiled out of a home office, scrounging clients, breadcrumbs, leftovers, whatever work he could find for his fledgling chemical marketing firm. He had just left a meeting at Cormex Corporation during which the door had been closed on him and his marketing pitch for the last time. He stopped at the payphone to break the news to his wife, who told him he might as well not come home if he hadn't closed the deal.

As he smoked, he leaned his tall frame hard against the booth. The exhaustion brought on by the last few hours of the intense and failed presentation grew in him. He inhaled deep breaths, knowing that the smoke and the nicotine it carried into his bloodstream would help him think. What now? Mr. Kirkwood waited for a smiling couple to pass, then crossed the sidewalk, set his briefcase down, and sat on a bench that had been set out by the owner of a Chinese restaurant, no doubt under the delusion of potentially having more diners than could fit in the small waiting space. Recognizing a superstitious private custom, he dropped the final unburned half-inch of his cigarette to the sidewalk, extinguished it with the square toe of his shoe, and vaguely watched each passerby.

He had only sat for three minutes when he heard the ding of the dry cleaner's door adjacent to the Chinese restaurant. A thick, upright man in a mechanic's shirt emerged, took a few steps down the sidewalk, then stopped right in front of Mr. Kirkwood. The man didn't look up. He stared at the sidewalk, clearly lost in thought. The mechanic, whom Mr. Kirkwood noticed was missing the tips of three fingers on his left hand, held a case of Hoerburger's TCE stain remover under his arm. He was close enough that Mr. Kirkwood could have greeted him without raising his voice, and for a moment he entertained the idea, but had little interest at the time in any more small talk. Mr. Kirkwood sat still on his wooden bench and watched the man stare at his feet, briefly look up, then stare again at the sidewalk. After a long minute had passed, the mechanic turned and went back into the dry cleaner.

Noah Kirkwood, who took pride in his intimate knowledge of chemical industry retail products, didn't recognize the Hoerburger brand on the case of stain remover. He stood to get a closer look at it as the man set it on the counter inside the dry cleaner. Through the glass front of the shop, Mr. Kirkwood watched as the mechanic spoke to the round-faced strawberry blonde, who stopped folding clothes and turned to face him. They smiled and the mechanic did most of the talking, while she kept nodding and saying yes, then the mechanic lifted the case once again and went back out onto the sidewalk. Mr. Kirkwood greeted the mechanic with a nod as the smiling man passed him on the sidewalk.

Maybe luck favors the prepared, or maybe he was just curious, but Noah Kirkwood's recent failures could arguably have been the reason why he decided to enter the cleaners and inquire as to why a mechanic was buying a case of cleaning chemicals. After a short conversation with the jovial woman behind the counter, who kept smiling and looking out the glass door, Mr. Kirkwood discovered that this particular brand of high-quality trichloroethylene, which was sold as an effective stain removal agent, was coveted by local mechanics for parts cleaning and degreasing.

In less than a month, he was standing in front of Stanley Hoerburger's desk in the tiny wood-paneled office that sat on the metal railed mezzanine above a factory floor. The Hoerburger Chemical Company was a lean, one building outfit on the edge of Burbank, specializing in purified trichloroethylene. For nearly twenty years, Hoerburger and his few employees had made only one chemical, intended for sale to the Southern California dry cleaning industry. What they didn't sell, they stored in old metal tanks on the lot behind the building. That first meeting between Noah Kirkwood and Stanley Hoerburger, a reticent and skeptical man who loved to say, "If it ain't broke, don't fix it," didn't go well. Hoerburger, however, conceded a second meeting, then a third.

Stanley Hoerburger was hard-headed and prided himself on unreasonable frugality and staunch opposition to change. Those tense early meetings eventually yielded a partnership between Noah Kirkwood and Stanley Hoerburger that would result in the Hoerburger Chemical Company successfully marketing TCE to mechanic shops nationwide. As their profits soared, Mr. Kirkwood eventually convinced Hoerburger to rebrand and rename the company, and within ten years of their initial meeting, Solina brand degreaser was carried on the shelves of every auto parts store from Seattle to Coral Gables.

Noah Kirkwood, who quickly abandoned his failed firm to become the vice president and marketing director at the rapidly expanding Solina Chemical Corporation, became a wealthy man. In those years of prosperity, he often thought back on that stocky mechanic and his case of Hoerburger stain remover. Twice he returned to sit and smoke on the wooden bench on the sidewalk outside the Chinese restaurant and Jaimis Dry Cleaners. He never saw the mechanic nor the woman behind the counter again. While superstitiously leaving the last half-inch of his cigarette unsmoked, he was overwhelmed with gratitude and at the same time deeply bothered by the idea that seemingly random coincidences in timing were all that separated him from a life of failure.

75
Beverly Hills, California
Present Day

Phone calls were made, then radio calls went out. The first police car to arrive did so ten minutes later. Caution tape was pulled across the street, photographs and statements were taken, and interviews were conducted.

Jorge Vargas stepped out of his car in the middle of the blocked-off street, tucked in his shirt, and shivered as the cool canyon air engulfed him. In the early morning light, he and Jack stood outside the open garage doors. They both looked old and tired in the blue glow of the fluorescents.

"You going to be alright?" Vargas asked. "You look terrible."

"Long night. That's all. I'll be fine."

"And the professor?" Vargas asked, nodding across to where Marcus sat on the steps near the front of the mansion staring blankly at the birds of paradise as they opened for the day.

"He's pretty shaken up. I wish Elizabeth Shackleton hadn't got mixed up in all this."

Two shiny black body bags lay on the floor in the garage. A few feet away, Lars was shackled to the metal bar of a gurney in the bright light of an open ambulance where an apathetic EMT in blue gloves was attending to his neck. His giant older brother was handcuffed in the back of a squad car, muttering quietly to himself in Danish.

"What a mess. Two stiffs and neither of these guys are Americans."

"Could've been a lot worse I guess," Jack said.

"Yup. Look who's here."

Ana Zaragoza stepped out of her vehicle, slammed her door, and pulled her necklace badge over her head. The bun in her hair was high and tight, and just a little wet. Even though it was early in the morning and she'd probably been asleep less than an hour earlier, she looked as put together as always. The passenger door opened, and a large black man in his mid-forties got out, looking groggy and swollen. He stood, bent back down, and fumbled for something inside the car, then pulled a badge necklace over his sweatshirt while closing the door with his elbow.

"Gentlemen," Zaragoza said as she approached.

"Where?" Vargas asked, pretending to look around.

"This is Special Agent Tom Mullen. Tom, these are Detectives Jack Bratton and Jorge Vargas." Everyone shook hands.

"Heard you barely scraped through one here," Zaragoza said to Jack.

"Everything turned out fine," Jack replied, rubbing the back of his neck.

"For you, maybe, not them," Agent Mullen said, looking at the body bags. "Is Jeff Hoerburger in one of those?"

"Yup."

"Bring me up to speed on what happened here," Mullen commanded Jack.

Jack turned to Zaragoza and asked, "Why is the FBI involved in this?"

"Let's just cooperate and we'll get to that later."

Ignoring Jack, Mullen said, "Let's take a look at the bodies." He pulled a pair of latex gloves out of his pocket and put them on while looking at Jack the entire time. On one knee, he unzipped one of the bags and stared at the body in silence. Eventually he said, "What'd you do, slice his throat?" Steve Duarte's face was blue and shrunken, and one eyelid was partially open. A filmy, glazed, black eyeball stared back at Agent Mullen. His neck was a mass of purple flesh and dried blood. "Whoever that is, it's not Hoerburger."

"Steve Duarte," Jack said.

Mullen looked up at Zaragoza, then to Jack. "The EPA guy?"

"That's him."

He unzipped the second bag, and with a gloved finger, touched the half of Jeff Hoerburger's mustache that remained on his face. The other half was gone completely where Lars's bullet entered the side of his face.

"Will you call the professor over?" Zaragoza asked Jack as Mullen snapped off his gloves. "We'll need to get all the details from both of you."

"It'll all be in my report," Jack said.

"Come on," Zaragoza said, rolling her eyes.

"Marcus." Jack gestured toward him.

Mullen and Zaragoza stood there silently backlit by the cold blue light of the garage while Jack told them everything and Marcus filled in his part. Simple, short sentences, grunted by tired men weighted down by lack of sleep. For the entire debriefing, Mullen wore a look of thinly disguised disapproval.

"If you check Rem's gun," Jack said to Zaragoza, "the ballistics will match with the bullet that killed Elizabeth Shackleton."

"Those two will be in a prison in Europe in no time. Is there anything else?" Mullen asked.

"That's pretty much all of it."

"Where's the EPA assistant girl?"

"She's lying down in my car," Jack responded.

"Has anybody interviewed her yet?"

"No."

"Alright, I'm going to need to speak with her," Mullen said.

"What's this all about?" Jack asked.

Mullen looked at Zaragoza and seemed to consider the next thing he said carefully. He started to say something, stopped, then started again.

"You guys killed an FBI informant. We'd been working on Jeff Hoerburger for a couple weeks now. We have undercover agents working in the EPA and he tried to bribe one during a site visit a few months back. We were planning to negotiate an arrangement for his help with a large government corruption case involving Duarte and others like him."

"Damn," Vargas said.

"When you guys discovered that Hoerburger owned the house we found Lindster in, the FBI started to monitor the case," Zaragoza said.

"None of us thought it would go this way so quickly," Mullen said.

"Neither did we," Jack said.

"Now this sets us back pretty far. As you can imagine, my director is very upset," Mullen added.

He turned to Jack and Marcus, who returned his stare, but said nothing.

"He says this can't look like a police investigation or our entire case is completely shot."

"Your case?" Vargas said.

"There's a bigger picture here," said Zaragoza.

"Bigger picture? We're talking about two bodies and the murder of an innocent woman. Who cares about EPA corruption?" Vargas asked.

"EPA corruption means more than a few lives. We're dealing with thousands of sick and dying Americans, and people who get away with murder every day." Pointing to Jack and Marcus, Mullen continued, "You two were never here. The Danish brothers are going to disappear, and Vargas, you have to quietly close the case on Lindster."

"This is bullshit," Vargas protested. "We worked hard on those cases. Look at Jack. He got knocked out, for God's sake." He continued with a slight smile, "Twice."

They all turned to Jack, who was looking like a swollen prizefighter the morning after the big fight.

"This is for the best," Zaragoza said. "It can't happen any other way."

Marcus gently rubbed the swollen part of his cheek. "What about Elizabeth?" he asked.

"Random violence happens in this city all the time. Sometimes perpetrators aren't caught," Mullen said.

"Vargas you're right," Jack said. "This is bullshit. She got killed and her family and friends aren't going to get any closure. Put the Danish brothers on trial."

The five of them sat in silence, trying to read one another.

"Jack, you have to get okay with this. It's the way the case is going," Zaragoza said.

"I guess it doesn't really matter if I am." Jack looked at Marcus who made an almost imperceptibly small shrug. "Whatever; I just want to go home. Are you two ready to talk to Bridge now?"

"Sure."

Vargas looked at his feet. "Alright," he whispered to himself, and there was nothing left to say.

76
Event Six of Six

Willie began to cry. Something like this was always going to happen to him, and somehow he knew it. It felt vaguely familiar.

"Please," he begged with a cracking voice.

Fourteen minutes earlier, Willie and Jack were driving down Sepulveda Boulevard as the mid-afternoon sun burned its way through the San Fernando Valley overcast sky. Willie took a break from tapping his finger on the steering wheel to look over at Jack as he played with the center console on the front bench seat.

"Hey, bud, have you thought about what you want for your birthday?"

"No."

"Well, you're going to be a big eight-year-old, so you should think about something special. What about a bike?"

"My bike is fine."

"Alright. Think about what other things you might want."

"Do you like your new truck?" Jack asked.

"Yeah. Do you?"

"I like the drink holders in the seats."

"I never had a new truck before, always fixed up old ones. Someday, I'll show you how to work on cars."

Jack nodded.

"Your grandaddy was a mechanic, too," Willie said.

"Did he work on trucks?" Jack asked.

"I don't know, I never met him. He died before I was born."

"How?"

"I'm not sure. When Grandpa Tom was alive, he said he died in an accident. But that was a long time ago."

"What was his name?"

"His name was Levi, Levi Bratton. Same last name as you and me."

While Jack silently mouthed the name Levi, Willie turned into the parking lot of a convenience store.

"Wait here a minute, bud. I need to grab some things."

"Can I have a popsicle?"

"Sure. I'll bring you one."

At the same moment that Willie closed the door of his new truck and headed toward the glass entrance of the mini-mart, Juan "Angel" Santana Jr. slammed the thin wood door of his girlfriend's apartment in the complex a short distance away.

Angel Santana had been released from Chino State Penitentiary five days earlier after an eight-month stay for parole violation. In the second week of his sentence, his right eye was gouged out with a plastic spoon in a medium-security cellblock lunchtime fight. After his recovery, Angel had his cellmate tattoo the word karma in sloppy cursive over his eyebrow above the empty socket using a guitar string as a needle and dye made from a mixture of soot, shampoo, and pen ink.

Angel was home for three days before he began to suspect that his girlfriend had been cheating on him while he was away. She had left for work earlier that afternoon, and upon discovering an unfamiliar pair of men's jeans in the apartment, Angel worked himself into a jealous rage. Thoughts raced through his mind. Everything's been taken from me. My job, my money, my eyeball, and now my woman. She can't even look at me without looking away. Nobody sees me anymore. They think they can take whatever they want from me. It's time for me to do some taking.

After beating the couch with his fist, Angel left the apartment with a Beretta .40 caliber handgun and a poorly formed plan to steal a vehicle, go to the hospital where his girlfriend worked, confront her, then go find the other man.

Moments later, Angel was crossing Sepulveda Boulevard when a new blue F-150 Ford parked in the lot of the convenience store caught his eye. His uncle had picked him up from prison in the same truck.

As they drove to Angel's welcome home party, he played with the center counsel on the front bench seat.

"¿Te gusta?" his uncle asked him.

"This is a pretty sweet truck, tío."

"It's nuevo. Straight from the dealer."

"How'd you get it?" Angel asked.

"I got some new things I'm working on. You keep your head down, do some trabajo, you could get a truck like this."

Willie held the popsicle awkwardly while fumbling for his wallet. He looked up at the attendant who wasn't looking at him.

"Is that your truck, sir?" the man asked in a thick Indian accent. "There's somebody waiting."

Willie stepped back from the counter and looked through the windows where Angel paced back and forth in front of his truck. The sun shone through the overcast sky and Angel's shaved head was brown, knobby, and glowing. One hand was tightly clenched into a fist, and the other held a silver handgun. He stopped and stared straight at Willie with his remaining good eye.

Willie was paralyzed and felt the familiar feeling of fear gripping his legs and quickly overtaking the rest of his body. He reached out to hold onto the counter. He wanted to hide or run out the back of the store.

"There is a boy in the truck, sir. You should go out there, sir."

Willie looked past Angel and saw Jack waiting for him in the truck. He tapped his right thigh as if to get it to work and returned his wallet into his back pocket.

"You should call the police."

"Already have, sir."

The bell on the door rang as Willie exited the mini-mart.

"Can I help you?" Willie asked as he approached, but was interrupted.

"Is this your truck?"

"Yeah, it's my…"

"Give me your fucking keys," Angel commanded, lifting the Beretta directly at Willie's face. Willie stepped back and put both his hands up.

"Hold on."

"Don't fucking tell me what to do." Angel lunged forward and hit Willie with the pistol on the side of his head. Willie fell to his knees on the sidewalk. Angel looked around agitatedly.

"My son's in the truck."

"You think I'm stupid, vato." Angel kicked Willie in the side. "Get the fucking keys out of your pocket."

Willie lay face down on the sidewalk, silent and not moving. His thighs felt as if they were in a vice.

"Please," Willie said with a cracked hoarse voice.

"Hey," Angel kicked Willie again. "What the fuck is wrong with you? Just give me the keys and stop your fucking whimpering."

Willie could hear sirens in the distance.

"Dad," Jack yelled and pounded on the window of the truck.

Willie looked up, made eye contact with Jack, and lifted his hand toward him.

"You motherfucker," Angel snarled and fired two bullets into Willie's upper back.

As Angel crouched to search through Willie's pockets, the sirens grew louder and a police car raced around the corner. Angel stood up and ran in the direction of his girlfriend's apartment.

When Jack got to his father, Willie was no longer breathing.

"Dad. Dad. Dad," he kept repeating and pushing on him as the blood wicked into Willie's shirt and formed two oblong blotches.

When Officer Gretchen Shultz lifted Jack up from behind, he started screaming. Jack sobbed while she held him in the back seat of a patrol car, until all he could see through his blurred eyes was the silver badge on her chest. His finger traced around its edges and down over the chevron-shaped front pocket flap of her uniform.

Jack watched the officers arrive and grew more and more calm. They swarmed the scene, congregated, and spread out again, each with their own crisp dark blue uniform. They talked to each other and witnesses, looked over at him with concern, pointed into the distance, and took control of the situation. In the forty-three minutes before his mother arrived, Officer Shultz held Jack, petting his head and neck while he watched the police officers do their job. As his mother took him from the back of the patrol car, he was strangely calm, and stared at the police officers as they went about their job.

77
Laguna Beach, California
Summer and Fall, 1962

After he had gone, the tattered pages of Alex Melter's abandoned Life Magazine lay on the sand for two days. A sickly Cooper's hawk in the midst of building a nearly failed nest discovered it in the early morning hours of the third day. The well-worn pages, damp with the morning dew, tore easily with each skittish jerk of her sharp beak. Had the magazine not been available, the hawk and her mate would not have constructed a nest that summer, but as it were, Alex had accidentally relinquished the only building material that would enable her to finish the structure.

High on the smooth branches of a towering eucalyptus tree, with the entire beach town visible below, the hawks established a conspicuous courtship, a grotesque entanglement of fiber and dried roots, woven together by torn pages featuring scantily clad women. That old and ailing tree, which effortlessly supported the hawk's elaborate roost, was growing too close to the expanded Pacific Coast Highway and had been slated for removal by city public works officials two weeks prior to Alex arriving at the beach. In a tense and often unfriendly debate that raged through the summer, the town's residents argued over the removal of the prominent and well-loved tree, which was ultimately saved by local environmentalists based on the presence of the visible hawk's nest.

On the Indian summer morning of October 15th, 1962, the old and embattled eucalyptus tree toppled, without warning, onto Deborah Karcher and her son Danny as they paused at a stoplight below the tree on their way to Danny's high school. The impact of the heavy branches crushed the back half of the car, killing Danny instantly and maiming Deborah, who would never walk again.

As a child, Danny had spent part of each summer with his godfather, Terry, at the Lockheed airport hangar in the San Fernando

Valley. Terry was a bachelor in his early thirties who loved children, and Danny was his favorite. Terry had looked forward to teaching Danny the art and science of mechanics as he aged, and was deeply disturbed by the senseless tragedy. The news of Danny's death and ensuing memorial inadvertently caused Terry to evaluate the relationships, or lack there of, in his own life. He drifted through the five Kübler-Ross stages of grief, eventually stalling out somewhere between anger and depression.

Six months after the accidental passing of his godson, Terry Ogden enlisted in the military. After many discussions and pleadings, Terry failed to convince his young mechanical assistant and only real friend, Willie, to not follow him into the Army.

78
Western Los Angeles
Present Day

Jack and Marcus rode through the blue streets of Beverly Hills, while Bridge Gardinier reclined in the expansive back seat of the Crown Victoria. A cloud rose from the sprinklers like valley fog in front of the mansions, and the bright green lawns had an olive hue in the early light. Excess water ran into the gutters and reflected the overcast sky in shallow pools on the sidewalks.

Jack drove the empty streets, numb and tired, staring into the distance. His lower lip and jaw had come completely untethered from the rest of his face, and his mouth hung loosely open.

He looked at Marcus briefly, but didn't say anything, then turned back to watch the opulent gardens as they passed.

"What's up?" Jack asked, still looking forward and concentrating on the road.

"Nothing. I just wanted to say thanks for coming to get me up there."

"No problem, man. It turned out fine. Could've gone better, obviously, but oh well. Get some rest and you'll feel better."

"We got lucky. We weren't really in control of the situation." Marcus rubbed his swollen cheek.

"You're right about that." Jack turned briefly away from looking at the road to Marcus. "Thanks for all your help with this case. Nice to figure things out, even though it won't lead to a single arrest."

"Or any closure for Lindster's family or Elizabeth," Marcus said.

"I'm so sorry I got you into this, and for Elizabeth."

"It's not your fault."

"You okay with us dropping everything? I'll fight Zaragoza on this one if you want."

Marcus sat in silence for a moment. "No, I think we should leave it alone. Rem will get what's coming to him."

"I'm really sorry about Elizabeth."

"There's also still some unidentified dead hit man run halfway through a chipper."

"That's all Zaragoza's problem now," Jack said as he stopped at the curb in front of Marcus's house and put the car into park.

"You going to be alright?" Jack asked.

"Yeah. I need sleep. I hope I can sleep."

"You will. I'll call in the afternoon. We'll have a slice at D'Amores and debrief. It's okay now. We're alright." Jack said, nodding and talking to himself as much as Marcus.

"Thank you."

"No, thank you."

Marcus stepped out and tried to quietly close the door behind him.

"What happened to the back of your car?" Marcus asked.

"Just a lucky little accident. Oh, by the way, happy birthday. I forgot to say so earlier."

"Thanks. I guess that was just yesterday. Seems so long ago now." Marcus said and limped off toward his house.

Jack looked into the back seat where Bridge slept. She seemed pleased, peaceful, no signs of disappointment on her relaxed face. He watched her torso rise and fall as she breathed, then placed a hand on her shoulder, the weight of which caused her to wake abruptly. She stared at him for a moment, then sat up, rubbing the side of her face.

"Hey, where am I taking you?" Jack asked.

"Will you take me to my house in Silver Lake?" Bridge responded.

"Sure. Do you want to ride up front?"

"Alright." Bridge gathered herself up and came around to the front seat. As Jack drove, she absentmindedly pulled on her wild red hair, eventually getting it tied up into a short ponytail. Jack watched her unconscious ritual in his peripheral vision and tried to concentrate on the road. He felt self-conscious and lucky to have been able to see her do it.

"Everything go okay with Zaragoza?" Jack asked.

"I told them everything I told you. About James and about our cases."

Jack drove on in silence. He didn't want to disappoint her, but eventually said, "I'm sorry it can't become public. I guess it's for the better. The FBI has a larger case."

"I think his death was vindicated tonight." She smiled, and Jack realized that he had never seen her smile before. "Thanks for what you did in that house. James's murder is part of something larger now. I feel good about that. I think he would, too."

"I'm just glad you didn't get hurt."

Bridge reached across and put her hand on the back of Jack's neck. It was red from rubbing it while he drove.

"Does it hurt?" she asked. Touching him was an unexpected gesture, and it caught him off guard.

"It'll be fine. It's alright. Burns a little." He stumbled on the words and she smiled again.

"Take a right here and it's the third one down on the right," Bridge said.

The sun was cresting the San Gabriels when Jack skillfully squeezed his Crown Victoria into Bridge's narrow driveway. He turned the ignition and the purr of the engine and the stream of warm air from the heater vent ceased. They sat in silence. Jack couldn't tell if this was the beginning, the complicated and crowded middle, or the end.

The city was just waking up, ready to cause another commotion, to scheme and swarm in the heat of the day, and glisten in the dark of its night. Shootings, murders, deadly assaults, robberies gone wrong, arson, these terrible occurrences don't all happen at the same rate throughout the day. In most of the world's cities the crime rate dips at around five in the morning. 5:00 AM is the safest time in the world. However, thirty-eight minutes earlier, as clocks all over the Pacific seaboard struck 5:00 AM, a few miles away, a woman killed her husband in their bed before he awoke. Within a week she would be face to face with Jack and Marcus, but for now, she sat in silence at the foot of the bed, plotting her intricate plan to cover up the true cause of his death.

"Can I see you again?" Jack asked Bridge before she got out of the car. The words came out unexpectedly.

Bridge looked at him for an uncomfortably long time, then looked away. "Do you ever wonder if there's a different life you could be living? Some insignificant event or unexpected change and you'd be down a completely different path? What if you got a glimpse of it, and it was way better than what you currently have?" She was silent and Jack didn't know what to say. "I guess that's where sadness comes from, knowing you're missing out. Knowing something or somebody, some kind of life exists that you can never have."

"I try not to think too much about those things," Jack said and wondered if he should repeat his original question, but didn't.

After a long contemplative silence in which Bridge stared blankly at the dashboard, she said, "Sure, I'd like that."

"Alright then," Jack said with a smile. "I'll be in touch."

Bridge opened her door and stepped out into the driveway. The morning temperature was already warming, and the sound of a leaf blower droned on in the distance. Jack glanced at the quarter moon, still bright on the fringes of the western skyline behind Bridge's head.

"Thank you again," she said to Jack, leaning down and stretching out her hand to him. He took her hand into his and wrapped his second hand around her forearm.

"It was nothing," Jack said.

As he said the words, the cool softness of her forearm came through the rough pads of his large fingers. His thumb landed directly on a hidden birthmark of sorts, put there partly by Bridge's own hand. The mark was raised above the rest of her skin, below the elbow, yet not fully out of the inside crook of her arm, a freckle inside a dark ring, a droplet of melanin encompassed by a reddish-brown circle.

For years, she watched that mottled freckle, studying it as it gradually morphed into what she thought looked like a mirror image of the full moon. On the night of her twenty-second birthday, with a clean single-edged razor blade bought specifically for the purpose, she laid the freckle under a bright light and meticulously cut a deep and enduring halo around it.

THE END

CPSIA information can be obtained
at www.ICGtesting.com
Printed in the USA
LVHW101553150922
728481LV00017B/621/J

9 780999 896051